MARIE-HELENE BERTINO

Marie-Helene Bertino is the author of *2 A.M. at The Cat's Pajamas*, *Parakeet* and *Beautyland*. *Beautyland* has been named a best book of 2024 and a must-read by the *New York Times*, *Guardian*, *TIME*, *Elle*, *Esquire*, *Goodreads*, *Nylon*, *Boston Globe*, *Literary Hub*, *San Francisco Chronicle* and *Chicago Review of Books*. It was a finalist for the 2024 National Book Critics Circle Award for Fiction. She has received the O. Henry Prize, the Pushcart Prize, the Iowa Short Fiction Award and the Mississippi Review Prize. She is currently the Ritvo-Slifka Writer-in-Residence at Yale University and lives in Brooklyn.

ALSO BY MARIE-HELENE BERTINO

Exit Zero

Parakeet

2 A.M. at The Cat's Pajamas

Safe as Houses

'Bertino's weightless, joyful prose style nevertheless freights huge emotion. As much about acceptance and community as it is about yearning and divergency, it's a wonderful novel about making a life on Earth. This is one of the best books I have read this year'

Kaliane Bradley, author of *The Ministry of Time*

'A book that I will recommend to people for the rest of my life'

Dakota Johnson

'Marie-Helene Bertino's delicious, uncanny vision throughout *Beautyland* makes everything feel brand new. The chapters are so propulsive one doesn't even fully notice the way she's subtly deconstructing the world. One page swiftly returns ubiquity to wonder, while the next reminds us that cruelty is a choice, that nothing is inevitable but death. It's impossible for a book to feel this fun and this urgent. *Beautyland* is a miracle. I'll be rereading it forever'

Kaveh Akbar, author of *Martyr!*

'This book is endlessly surprising on the sentence level, but also as a story, and also in its tenderness. We might all need the unexpected love and perspective of a child alien at this point in human history. *Beautyland* is beautiful and hilarious and transcendent. It honestly feels like a message from another planet. Marie-Helene Bertino is an otherworldly talent'

Tommy Orange, author of *There, There*

'[A] remarkable funny-sad novel . . . Astonishing'

New York Times

'So surprising and so delightful'

New York Times Book Review

'The heroine of Marie-Helene Bertino's strange, engrossing third novel is at once fully human and entirely otherworldly . . . Underlying these paradoxes is the poetic observation that there's nothing more human than the experience of gazing out at a planet full of incomprehensible people who look just like you and deciding that you must be from outer space'

TIME

'Within moments of cracking open the cover to Marie-Helene Bertino's *Beautyland*, I was sold . . . A landmark work of literary science fiction . . . A wonder . . . as tender and intimate as it is conceptually courageous'

Elle

'Warm, witty and touching, *Beautyland* is an out-of-this-world exploration of loneliness and belonging'

Esquire

'A startling novel . . . I read *Beautyland* in forty-eight hours and was so distracted by the ending that I left my passport on the plane'

Bustle

'Wry, melancholy, utterly bewitching . . . Deftly blurring the line between reality and metaphor to create a work of exquisite beauty, joyfully off-kilter humour and aching sorrow, *Beautyland*, and Adina's lonesome journey, will fill and then shatter your heart'

Literary Hub

'Wise, lyrical and unwaveringly original . . . A tender coming-of-age story, an imaginative thought experiment and a moving depiction of the pain and power that come with being an outsider'

Shondaland

'A compelling, touching story that weds Bertino's masterful eye for the poignant detail of the everyday with her equally virtuosic flair as a teller of the tallest kinds of tales – so tall, in this case, they are interplanetary. A heartbreaking book that staggers with both truth and beauty'

Kirkus (starred review)

'The triumphant latest from Bertino offers a wryly comic critique of social conventions from the perspective of a woman who also happens to be an alien from another planet . . . Bertino nimbly portrays her protagonist's alienhood as both metaphor and reality. The results are divine'

Publishers Weekly (starred review)

'In *Beautyland*, Marie-Helene Bertino's Adina (maybe an alien, maybe a troubled human, always both) takes the tired old world and describes it so perfectly that we see it as if for the first time. Sparkling and alive, funny and magnificently true, this book woke me up. It made me weep with appreciation for the hard, strange, small-but-huge lives we lead. It made me fall back in love with this universe'

Ramona Ausubel, author of *The Last Animal*

'*Beautyland* is both an otherworldly and completely human look into one girl's life, written in concise, lyrical prose. It is richly allusive, funny and hypersmart. Marie-Helene Bertino has knocked it out of the park with this one. I loved it'

Brandon Hobson, author of *The Removed*

MARIE-HELENE BERTINO

Beautyland

VINTAGE

3 5 7 9 10 8 6 4 2

Vintage is part of the Penguin Random House group of companies

Vintage, Penguin Random House UK, One Embassy Gardens,
8 Viaduct Gardens, London SW11 7BW

penguin.co.uk/vintage
global.penguinrandomhouse.com

Penguin Random House UK

First published in Great Britain in Vintage in 2025
First published in the United States of America in 2024 by
Farrar, Straus and Giroux

Background art on title page and part openers by Crisis

Designed by Abby Kagan

Printed and bound in Great Britain by Clays Ltd, Elcograf S.p.A.

The authorised representative in the EEA is Penguin Random House Ireland, Morrison Chambers, 32 Nassau Street, Dublin D02 YH68

A CIP catalogue record for this book is available from the British Library

ISBN 9781529964394

Penguin Random House is committed to a sustainable future for our business, our readers and our planet. This book is made from Forest Stewardship Council® certified paper.

FSC www.fsc.org MIX Paper | Supporting responsible forestry FSC® C018179

For every Adina in the universe

STELLAR NEBULA

(BIRTH)

In the beginning there is Adina and her Earth mother. Adina (in utero), listening to the advancing yeses of her mother's heart and her mother in the labor room, vitals plunging. Binary stars. Adina, swaying in zero gravity. Térèse, fastened to the operating table. The monitor above the bed reports on their connected hearts: beating heart, heart, beating heart, beating. Térèse's blood pressure plummets as Adina advances through the birth canal; she has almost reached Earth. At this moment, Voyager 1 spacecraft launches in Florida, containing a phonograph record of sounds intended to explain human life to intelligent extraterrestrials.

It is September 1977 and Americans are obsessed with *Star Wars,* a civil war movie set in space. Bounding to the stage after hearing her name, a *Price Is Right* contestant loses her tube top and reveals herself to a shocked Burbank audience. In the labor room of Northeast Philadelphia Regional, no one notices Térèse's plummeting blood pressure. Something lighter and more conscious detaches and slips beneath the body on the table, underneath the floor and sediment, landing in a corridor of waist-deep water. Behind her, unembodied darkness. Far in front, over an expanse of churning waves, a certain, cherishing light. Térèse wants the light more than she wants health, more than she wants this baby's father to become a shape that can hold a family. She forces one leg through the water then the other, trying to paddle herself like a vessel.

*

The contents of Voyager 1's record were chosen by Carl Sagan, a polarizing astronomer who wears natty turtleneck-blazer combos and has been denied Harvard tenure for being too Hollywood. Carl and his team have assembled over a hundred images depicting what they decided were typical Earth scenes: a woman holding groceries, an insect on a leaf. The sounds include Chuck Berry's "Johnny B. Goode," the sorrowful cries of humpback whales, and recordings of the brain waves of Carl's third wife. Footsteps, heartbeats, and laughter. Destinationless, Voyager 1 will travel 1.6 light-years: farther than any human-made object. At a press conference Carl says that launching this bottle into the cosmic ocean is intended to tell "the human story."

*

The astronomers hoped to include the Beatles' "Here Comes the Sun," but Columbia Records asked for too much money. It's hard to make human beings believe in things.

Also not included is 1977's top hit "Barracuda," though every story hummed that year over the upholstered dividers of United Skates of America or yelled between cars pinned atop Auto World pistons or delivered through the eldritch mists of

Beautyland's perfume section is told over the twinned guitars of the two-sister band from Seattle. It plays on the radio in the nurses' station at Northeast Regional. A speck of Panasonic rustle between songs.

*

The current is too strong; Térèse makes no progress. The light remains distant. She cries out. The fright of a huge suck pulls Adina through to big white. Térèse regains consciousness under unfriendly lamps, baby on her naked chest. The baby is too small. Her skin and eyes appear lightly coated in egg. She is placed under a phototherapy lamp. Lit blue-green by the mothering light, yearning toward its heat, she appears other than human. Plant or marine life, maybe. An orchid or otter. A shrimp.

*

Adina: *noble*
Giorno: *day*

*

Térèse watches through the nursery window as her new daughter fails to reach the light.

Adina will hear this story several times in her life and in her imagination Térèse will wear a strapless red corset and capelet like Ann Wilson on the cover of *Little Queen*, only Sicilian, and with roller skates, humid late-season wind blowing through the doors. Her hair will glisten darkly with Moroccan oil, too coarse to relent to the popular feathering style.

In reality, Térèse has been arranged into a wheelchair by the nurses, feeling retracted to Earth by an unkind thread. The collar of her hospital gown falls beneath her collarbone. Her baby unrolls a tiny fist and she thinks of her unchained friends, Adina's father among them, on their way to the club. She is too tired to realize that pursuing him is following the promise of a dead star. The nurses chat about the *Price Is Right* contestant. *Did it on purpose*, one says. The first part of Térèse's life is over. He will never again beg to hold her perfect nipple in his mouth. She will never again be wild Térèse dancing on the lit floor at Bob and Barbara's. Her parents will not support her. She is this tiny baby's mother, mother, mother. The *she* in Adina's head.

In Adina's imagination, her mother will gaze through the nursery window, electric guitar chevroning behind her. In reality, Térèse is perforated by exhaustion, parentless, barely returned from death's corridor. Even the hospital gown refuses to help; its foolish smile exposes half a perfect breast.

*

But the womb is Adina's second lost home. The first has already tumbled three hundred thousand years away. A planet in the approximate vicinity of the bright star Vega, in the northern constellation of Lyra. Intelligent extraterrestrials have sent their own probe in a form and to a location no academic—not even Carl Sagan—could anticipate.

It is an interstellar crisscross apple sauce. Two celestially significant events occurring simultaneously: The departure of Voyager 1 and the arrival of Adina Giorno, early and yellowed like old newspaper. If like a newspaper Voyager intends to bring the news, this baby is meant to collect it, though no one knows that yet, including her. Even as the spacecraft breaches the troposphere, the delicate probe stretches her fist toward a heat lamp in the pediatric ward of Northeast Regional, having just been born—or landed—depending on perspective, premature. Wriggling, yearning, recovering in heat, full head of thick black hair, at the moment she is still mostly salt and feeling.

*

This family, trying, lives across from Auto World in Northeast Philadelphia. Their apartment comprises the bottom floor of a two-unit brick building attached to another brick building, attached to another brick building, and so on, et cetera-ing down the highway. These are starter row homes. This is a starter family. The complex's lawn, newly mowed, emits a pleasant fecund smell to the cars speeding by and to Adina's father, where he crouches, glaring at a screwdriver. If he keeps his city job they'll move to the suburbs where within years he will not rent but own an unattached house. They'll have a yard that's only theirs, a grill, a tree, and enough space for each family member to do things alone. There is no solo activity in the row home across from Auto World. Being a father is alien to this man but he's trying. Today, he will use metal to add wood to wood and produce a swing, the way a man plus a woman and baby makes a family.

Each row home is designed like a cadaver lying flat on a table: at the prow of the apartment is an abbreviated entryway that normally holds Adina's kicked-off boots and her mother's neatly arranged work pumps, hallway like a throat leading to the open kitchen, the torso a family room big enough to hold a couch and a half-moon table covered in the open faces of their books, a fart of a bathroom, two small back bedrooms. Wood paneling. Everything possible painted beige. In front of Auto World a flying man twists and gyrates, making Adina and her mother giggle as they pull into their driveway.

Four-year-old Adina wakes from a nap and moves through the apartment, surprised to find the family room empty. Where are they? She believes she is the nucleus of every interaction and while she sleeps her parents pray for her to wake. She is still inactivated. She is still upturned to the sun. She cannot stop thinking about the bunnies she saw on the lawn the previous day under a bush, heads pressed together in a soft shamrock.

There are no cookies in the jar and the fridge is filled with off-limits bottles. Kid math: if her mother is rustling in her bedroom then her father must be in the backyard. There is still as much chance Adina will go to her father as her mother. She pauses. The home itself—every crock on the shelf, every bill—seems to pause.

The swing wins. Adina longs to sit weightless on a piece of oak fastened to rope. The vehicle of upward thrust. There is no reason to have a swing. This makes the swing an anomaly because in addition to its intended purpose every object in the apartment must also function in two or three other ways. Everything repurposed, everything salvaged. Even she, the child, was meant to fulfill several things at once: to be silent, useful, hardworking, a credit to her father.

That morning, her mother pulled a fax machine from a neighbor's trash and, holding it aloft like a prized marlin, engaged in conversation with herself. "Why would anyone throw this out? Probably because they want the latest model. But it could clearly be a planter!" (Anything about to be trashed was first tried as a planter.) "It even comes with paper!" (She unearthed the roll from the trash, brandishing it in front of herself and Adina.) "I'll bet it works. Paper! People are crazy." (People were always crazy.)

Her father said it was ugly and no one he knew had one in their home and it should stay in "the child's" room.

"Fine," her mother said in her not-fine voice and carried the fax machine to Adina's room where it claimed most of her bureau's top. Except for the paper tray, city-pigeon gray, the machine was the color of the orthopedic shoes the employees wore at her mother's job. A slim phone posed beside a bank of flat buttons with scripted numbers that glowed when her mother plugged it in. Portals to the business world.

Adina's mother slid a sheet of paper into the tray. "Who should we fax?"

Adina didn't know any phone numbers except her own. Her mother dialed: 215-999-1212. The machine whirred to life, trembled pleasantly as it pulled the paper through itself, went silent.

"What happens now?" Adina heard her father in the backyard, readying his tools. The woosh of cars on the street. A clicking sound from a private place inside the machine. A sheet of paper launched from an internal chamber Adina and her mother had not anticipated. An error message: NO ANSWER.

Adina's mother's eyes were wide. "Incredible."

*

It is impossible to be unhappy on a swing. Even at four, Adina knows this. She wants it to be finished so she can be as happy as she needs to be. She wants her father to swing her until she is high enough to reach the porch's tin ceiling.

"Is it finished, Daddy?"

But some immeasurable slanted expression over breakfast has dug a divot into him. Her mother thinks he's weak or unable to build a swing. She thinks she'd be better off alone. He is. He is. She would be. Even though the plates are his, the table his, the yard, the everything is provided by him. The nail's failure to find purchase in the flaccid wood has dug that divot even farther. Now this brown berry kid wants to check his progress? *Is he finished. Thank you*, how about.

Her father's neck bulges with veins in an unmatchable shade of red. He pushes Adina out of his space. Maybe he forgets the five concrete steps leading to the shared yard when he pushes her again. The concrete and the trimmed grass offer little to cushion her brief fall. Falls.

In the kitchen her mother lifts a glass of water to her mouth. She drinks eight a day, soundlessly, one after the other. She hears a neighbor call her name and hurries to the backyard where Adina is a quiet lump on the pavement.

How long does Adina stay outside the realm of human

voices? Seconds? A century? She wakes to her mother shaking her, screaming go back inside to a constellation of worried neighbors. Earth to Adina. Come in, Adina. Adina reboots. Some things return immediately and some take time. A tin taste sours her mouth. Her mother's steel grip on her shoulders, helping her stand. Her father's gaze locked on the abandoned tools on the ground.

Adina is activated.

✶

That night, Adina "wakes" in a room designed to appear as a classroom. The English alphabet borders the walls. An aquarium with blinking blue fish and a shelf filled with globes. The scene is stitched from what she has seen from classrooms on television and the visit she made to the grade school she will attend the following year. They are using human objects so she will understand.

Her superiors are an area near the front of the class that shimmers and evokes the sense of the singular plural. Multi-souled, multi-personed Shimmering Area. The closest human word for how they communicate is *intuiting*. They intuit toward Adina and she receives the message. This is her native tongue. It makes sense that she dreams in it and that using it fills her with ease. She intuits the Shimmering Area is both a location and a doorway.

The lights dim. An ivory screen descends from the top of the chalkboard and fills with projected images. A switchboard operator pulls a line from a connection. Two housewives talk on the phone. A formally dressed man ducks into a telephone booth to make an emergency call. Adina consults the Shimmering Area for whatever is next.

A familiar object flashes onto the screen, the fax machine her mother pulled from the trash. A disembodied hand feeds a sheet of paper with nondescript handwriting into it and presses the large green key. The paper churns through the mechanism. As it emerges on the other side, the machine and paper glow. Joyful sparks beam out.

*

Adina wakes in her Earth bedroom, nostrils filled with the tang of cleaning supplies. She lazes in and out of sleep, considering a space near the door where morning light has collected into the shape of a ship. Seeing the fax machine on her bureau, she remembers the images from her dream.

She writes on a sheet of paper:

I am an Adina.

After thinking about it, adds:

Yesterday I saw bunnies on the grass.

She feeds her note into the machine and presses the green button. The paper jolts through the tumbler with a robotic scanning sound.

It is so early even the boulevard is silent. Her mother is asleep in her bedroom and Adina is awake in her own, hovering next to an office machine, unsure what to hope for. After a moment, a red light she hadn't noticed activates. Incoming fax! A sheet of paper squeaks through the tumblers.

DESCRIBE BUNNIES.

*

In the kitchen, Adina's mother prepares what she calls her special Lipton tea. Her voice is calm though she plunges the tea bag into the steaming water as if angry at the bag and the water.

"Listen, Adina, your father is gone. This is one of those good and bad things. There are so many hard times you may as well celebrate them," she says. "Most are. Even if you haven't figured out how. Good, I mean. Even if you're sure they're not. Like that car I ended up not buying. I found the VW and even though it's not great on hills it still has way better heat. So, no whining. No, why is this happening? It's better for him and us."

Her mother's face is mapped with tears. Adina knows what she is seeing is the composition of bravery. They sit at the half-moon table, the tea too hot to drink. Every so often, her mother stops herself from saying more. The man who had been living there, her father, is gone. His hair gel, his rigid combs, his work shirts spiced with earth smell at the pits. The apartment is filled with the scent of California lemon trees: He has been Pine-Sol-ed off the surfaces. Adina doesn't cry. She is already mentally describing the tea to her superiors; bitter because she is not allowed sugar—or anything sweet.

*

Beautyland is a dash-to-in-a-pinch supply store that contains what humans believe are necessities. The bottle of rubbing alcohol they never use that haunts the hall closet like a pale ulcer, the sponge curlers her mother forces her hair into, good for two occasions though she's used hers for going on ten. They are belted into the car, their eggplant-colored VW bug, the car they pray up hills on cold mornings. It is winter and the car's heater is busted, the windshield fogged with their breath. Beautyland's abnormally pink roof juts out from a gyre of row homes near the boulevard where big rigs haul supplies to New York. Concrete divides each small lawn where kids play. The grass is dead scratch.

Adina has been invited to join her school's accelerated learners' program and her mother, after being assured there's no cost, is stiff with pride. "Gifted," she says, as they drive. "We knew that. Lucky they caught on."

They have been to this store many times. Adina has already faxed notes about the clerk whose job it is to patrol the upper, sacred perfume floor, cordoned off by important carpeted steps and a sign reading HAVE GOOD SCENTS. She has explained how his careful, even vacuuming switches the carpet's threads to a darker tone. But on this day Adina realizes the aisles of beautystuffs can relate to her, a six-year-old earth girl. That she too has parts these items can clamp on to, curl, plump, redden, or whiten.

On every other visit, they've stayed on the necessity floor but today Adina is gifted so her mother says, "Let's live a little for the love of Christ."

Upstairs, perfume bottles pose on mirrored shelves like odd-bellied birds. A display of items sold on television: a set of sin-sharp knives, Chia Pets, and the Flowbee, a combination vacuum–hair cutter. The clerk is sliding open the doors to the glass case behind the counter that protects the rarer creams most likely to be stolen. He hands a purple vial to a woman from their church who twists it open and applies a few drops to her pulse points.

Her mother knows where to find her Jean Naté eight-ounce bottle, at the end of the aisle, bottom shelf, amid the Jean Naté body powder and after-bath splash. Each visit to Beautyland comes after weeks of adding water to the existing bottle then, if Adina is in the room (she normally is, transfixed by her mother's preparations), holding out her anointed wrists and announcing, "See? The same, just lighter." If Beautyland doesn't have her eight-ounce bottle she will not substitute with another. If they have changed the formula, promising a cleaner or muskier scent, she will not buy it. If they have the right perfume but not in eight ounces—for example, the twelve-ounce bottle—she will not buy it. Even though the twelve-ounce bottle costs less per ounce. They cannot afford to be smart with money.

Adina's world begins at the waistband of her mother's Burlington Coat Factory control-top pantyhose in Misty Taupe (at the end of the laundry rotation, Wild Rice) and ends near the giant golf ball on the Garden State Parkway that heralds the Atlantic City entrances. Adina is a student and her mother is her major concentration. Every night, Adina watches her remove her work dress and place it on the ironing board, ready to wear the next day. After boiling a chicken or making stew from whatever's about to rot, she types time cards for a paper factory near their apartment. She says a lot of women would pay good money for her deep-set eyes and Roman nose. Mark at work told her she belongs on a coin. Anything that's different from everyone else in the neighborhood she swears women would pay good money for. So far this includes their eyes, hair, the dark olive skin that deepens in the summer. She does not like to hug—Adina can usually only get perfume-close, which is why she loves the bottle so yellow she could see it from space.

"Jean Naté." Her mother waves the bottle, correct in weight and formula. "Very fancy." She pretends to consider a different bottle, impersonating the voice of Julia Child. "This is a pretty bottle," she says. "But it's the color of snot!"

Adina has never seen her mother this carefree. She sprays the tester over their heads and demands Adina step into the mist.

"Well," she says. "How does it smell?"

"Like eggs!" Adina frowns.

Her mother selects another bottle, the color of Adina's favorite betta fish in Martin's Aquarium.

"Well?"

Adina says the name of the only flower she knows.

"Daffodils! My daughter is gifted," she announces to the shelf. "You couldn't possibly understand. May I borrow your notebook?" She's joking. It is a family fact that Adina won't let her touch the red notebook that peeks out of her coat pocket like a perpetual tongue.

Her mother pretends to scribble notes on her hand. "This is you." She laughs. She sprays a few more. They evaluate down the aisle.

"The human nose can only process seven scents," a voice says. The clerk stands behind them, lips curled away from his teeth. A vault of a face. "You're wasting perfume."

Adina is surprised he'd be this curt in front of the churchwoman. But she has completed her purchase and left. They are alone. Her cheeks heat.

"Thank you." Her mother's tone is brisk. She replaces the bottle. It clicks against the mirrored shelf.

"Can I help you with anything else?" The clerk turns and walks back to his counter.

Her mother uses Adina's elbow to steer her out of the section, down the steps, through the first floor. "Adina," she warns. She knows tears are coming because her daughter cries at the lobsters in the tank at Seafood Shanty, their claws constricted with black bands. "He's just a stupid man." She pushes Adina past the main counter, the front door, the quickness of lawn, into their car. She is more frustrated with Adina than with the man because Adina is who she is supposed to be able to control.

Their neighborhood has turned winter blue. They still have to go to the store to find a chicken to boil. "Sit up straight." Her mother's expression is the one she uses when readying herself to plainly state the truth. "Sometimes people don't like when other people seem happy." When this doesn't stop the tears, she slams the car into gear and drives home. No perfume. No brush. No chicken. They pass the famous Sandwich Castle, the famous Putt-Putt Station, Martin's Aquarium, Auto World.

✶

Later in her bedroom Adina feeds a sheet of paper into the fax machine.

Human beings don't like when other humans seem happy.

A reply arrives the next morning: WE ARE SORRY.

Adina imagines someone on the other end cheering for her, worried on her behalf.

✶

Displayed along the road extravagantly, it is the first and only Auto World in the neighborhood—a "Super" World because it not only sells car products but also fixes actual cars. Mid-sizes, compacts, and sedans levitate in its bays that yawn along the expanse.

The Flying Man in front of the Auto World is father-red. After homework, Adina sits on the front step and watches him gesticulate over the cars heading to Route 95, which leads to the ineffable: New Jersey. The Flying Man says, *Come! Go? Adina! Hooray! Adina!*

✶

Adina's hair is crimped in places, succinctly spiraled in others. Attendant curls fuzz the back of her neck. John Frieda is years away from inventing anti-frizz serum, she uses gel to control what she can. Most days it creates a black arrow jutting forward from her stiff school collar.

The patterns of the tiny apartment streamline and deepen. Mother to work and daughter to school. Mother, returning home, hurls pocketbook onto the half-moon table. Daughter penciling geography answers. Mother in the kitchen, singing. Daughter in the bedroom, waiting to be called. Mother slamming a cabinet. Daughter alert. Mother counting chicken cutlets, figuring how they'll last the week. Mother math. Daughter complaining, *Chicken again?* Mother shelving important parts of herself into places even she'll forget. Daughter reading a book a day from the Roosevelt flea market stack. Daughter's desire growing into the shape of ski trips, libraries, meadows she reads about. Mother and daughter in line at House of Bargains, concocting stories so they'll allow a return. Daughter thinking how the word vestibule does what it means, circles around and makes a space to hang Mother's gross puffed coat and her pink one. Vestibule. These pantyhose are supposed to be on sale. Daughter asks questions, eats ice cream cone. You cannot go on the ski trip. You don't know how to ski! Daughter will never learn if she's not allowed to go. Mother's sound is, *Don't start, you don't even wear the ones you have, I could make that for half the price, anyway, it's ugly as sin.* Daughter's sound is, *Chicken again?* Their routine changes so infrequently they don't need much language. The reprises, laments, and interludes become famous to them. A song in two parts they sing together.

"I'm cutting my hair off," Adina says.

"Women would pay good money."

"I'm cutting it off."

"You don't know how lucky you are."

*

The name of the planet Adina is from does not have an English equivalent. Roughly, it sounds like a cricket hopping onto a plate of rice. She has been sent to Earth to take notes on human beings. This will help the people of Planet Cricket Rice, glimmering on their troubled planet centuries away.

Every night, Adina falls asleep and "wakes" in the Night Classroom, superiors shimmering in front of her. The room's charts and dioramas update to reflect whatever she studies in Earth school. The Revolutionary War, verbs, the solar system. She intuits this is to create continuity. She acclimates to the double load but is always tired.

*

In fourth grade, a girl with short black hair and bangs joins the school. She is introduced as Antoinette-Maria and sits silently at the front of the class under the weight of her giant name.

It's milk day. Every student receives a container of either plain or chocolate milk based on what their parents specified on a permission slip weeks before. That the milk is not distributed during lunch but in afternoon Science class is never explained. Students whose parents fail to fill out permission slips default to plain. Every student wants chocolate, but the parents of loved children choose plain. This is what Adina's mother tells her to excuse why she forgot to sign her slip. Antoinette-Maria wasn't around when the slips were distributed so she gets plain. The Science teacher helps them open the tough-skinned cartons then pulls a wheeled dais containing a combo television-VCR into their classroom. She announces that the students should put down the milk they only just received. Unlike their Art teacher who hops in place whenever someone uses pipe cleaners in what she calls a "unique way," their Science teacher is not prone to enthusiasm. This must be big. She shuts off the lights.

The TV screen fills with the image of a rocket ship in space. A man with friendly-looking hair appears. He wears a prim three-piece suit and assures her there is life on other planets and they will find it. His coppery voice presses a button in Adina. She leans forward, flipping the carton of milk into her lap. White liquid releases itself over her skirt. The classroom explodes into chatter. The Science teacher turns the lights back on, runs for paper towels.

Later in Art class, the prompt is: *Draw your home.*

"What are you?" the new girl asks Adina.

"Adina," she says. "You have the longest name I've ever heard."

"My mom wanted a girlie name because I have a hundred brothers." She smiles. "But everyone calls me Toni."

"Where are you from?" Adina says, and Toni says, "From very far away."

A stab of hope. "Me too," Adina says. "Past Neptune."

"Philadelphia," the teacher says. "Rhawn Street and Verree Road."

"I'm from Neptune," Toni says.

"Kensington." The teacher sighs toward Adina's paper where she has drawn ten royal-blue dots. "Adina, the assignment was to draw your home."

Toni does not glance up from her paper where she has drawn a girl surrounded by a firework of boys. "They're stars."

*

Adina checks out every book in the library about Carl Sagan and faxes what she learns.

Carl Sagan is a polarizing astronomer who wears natty turtleneck-blazer combos and has been denied Harvard tenure for being too "Hollywood." He says human civilization is so far behind that if extraterrestrials were to make contact, they'd have to speak slowly. Is that why you sent a fax machine? Is that why you sent me here instead of somewhere like New York City? He says Voyager 1 launched a cosmic message in a bottle into the universe. He is looking for us! This statement does not convey the wealth of joy this brings. She adds: *He believes in me.*

Even the squeaking tumbler sounds disinterested when the reply arrives:

YES WE KNOW ABOUT HIM AND HIS TURTLENECKS.

*

Except for the parrots that yawk above the litter bags, everything is liquid and quiet in Martin's Aquarium. The sound is early morning on a snow day, the tone in utero. Her mother's mouth noises and the scritching of her classmates' pencils create chaos in Adina's mind. In Martin's Aquarium, she feels calm.

When the tiny show-off betta fish reaches the end of its aquarium and turns, its tail fans out in a razzmatazz. Luminescent blue skin and a bright pink tail. Do fish have skin? She makes a note in her copybook to look it up.

Her mother winces into the box's fluorescent light. "Hard way to live." She has assented to this post-work visit because

Adina seems beleaguered, as if she's responsible for a factory of workers and their families. She worries the gifted program is too much pressure. A little girl should not retreat so often into thought, a space a mother cannot breach, no matter how many times she calls her name.

Adina doesn't like when her mother says adult things when she's trying to listen to fish. She is relieved when her mother loses interest and walks away to chirp at her favorite, the birds.

She places her ear against the cool, thick glass.

Ooo moo a moo a, the water says. She hears: *Mom, mom, mom*.

*

Adina's mother coaches her into the 7-Eleven: "You will walk into the store and ask the man at the counter for a pack of Marlboro one hundreds. He will turn and get them and you will hand him this five-dollar bill. Wait for the change, which will be around three dollars."

"What if it costs more?"

"It won't. I'm overestimating by a lot."

"What if they raised the prices last night?"

"They didn't," she says. "I checked."

"What if they don't have Marlboro . . ."

"One hundred's," she supplies. "Then you ask for Newport one hundred's."

"And what if they don't have those?"

"Then I'll quit smoking."

Adina tests the bill in her hand as if it's counterfeit.

Her mother gestures to herself. "I'll watch from here. You can see me through the window." She waves to an imaginary Adina.

This calms Adina the necessary amount. She gets out and circles the front of the car. She worries that someone will push her out of the way at the door but no one does. She walks to the counter and asks the man for the cigarettes.

He pouts. "Are you eighteen?"

Adina stammers. "My mother is outside. They're for her." She points, waves, but her mother is combing her bangs in the rearview mirror.

"Take it easy." The man chucks the box onto the counter. "I'm kidding."

The bill shakes in her hand. The change is $3.25. She returns to the car where her mother is glossing her lips.

"You weren't watching!"

She claps the lid back onto the gloss. "And look how good you did!"

*

Adina "wakes" in the Night Classroom to find that the alphabet has been replaced by a series of panels. In the first panel, a collection of microbes cluster against a dark background. In the next, an eyeless fish. The next, a fish with eyes. Then a reptile. A tree monkey. A baboon. A caveman. Toward the end of the series, a panel debuts the first human. As humans evolve over the next few panels the body shears what it no longer needs, like wisdom teeth. The last panel features a contemporary man holding a briefcase. The chart stops.

Adina consults the Shimmering Area. She intuits, more to come.

Another panel appears. In it, the man with the briefcase poses mid-stride. It is the same panel only his head is bigger. Another panel appears—the same man with an even bigger head, shoulders and legs thinning. Adina understands she is witnessing the future of human evolution. She thinks of her Earth body, asleep in bed, scanned by gradations of light.

More panels appear. The man's head grows while his body diminishes. In the future almost everything on a body will prove itself to be wisdom teeth. The brain grows. Gender is no longer discernible. The eyes and nose, unnecessary in the presence of profound intuition, narrow. In the final panel, the man with the briefcase has transformed into a gray, waxy-skinned giant-headed being with slits for eyes and an inconsequential body. Adina recognizes the image from the photos on her mother's *National Enquirer* magazines that run alongside headlines like UFO LANDS IN NEW MEXICO CAMPSITE UPSETTING LOCALS.

Adina considers the first and last panel. Extraterrestrials are humans, visiting from the future. Us, later. She cannot reconcile the man standing with the briefcase with the bobble-headed creature. The Shimmering Area registers her unease. It appears to consult itself and decides she's seen enough. Adina wakes in her bed, shivering with reverberations of the important instruction.

*

The next morning, her mother pokes at sausages on a skillet. "You look like a cabbie at the end of her shift."

*

There is nothing uglier than sin. Sin: Dirt on your mind's floor you must always be sweeping. Everyone is obsessed with it at Adina's school, which is based on one of the major Abrahamic religions, Roman Catholicism. They are taught that God's major sin concerns include whether your parents are unmarried (mortal), whether you are attracted to a member of the same sex (mortal), if you kiss someone with tongue (mortal), if you lie about it (venial). The best way to avoid sin is to do without. Adina and her mother do without new coats in the winter and full tanks of gas and air-conditioning and full-price chicken and vacations. Her mother steals reams of paper from her work. This is not a sin, she says, because Adina needs it.

Adina faxes a sin breakdown to her superiors and receives an immediate reply. At first she assumes the two dots and squiggle line are a code, then realizes: it is a smiley face. They are amused.

*

"Mark" has a degree in art therapy. "Mark" likes diet soda. An unresponsive student at their work was able to eat only when "Mark" played a Schubert record.

One Saturday afternoon, Adina's mother announces that they will go to see Adina's first movie in a theater with Mark.

"Who's Mark?" Adina says, and her mother says, "Don't start."

Because of the transitive property of apartments and single mothers, Adina is supposed to pretend her mother has already told her about Mark. Her mother relies on her position at the top of the hierarchy to excuse the fact that she hasn't. Adina has heard her mother on the phone, has heard the name (the reason she let it pepper her conversation in the first place), and no further explanation is needed. They will put on semi-nice clothes and go to Boulevard Cinemas near House of Bargains.

When Mark's car arrives that night, Adina's mother yells "okay" so loud they are both startled. The man lit by the console of a Toyota Corolla appears similarly nervous when Adina slides into the back seat. Her mother and Mark smile at each other. He turns around and says hello and let him know if her seat belt is too tight. On the ten-minute ride to the theater Adina memorizes every smell in his car. Sweet peppers and metal. She is not accustomed to seeing her neighborhood at night. The soft-pretzel vendors are gone. The boulevard's sapling trees are inky and blue, the way she imagines they are in Wales, the setting for most of her fantasy books, only instead of in a forest they are isolated along the concrete wall that divides eight lanes of traffic. But they are still trees. They are still beautiful.

Adina tries to understand her mother's new laugh, marbles spilling from a jar onto a table. But when they reach the theater, Adina is entranced by the stand selling soft drinks, popcorn, and every candy she has ever heard of. Mark says he'll buy her what she wants. They get a tub of popcorn, buttered, extra salt. He chuckles as she digs her fist into it.

The theater is wide and smells like a new coat. Mark says

it is a special showing of *E.T.* The projector fwips on and the audience quiets. Even the sound of people eating popcorn recedes for one hour and forty-five minutes as Adina, heart hammering, watches the story of a gentle alien being helped by young humans. In a quiet moment toward the end, a woman seated next to Adina unwraps a chocolate bar. The sound of the wrapping and the woman's chewing snaps Adina out of her reverie. She can no longer focus, her arms heat, she leaves her seat and rustles past her mother and Mark into the aisle.

"What is she doing?" Mark says.

"Adina, sit down!" her mother hisses.

Adina walks to the back of the theater, her mother trailing. Adina explains that the woman's eating was hurting her ears. The movie ends and the audience files out, Mark's head bobbing among them. "That was quite a reaction," he says, rejoining them.

"Adina is sensitive," her mother says.

Returning home, her mother and Mark stay in the family room while Adina retreats into her bedroom, buzzing with information.

✶

When it was time to decide the official food of movie-watching, human beings did not go for Fig Newtons or caramel, foods that are silent, but popcorn, the loudest sound on Earth.

✶

In the 1980s the state of Pennsylvania switches from calling her mother's workplace a school to a facility and, instead of students, refers to them as clients. This is because, Adina's mother explains, the clients are unable to learn in ways state administrative boards can understand. She says many families don't visit because having a child with a severe disability fills them with shame. She prefers the clients, who think as clearly as anyone but live in bodies that cannot cooperate with their desires. Her own family cut her out too, after all, as cleanly as you'd snip a coupon.

Adina's mother collects everyone's time card at the end of the day and types them into a long sheet she turns in to Human Resources the next morning. One night that winter, she forgets the time sheets. She cannot leave Adina alone and she cannot do without them. They drive to her job.

Adina's mother hurries her up the path to a squat brick building. She opens the door slowly, as if afraid of disturbing whoever is inside. In the lobby, clients are seated in wheelchairs around a coffee table. A night nurse sits behind a windowed back wall, startled by the sound of the door.

"Stay here," her mother says. She moves through the lobby, greeting clients. One woman sits in an uncomfortable-looking position, head resting on her left shoulder. "Hi, Martha." Her mother smiles into her eyes. The woman's expression does not change but her hand reaches toward her mother's. Adina has never seen her mother hold hands with anyone or heard her speak so gently.

"I hear you gave them hell at breakfast yesterday."

The woman jostles in the chair which her mother interprets as affirmation. She presses the woman's hand between hers and calls hello to the night nurse who buzzes her into the back.

Adina hovers in the lobby's doorway. The walls glow with plastic domes that make the room appear sunken. A man on her right turns his wheelchair in the direction of the wall. The diagonality of his shoulders makes Adina worry he is in pain. She wants her mother to return so they can leave. Martha wheels her chair toward her.

"Hello," Adina says. "I'm Adina."

"This is my daughter." Her mother emerges from the back, holding the time cards. "The one I told you about. Gifted."

Adina has never heard her mother brag. She has never seen her give someone a side hug. She has never heard her raise her voice to address more than one person in a room.

"Be good, everyone. I'll see you tomorrow."

In the parking lot, her mother pauses before starting the car. "I know it's upsetting but they're safe and getting good care."

They drive the ten minutes home in silence. Adina's mind is filled with simple, unfathomable thoughts. Her mother touches people. The boulevard's trees wear string lights. Even the corner boys in their glitzy jackets are in concert with an agreement her mother's warmth has made with the world.

⁎

Human beings, Adina faxes, *produce water in their eyes when they are sad, happy, or sometimes just frustrated. Water!*

*

Adina develops a bad cold and is allowed to sleep on the family room couch, wrapped in blankets and reading. Her mother explains that she should blow what's in her nose into a tissue. Adina assumes she's misheard: Blast the most disgusting parts of her through her nose? Her mother re-explains, checks her watch, makes an excuse into the phone, grows impatient. She forces Adina's nose into the tissue.

"That's your mouth, blow through your nose."

She can't. The softest parts of her stay inside.

*

In school they learn that meteors sound like frying bacon. Adina stays awake until morning, listening.

*

Every Sunday they go to the Roosevelt flea market to sell clothes or shop the aisles. Her favorite vendor is Mrs. Goldman, who sells used books out of a Chevy van. On good days Adina receives two dollars to buy four books: three Nancy Drews (two quarters apiece), and whatever new book has arrived about a normal girl with a secret, royal identity. On bad days, when Adina's mother can't find a parking spot or Mrs. Goldman's van is not parked at the end of the fifth aisle, Adina is inconsolable. They leave early.

This Sunday, Mrs. Goldman pulls out a book she's been saving for Adina. Carl Sagan's *Intelligent Life in the Universe*. The sacred title hangs over an image of the Milky Way galaxy. Two quarters.

It is a clear, gray morning in Philadelphia. Hot pretzel stacks steam on the boulevard's divider. The vendors move among the cars like flamenco dancers, shaking their paper bags. At McDonald's Adina is allowed to buy a box of mini chocolate chip cookies. Before eating each one, she holds it toward the window and admires it like an emerald. Adina slides the book out of her jacket pocket to make sure it's still there.

Characters in books are always admiring gems against the light of windows, she faxes.

The smell of smoke pushes through the tiny window. Mother on the back porch exhaling smoke over the concrete walkways. Adina stays up late, reading about the universe.

✶

Adina's mother lectures while ironing: Nothing is more important than bringing substance to the table.

"What does she bring to the table?" she says, about the women at church, about neighbors, about Vanna White.

This is what Toni brings to the table:

Three brothers, Christopher, Matteo, and Dominic.

A de-crusted lettuce sandwich.

A hand-me-down pink-and-orange windbreaker she wears every day.

An art sponge she chews in a bathroom stall when she's nervous.

Silent eating. Not one throat or slurping sound.

A father who lives two states away with another family. A mother who works at a law office but is often sick.

Toni is the only person Adina considers telling her secret, royal identity.

✶

The news reports beat from a distant point in space. Adina enters a period of medical testing.

In the eye doctor's office, a panel on the far wall illuminates.

"First or third?" the ophthalmologist says.

"Third."

(Sound of plastic slides flipping)

"Second or first?"

—

"Would you like to see the first again?"

(Sound of plastic slides flipping)

The ophthalmologist swallows, making a disturbing over-wet sound.

"First," she says, repulsed.

"Please don't guess."

"I'm not guessing." She is guessing. She wants to say whatever will shorten the visit so she doesn't have to hear him swallow again.

Mechanisms slide away from Adina, a table with different

instruments assembles itself in front of her. A panel on a farther wall illuminates.

"Read the lowest line you can." The liquid in the ophthalmologist's mouth is so close to Adina's ear. She is certain he is making these sounds to aggravate her.

Adina lists letters, stomach roiling.

In the waiting room, her mother reads an article about a family of actors who've recently invested in salad dressing. "How'd it go?"

The ophthalmologist describes the astigmatism like a concave glass that makes Adina feel special and damaged. With a scribbled prescription, they drive, her mother sighing over the steering wheel, to Lens Kingdom, where the walls are lined with glasses. Adina selects a pair of round red frames. Her mother stares through the shop's window to where their mercurial car is parked under a streetlamp. Mother math. As if on cue, the streetlight turns on.

"It's okay," Adina says, "we can skip the glasses."

Her mother looks confused. She thinks she's kept their lack of money hidden. She doesn't realize how anxiety influences her posture, voice, the heaviness of her footsteps, the length of time it takes her to leave the car in the driveway at the end of the workday, so that even before she enters the apartment Adina knows her mother's mood.

They stand in Lens Kingdom amid orange plastic couches with a clerk who's mentioned twice they close at five. "These," her mother tells him, about the red frames, which will be outfitted with lenses and accompanied by a felt case, a cleaning cloth, and an instructional pamphlet. Like an adult, Adina will have things.

Even the Terwood Road Hill is not as big as her excitement.

"It's going to be boiled chicken for a while." Her mother taps the steering wheel.

The sun sets over Auto World's vaulted cars, as hulking as hard facts. Mechanics administer to their shining bellies.

*

Adina and the speech pathologist find her mother in the waiting room, sliding a magazine sample of perfume across her wrists.

The doctor hands her a tape. Her mother looks from it to the doctor, expecting a woman-to-woman candor that does not arrive. A pantyhose run peeks out from her short skirt, a line of gold under the office lights. Every woman in the neighborhood (except the old ones) wears her hair in a wild tease like her mother's. However, the doctor's hair is arranged in an unflattering bun. She wears a white coat and subdued glasses. Adina feels sorry for this woman's unattractiveness, her plain, fair face. She is years from learning understatement and believes the neighborhood rule of *If you got it, show it.* Adina longs to show it.

They drive to the Shop & Save where a hardy discount chicken beams under the produce light. At home, her mother places the tape into a machine and presses play. Adina's voice ekes out.

"Say rabbit," the nurse says.

"Wabbit," Adina says.

"Rabbit," he corrects her.

"Wabbit," she says.

Adina's mother pulls her into her lap where she can smell the magazine perfume sample. "Say rabbit."

"Wabbit."

"Rabbit," she insists. "Like the kind we see on the lawn. Hopping along the grass in the country."

Adina has never been to the country. She hasn't even done most things once. "Wabbit," she insists.

"Ruh."

"Wuh!"

"They want me to pay for speech lessons," her mother says. "You'd go to some office after school. Why does everything cost money? Let's pray your teeth stay straight."

✶

I require speech lessons and corrective lenses and most likely teeth braces. I am an expensive extraterrestrial.

The reply: DESIGNED TO APPEAR NORMAL.

What's normal?

YOU TELL US.

✶

Amadeo Calvi walks on the balls of his feet. Each step, a pulse. His skin tone is fish green, an ill pallor that Adina has questions about. In seventh grade, the muscle in the center of her chest reveals its purpose—to pump desperately whenever Amadeo bounces by. Sometimes he appears when she's not expecting him, clapping erasers when he's supposed to be in the gym or running an errand in the rectory and Adina's heart has to catch up with itself, takes minutes to regain its rhythm. His butt protrudes like a cherry in the standard-issue uniform pants. She wants to know if he has siblings and if they also have cherry butts.

Toni says the word for Adina is *boy crazy*.

✶

Adina "wakes" in the Night Classroom, superiors shimmering at the front of the class.

The last time she saw the evolutionary panels, they'd evolved into a *National Enquirer* sketch of a bobble-headed creature. A progression of new panels has appeared. The bobble-head shrinks. A light becomes visible at the center of the "body." Adina intuits this is what humans call a "soul." New forms enter the frame; other humans with "souls" whose bodies diminish, then combine. In one panel, a "body" contains three "souls." Other "souls" are added until the "body" is no longer and only the "souls" remain. Planet Cricket Rice is a single, polyphonic blanket made from billions of sentient what-humans-would-call souls. Her people have evolved past the body.

The Shimmering Area undulates, pleased with her comprehension.

Adina asks if Carl Sagan knows about this and intuits they are not interested in discussing him. Their planet is in danger. She has been sent to Earth to take notes and decide whether they can survive there. One day she will be called to deactivate and return home. The word hovers.

"What is deactivate?"

Adina wakes slick with sweat, blood pounding, as if after a nightmare.

She does not want to inhabit a body with other souls; crowded and intimate, like an internal city. She likes her body's solitude and privacy. Her belly button. Her glasses placed over her one set of eyes. She is grateful to be in her own bed breathing into distinct lungs, to have two personal arms that taper into hands with five digits she wriggles in front of her singular face.

✶

New routine: Hasty, tasteless dinner, clearing the dishes, Adina's mother unhooks the phone from the wall, disappears into her bedroom, succinct thunk of the bedroom door. Adina does her homework at the table. Every so often, tumbling into the room, her mother's equine laugh.

✶

Teachers are for the most part the same with interchangeable parts, like some have ponytails and some wear bangle bracelets. Students can only guess what they do during off-hours. Once in a while a teacher shows up brandishing evidence of outside life like a tan or a non-Philadelphia hairstyle. Mr. Texler is the only male teacher. Toni says he looks like the answer to the assignment *Draw the most average man alive.*

But the students love him because he is the only man they know who is older than their older brothers but not ancient like their fathers. Once they hear the Science teacher call him Thierry, and consult one another with holy eyes. Thierry! The sound of a foreign land in one of Adina's fantasy books.

"Relax," the Science teacher says, fingering the new bracelet the origin of which they've spent hours discussing. "Do you think we don't have first names? We have lives and families like you."

*

Sunday at the flea market, Adina tells Mrs. Goldman about her glasses. Will she be able to see through walls? Possibly. She describes the dance move Amadeo did in the yard at recess as she helps unload boxes of books from the van. Mrs. Goldman listens, arranging books by size on her foldout table. When Adina is finished pantomiming the Roger Rabbit ("Rabbit," she repeats, with pride), the woman plucks a book from her stack and places it into her hands. It is called *Honey*. A miserable girl Adina's age stares out from the paperback's muted cover. Her mother is far down the aisle, chatting with a man selling toilet seats. "I don't have any money right now," she tells Mrs. Goldman, as if she's waiting for a deal to go through.

"Take it," Mrs. Goldman says.

*

In the book, Honey creates a father pie. Comprised of her neighbor, a teacher, the postman, she uses each man as a slice in her understanding of what a father can be. Anyone can be a slice. Some have bigger slices. Some are women. There are endless ways a human can achieve connection if they broaden their perception, Adina reasons. You could make a mother pie or a friend pie.

HOW MANY FATHERS CAN A HUMAN HAVE? reads the reply fax.

Infinite.

✶

Adina's mother flips through a *National Enquirer* and mm-hmms while Adina lists reasons she should be allowed to get her ears pierced.

The other girls have theirs.

The only reason she's not allowed is because her mother doesn't want her to be happy and this is upsetting on various levels, seen and unseen.

It will connect her to the world of adolescence in a way that will allow her to feel more comfortable in middle age.

Her mother shuts the magazine. "When you were born, your earlobes were stuck to the sides of your head."

"What does that have to do with—"

"You have your whole life to wear earrings. Why don't you enjoy your perfect ears while you have them."

The phone rings. It is Lens Kingdom. Adina's glasses have arrived! Her mother gazes at the dishes in the sink, the phone, her slippered feet, the window that blocks an unfair wind-chill. If they don't go immediately, Lens Kingdom will close and they'll have to wait an entire school day.

"Fine," her mother says. "But you're running in."

At Lens Kingdom, a few workers gather behind the counter in an end-of-the-day relaxation Adina won't understand for years. While one of them sorts a file of glasses, Adina raises herself to her toes. Raises and lowers. Finally, the clerk pulls a dark pouch from a folder and slides it over. Adina opens it to reveal the body of her first pair of glasses. Smooth, cardinal red. She slides them on. The room's plastic furniture takes one step closer. She can touch anything. The clerk measures the bridge and declares them a fit. Adina sees every filament in his grass-green eyes. She receives the pamphlet and a polishing cloth.

The VW steams in the parking lot. The sun is gone but Adina can see where it peaches the horizon. The writing on the side of the Fotomat: ONE DAY PHOTO SERVICE. Every wrinkle on her mother's face as she exclaims, "They're so cute!" and leans over to deliver a quick kiss to her bespectacled face. The affection happens quickly, startling both of them.

*

Dominic says, "It's when you put your tongue in someone's mouth."

They are drinking glasses of iced tea at Toni's kitchen table waiting for Adina's mom to pick her up. In the book Mrs. Goldman gave her, everyone is making out and she has asked Toni's brother Dominic what it means.

"And just, like, leave it there?" Toni says.

Dominic is who they go to for answers because unlike Toni's other brothers he speaks to them with patience, even when they list things a tongue can do because he is for sure messing with them. "Here, put my tongue in your mouth. Special delivery! I mean, Dominic! A tongue? What?"

He waits for them to settle, then says, "You each put your tongue into the other's mouth and roll it around."

They are stunned quiet. They don't even notice when he collects their empty glasses and takes them into the kitchen.

*

On a class trip to the planetarium, Adina sits in the hushed auditorium, thinking about making out. She understands she should want to be making out constantly. Her teachers make out, and their parents, and when two girls ask permission to go to the bathroom she assumes it's to make out.

Across the star-shaped auditorium, Toni talks to a girl named Audrey whose calves are shaped like two oranges. Since every student wears the same uniform, the class must base popularity on watches, bracelets, rings, hairstyle, eye and skin color, and calf shape. Adina worries that Toni will become better friends with Audrey and that they will make out together forever into high school and college, a concern that disappears when the show begins. Constellations are projected onto the dome's ceiling. Adina scans for a planet that feels like hers. She is certain she'll recognize it the way she knows when they pass the Parkway's giant golf ball they've almost reached the beach.

"Sit down, Adina," her teacher hisses. "All the way."

At the end of the film, they pan through the universe. A song begins. Made out of choppy, repetitive phrases, sturdy in the middle and fragile around the edges, so soothing she can't believe a human has made it. Every nerve and question she has settles by the organizing effect of its tones. In this moment, Adina understands what making out is. The music, every fuzzy chair in the auditorium, even the metal water fountains have made out with her.

Homesick and wild, she locks herself in a bathroom stall and breathes, trying to keep the song in her memory. When she emerges she can't find the nice teacher so she has to ask the mean one who is wrangling students into line.

"What was that song?"

"I don't know every song on Earth, Adina."

"I know it." It is the voice of Tamara Welsh, a buttoned-up smart kid with no friends. This is the only night Tamara will appear in Adina's notes and faxes though she gives her one of the most important details of her life:

"It's Philip Glass."

*

The next day in the classroom, the students ask what the planetarium jerks are trying to get away with.

"Why were there so many stars?" Amadeo says.

The Science teacher is unprepared for their collective disbelief and does not understand why she is under suspicion. She answers the wrong question. "We don't know how many stars there are."

"But why did they guess so many?"

"They are endless."

Adina knows there are at least 250,000 observable stars in the galaxy. She feels Toni's serious gaze.

Patrick, who everyone assumes will one day head to the NBA, says, "I see the stars every night from my window on the top floor. There are, at most, thirteen."

Amadeo agrees. "I've only counted nine."

"At most," Patrick says.

The Science teacher appears to remember that city kids are wary of anyone asking them to believe things they can't see. "Let's talk about light pollution." She draws a giant chalk circle on the board.

*

That night when her mother retreats into her bedroom with the telephone, Adina knocks and asks for homework help. She does not need help. Her knock goes unanswered. Adina opens the door. Her mother is crouched on the floor in her slip, ivory telephone cord wrapped around her fingertips.

"Adina!" She is shocked. Entering her room is verboten.

"I need homework help!" Adina says with an insistence even she doesn't believe.

Her mother speaks into the phone using her barely controlled-anger voice. "Mark, give me a minute." She places the receiver onto the carpet, ushers Adina out of the room, silently closes the door behind her, ushers her into the family room, leans into her, and whispers, "It is your job to figure out your homework by yourself. If you need help, ask one of your goddamned teachers." Adina can tell there are two contradictory impulses at work, fury and regret. Without apologizing for cursing her mother turns and vanishes into her bedroom, leaving Adina alone with the failure of her only tantrum.

*

Mark: the sound of dust fouling up the microchip of mother to daughter. Residue left on a mirror when you use the crappy glass cleaner. The sound Patrick made when during gym he was gut-hit by a softball.

Pollution is human pressure weighing upon the earth, she faxes, and climbs into bed early.

*

Hair and nails grow and are cut. Limbs lengthen. Daughter asks for a dog and mother says no. Daughter asks well how about pierced ears then IF SHE IS EXPECTED TO LIVE IN THIS DOGLESS HELL. Daughter believes Auto World Flying Man is trying to deliver a vital message only she can understand. Daughter attempts to divine this message while Mother boils chicken. Treasure! Here, Adina? Long buried! Historical secret! Up! No, down! Mother yells dinnertime and everyone will die if chicken gets cold so Adina forgets Flying Man until the next morning when he lies unglamoured on the lawn and walking to the bus stop she is tagged by shame. Mother gets a manicure: clear with white tips. She wraps the phone cord around these delicate crescent moons. Having been invented years before in a Queens basement, hip-hop reaches Northeast Philadelphia, trickling from its teenagers' boom boxes. LL Cool J pins line Toni's jean jacket. Every Tuesday from 5:30 to 7:00 p.m. is grade-school night at United Skates of America. Social groups on wheels flash by, pulsing to Whitney Houston and Bell Biv DeVoe. Daughter clings to the upholstered wall. Muscles appear in her thighs. Her favorite event is when her mother turns to her and says, "Do you like her?" about an actress on TV. Daughter rarely pays attention to the screen, preferring to scribble notes into her copybook. But she focuses on the actress as if she is the most important human before she answers. She wants her mother to value her opinion. She wants her mother to always ask, *What do you think of her? And her? And her?*

Daughter is always digging her pencil out from the couch's creases. Every night the Flying Man reaches for her from his pulpit and every morning he lies dead on the grass.

*

One weekend in the deepest chamber of seventh-grade winter, Adina's mother says they will go to Seafood Shanty to celebrate and when Adina says, Celebrate what, her mother says, Mark's promotion. He has apparently done whatever his job is well enough to receive a reward for which they will eat Alaskan snow crab legs.

Mark: the sound of the neighbor's dog's bark, post-surgery.

*

That Friday night, wearing dresses, Adina and her mother wait for him to arrive. Adina's mother is nervous and over-perfumed.

In the Seafood Shanty lobby, they receive a remote control the host promises will cluck when their table is ready. Adina's mother and Mark discuss a client who will only eat if Mark plays a certain version of "Greensleeves." In the corner aquarium, lobsters click and scrabble over one another, claws confined by thick bands. Adina tries to ignore their ululations of sorrow. She focuses on the bursts of talking in the dining room she can see from where she sits, swinging her good shoes over the lobby's floor. Babies in high chairs thrash their limbs and produce water from their eyes. Bibbed families lift buttery carapaces to their open mouths. The glushing language of the tank: *What will happen to me?* A diner cracks out a hank of meat, boiled rage pink, smothers it in sauce, and holds it aloft to her family, who congratulate her on a fine pull. Adina's glasses bring this agony breath close. She twitches on the plastic seat. Smothered in butter.

Adina comes to with her cheek pressed against the cool aquarium. She resists her mother's attempts to pull her away. The lobsters quibble. The way the waiting families in this dark-paneled vestibule react means she must be making a scene. She and her mother are wet. The hostess clicks a pen in shock. Her mother, eyes pleading, Please let go of the tank. Mark stands away from them as if he is there alone.

*

The silent ride back to the apartment is long enough for Adina's indignation to grow. Every so often Mark drives over a pothole or idles at a red light and her mother apologizes again, but Mark says he gets it, it's hard. Adina doesn't know what he gets or thinks is hard—it could be raising a daughter, eating a meal, or her, specifically. She wants her mother to ask but she stares out her window, crescent-moon fingertips worrying a fake silver chain.

They've almost reached their apartment when Mark realizes the restaurant's buzzer is still in his pocket. It never clucked. He will drop them off, then drive back and return it.

"Come back after and have a drink?" Her mother on the verge of an emotion Adina does not recognize.

He says he will. They reach the row homes and Adina opens her door. "Thank you, Mark."

"It's okay," he says, though she hasn't apologized. "It certainly was an adventure."

Inside, her mother says, "Bed." Her eyes are lined in red.

Adina retreats into her bedroom, torn by twin feelings of righteousness and regret. She hears her mother kick her pumps off—two hard clunks on the floor—and settle onto the front couch, legs drawn underneath her, elbow braced on the cushion top, palm digging into her powdered cheek, staring at the street.

*

A motorcyclist in a television commercial pulls up to a local bank, removes a helmet, and shakes out a head of long hair, revealing themselves to be a woman. *PNC Bank: Expect the Unexpected.*

Motorcyclists, Adina faxes, *are not expected to be women. Women who ride motorcycles do not want you to know they are women. Women,* she faxes, *have long hair.*

*

In the summer before eighth grade, the students at Adina's school trade RUN-DMC tapes and practice dance moves learned from MTV. Music in Adina's Earthtime could best be tracked in the evolution of pants, specifically where the fabric blooms on the leg. Sometime in the 1980s the neighborhood abandons bell-bottoms for Z. Cavaricci jeans and pretend to beatbox.

Everyone in Adina's neighborhood can dance. Everyone knows how to turn their stomachs into a snake and let that snake move up the neck then back down to the ankles. How to figure-eight their hips. Reverse that figure eight. Everyone except Toni. Rare ones like her develop survival methods. At dances they hand out juice or hang coats or go to the bathroom even though they just went.

*

Jen, Jen, Janae, Joy, and Jiselle roam the halls like a school of predatory fish. Their parents sit together at every First Friday mass. The sheer coincidence of the *J* names—as if they were marked at birth to find one another and control the eighth grade.

Jen, Jen, Janae, Joy, and Jiselle's faces are wide, pale, set off by inconsequential noses, skin color from the favored side of the makeup color wheel: corals and palm pink. They wear ponytails at the top of their heads that have been caught edgewise in the looping process, making them look like gorgeous turnips yanked from the ground. These slight and tipsy piles shouldn't work yet the constructions are captivating. Performed sloppiness is a feature of beauty. Adina has memorized every cuffed jean jacket, every pair of carefully untied high-tops, how each of their diamond-shaped calves slips into their slouch socks. She longs to have turnip hair. As it is she's inherited her mother's coarse curls that when pulled through an elastic three and a half times creates a confusion larger than her head.

Toni is unimpressed by how impressed she is. "They look like the answer to the assignment *Draw if milk were people*." Toni's hair is too short for a ponytail. Sometimes she controls it with a headband but most days it falls into her eyes.

When Jen, Jen, Janae, Joy, and Jiselle love something they say it needs to stop. That skirt needs to stop with those sequins. That piece of pizza needs to stop with that crust. Some things they hate also need to stop. She needs to stop with that fugly bracelet. The listener detects from context clues as to which usage is at play. This nuance of grade-school linguistics is challenging to articulate, though Adina tries in several faxes until her superiors reply: STOP.

*

Adina asks her mother if she is beautiful and she says she is unique. She does not say Adina is not beautiful. She does not say the word *beautiful* at all. Adina is adept at drawing lines from her mother's language to hidden meaning. She knows what she is: ugly as sin.

*

One night after dinner, Adina's mother retreats into her bedroom and emerges moments later, cheeks mottled with emotion. She fills a tumbler of water in the kitchen and stands at the counter draining it in a long, faultless take. She refills it and does the same. The half-moon table is piled with books and tea is arranged neatly in the cupboards but something is happening in the room. Adina straightens to meet whatever it is.

After draining a third glass, Adina's mother sits beside her. "So," she says, in her formal voice. "We're probably not going to see Mark anymore. Which is for the best, I guess. He wasn't exactly . . ." A gust of wind shakes the front screens. A storm has threatened for days. Adina guesses: Nice. Handsome. Rich. "Single." Her mother clears tears with two quick swipes of her fingertips. "Anyway. Never date a man who lies. If they lie to one person they'll lie to anyone." Adina is still processing the word single when her mother calls, "Good night," from inside her bedroom, then, "Sorry!" when the door shuts more loudly than she intended.

*

The next morning, Adina's mother frowns over a skillet of eggs. "This weekend," she says, "we are going to plant a goddamned garden."

*

Mother and daughter push a borrowed wheelbarrow filled with earth and rocks down the city street, cars whistling by. In the back lot of the row homes, Adina's mother argues a two-square-foot patch of dirt out of the ground, between the first and second telephone poles, cordoned off by rocks they stole from Pennypack Park.

"Ignore them," she says, when men driving by jeer. "Take this dirt and spread it around. Use this trowel to make sure everything is tilled."

She says she learned how to garden from her father before he died. Mentions of Adina's grandfather are rare. "Was he a gardener?" she asks. But her mother's face closes and she humps the shovel into the ground.

Adina imagines stems. She wants to wake up thinking of plants and run outside in her slippers. Did the bud destroy itself into a flower? Is there color yet? How many? Will they stay?

"Drag the hose from the side of the building," her mother says. "Dig the hole big enough so there's room not only for the roots but for the roots to grow. Water evenly, not too much."

They drive to the nursery and pay for the plants using the new credit card her mother said was for emergencies. "Emergencies take many forms," she says.

They spend the afternoon tilling and planting and watering and arranging, neighbors coming by to admire and offer advice, the hose dancing and pumping into the ground, until the streetlights snap on and her mother's arms are covered in soil plus her forehead where she dragged one hand across her face, leaning against a borrowed rake, surveying what they made. A square of earth ringed in portulaca, daylilies, one basil plant, one oregano, and a rosebush because Adina insisted.

*

Toni and Adina are paging through magazines when Toni mentions she has accepted an offer from Audrey to come over and make slam books and listen to tapes.

Adina is confused. "I've heard her eat a bagel. So much mouth water. She needs to stop with that saliva. We get it. You're chewing."

"I never noticed," Toni says.

"But what does she bring to the table?"

"Chocolate chip cookies," Toni says.

"That does sound good," Adina admits.

"Anyway, nowhere near as much as you do."

Adina asks what a slam book is and Toni explains it's when you write a heading on top of every copybook page like, *When I'm older I want to . . . Hottest guy in school . . . My favorite outfit is . . .* and take turns filling them out.

It's a simple, brilliant idea. Adina heats with jealousy. She wants to give Toni something better than a slam book. She asks, Do you want the world's best lemonade? And Toni says,

Who doesn't? Adina walks to the backyard where her mother holds chive blossoms like pom-poms.

"Do we have any what?"

"Lemonade," Adina says.

Her mother squints at the sun. "Where do you think you live?"

*

At roller skating that Tuesday night, Toni and Audrey hold hands and skate. Adina clings to the upholstered side, heavy with grade-school cologne.

*

The Science teacher makes an offhanded comment that when it gets really cold, Arctic hares turn white. It is meant to be a casual, tranferring-papers-from-one-side-of-the-desk-to-the-other comment.

"Hold up," Amadeo says. "Arctic whats turn what?"

The only biographical information the students know about this teacher is that she spent a lot of time in Alaska and is teaching at their school to prove a point to her parents. She doesn't know what has made her usually disaffected classroom rapt. "Hares?"

The idea of hares changing color is so juicy, even the *J* girls are interested. Mary, who's never spoken in class, not even when Greg dropped a stack of books on her hand, doffs the constraints of her own shyness and says, "They turn what?"

"White?" The Science teacher still does not understand.

"From what?" Mary insists.

"Gray," she says.

The class is comprised of skeptics and lawyers. Patrick tests, "I'm a hare in the Arctic. I'm gray."

The Science teacher appears to weigh possible reasons for this attention, all a variation of, *Just how much are these kids messing with me?* What she doesn't understand is that a hare can be a faraway idea. That it could be one color on Monday and a different one on Tuesday is beyond their limited understanding of not only hares, but color, winter, and days. The students want to know just how much she is messing with them.

"I'm gray," Patrick says again. He has established the baseline circumstance: He is a hare. And, what may or may not be the variable: He is gray. Uncertain how to proceed, his fellow students come to his aid.

"But then the animal"—Adina avoids the word and its manipulative *r*—"gets cold?"

"In the Arctic, temperatures can fall below ten degrees." The Science teacher mistakenly guesses the source of their confusion is related to the weather.

"That's cold," Toni says.

Mary, emboldened by the first answer she's ever given in class, tries a second. "So, I turn white?"

The teacher realizes her students think this naturally occurring method of survival is magic. "Embedded into a hare's DNA are receptors that respond to the animal's awareness of its own safety . . ." She describes self-preservation and protection.

"But why white?" Patrick points out. "What about green or brown?"

Patrick! Perpetually undersold as only a basketball prodigy when he exhibits this smart person's tendency of *but what about?* Yes! Why not brown? The students shift in their seats, eager for the answer.

"Because," she declares, "white is the color! Of snow!"

Of course! There's a ton of snow in the Arctic and the hares want to blend in! The wild is weird and big and far away but they get it! They roll it around on their tongues, *the wild.*They are as thrilled as the teacher to find a subject to care about. Success loosens her storytelling, she twirls slowly, wagging her fingers to pantomime changing. The students who so many mornings seem unincorporated, collect and become a town. They ask all white or part white? What shade, Mary screams! They yell options. Ivory! Bone! Camaraderie allows them to tread into the sacred space of giving an adult a hard time. They begin to speak their language—use their currency—with her. As white as . . . they say, you? There is a hanging moment when all parties feel a form being drawn and whatever she says will determine its shape.

She braces her forehead with her fingertips to stop the laughter but cannot. "As white as me!" she says. "Next autumn, you'll see. I'll turn gray."

They've never experienced lightness from a teacher. The class is such a success that when the bell rings she stands in the doorway congratulating each student one by one. Repeating the funny parts so they can laugh again.

*

During the next class's lesson on photosynthesis, they attempt to find the same levity. But there is nothing interesting about the sun. A window snaps shut. They cannot re-access the tendernesses they've shown one another.

*

Her mother insists on Midnight Mass because it has "the lights and the singing." The student singers step-touch onto the altar, holding paper bags filled with quivering light. "Watch how they lower their chins when they sing," her mother says. She loves the canter and candles. She keeps string lights up in the apartment throughout the year. Tinsel circles the singers' heads, wrists, and hemlines.

Her mother doesn't have many friends. Neighborhood unmarried mothers are under constant suspicion of wanting to nab someone's husband, she says. Spending a minute too long conversing with the men in the family room while the women cleaned up the kitchen was enough to get you talked about.

"As if I'd want them."

Sometimes her mother acts like a single-sailed vessel on a giant sea. Adina anchors her fingertips on her mother's arm. In this moment, listening to the singing, she is not her mother but Térèse Giorno who could have been another in a line of Italian chanteuses if she'd had a different life.

*

A famous saxophone player who has a son in her mother's facility agrees to play their yearly Christmas lunch. The nurses decorate the lobby transoms with plastic holly boughs. The famous saxophonist stands in the center of the room and lifts his instrument to his lips. His son cannot move his limbs or communicate in spoken language. He sits in his wheelchair, angled toward his father playing "O Christmas Tree."

Adina's mother describes the scene to Adina that night while they eat the party's leftover gingersnaps. Adina knows if she shows signs of producing eye water, her mother will stop talking.

"Does he recognize his father?" she says.

"I'm not sure," her mother says. "He's unresponsive to most things. But when his father played he stretched out his arms like this." She raises her arms to shoulder height.

"How can you know?" Adina says. "If he doesn't recognize his father because of disability or because his father never visits?"

"That's the question." Her mother chooses a cookie, then decides against it. "Anyway." Dusts crumbs from her hands. "You tell me that's not dancing."

*

Once in a while Adina's mother goes into the city to have what she calls a "girls' dinner" and leaves Adina with the neighbor, Mrs. Leafhalter. Mrs. Leafhalter is a retired meter maid who unlike other adults doesn't feel responsible for keeping up conversation with a child. Though Mrs. Leafhalter's apartment is smaller than theirs it feels vast and cold. They eat canned soup for dinner then spread blankets over their laps and watch television.

During *Wheel of Fortune,* Mrs. Leafhalter asks Adina if she's ever noticed the different ways a woman can cross her legs. Soft cross is more like propping one over the other, so the calf and foot of the propped leg jut. The hard fold is when thin women cross one leg over the other so they are side by side. Hardest fold—only the flexible can do this—is when you form a hard fold and tuck the foot of the top leg under the calf of the other.

"Ankle cross explains itself," she says and returns to watching *Wheel of Fortune,* where a floral-shirted contestant guesses *R*.

When her mother arrives to walk them back to their apartment, Adina says, "Nice of you to return."

"Leave your mother alone," Mrs. Leafhalter says. "It's good for a woman to let loose once in a while."

Her mother gives her startled laugh. She is not accustomed to encouragement, especially from this woman. Mrs. Leafhalter chuckles, showing a surprising number of teeth, making her appear for a moment overexposed, until she closes her mouth and mother and daughter walk back to their apartment. They pause to consider the garden under the streetlights. Adina's rosebush did so well her mother will plant another. If the complex doesn't like it, she'll remind them she's raising the property value. "Next year, watch," she says. "Cherry tomatoes."

*

Human beings, Adina faxes, *show their teeth when they are happy, in pain, repulsed, disappointed, surprised. Animals in the wild show other animals their teeth (canines) when they want to appear menacing. I will hurt you with these right here.*

*

The homes on Logan Triangle were built above a creek bed a hundred years deep. Every year the silky mud parts and the creek claim another house. Adina and her mother watch alongside the rest of the neighborhood when the last one sinks. Some neighbors drag folding chairs from their homes, hand out beers from six-packs.

The house's left side descends first. Each of its windows shatter as if holding hands. The floors and beams pop. The splintering gas lines and plaster sound like the crack of baseball bats. Adina covers her ears. Sulfur fills her nostrils. A woman sitting on a lounge chair bounces a soft-crossed leg as if the house is taking too long.

Logan Triangle is actually a five-sided, thirty-five-acre piece of land bordered by the Roosevelt Boulevard. Adina is disappointed when the house stops sinking halfway. She has imagined the ground subsuming the house whole, then burping out a silty doorknob. Neighbors finish their beers, snap their chairs shut.

Adina's mother says, "That's all there is to that."

*

Everyone is accepted onto Northeast Philadelphia's Community Swim Team. On Wednesday nights in eighth grade, Adina and the other neighborhood kids drag their goggled, preadolescent bodies up and down the lanes of the hyperchlorinated pool. When the dismayed coach blows the end-of-practice whistle, Adina is the first one in the women's dressing room undressing and re-dressing underneath a well-placed towel, shoving her damp clothes into her duffel bag and running, when she has enough coins, to the vending machines where she pretends to mull but always selects vanilla wafers.

She takes her cookies to the lobby to wait for her ride along with the other damp swimmers. Their school forces them to wear uniforms to neutralize their understanding of class but they can't hide their parents' cars. They know exactly who has what kind of money.

On one particularly cold Wednesday night, Adina begs her mother not to fall asleep and be late picking her up because she wants to be home in time to watch *Cosmos*. One by one, kids identify their parents' cars and run into the cold night swinging their swim caps and goggles, breathing jagged with exertion and chlorine.

Every car turning into the gym's horseshoe-shaped

driveway is not the rotted VW. A lucky kid activates from the cluster of dwindling losers and pushes happily against the thick glass doors. Mom! Dad! The luckiest swimmers are the ones with aggravated older brothers or sisters careening into the lot and laying on their horns.

Eventually, Adina is the only child left. The secretaries, Gail and Gina, throw concerned glances to each other. Adina knows they want to get home to John and Eddie, who every Sunday distribute the church donation baskets. This is not the first time Adina has been forgotten.

"I'm sure she's almost here," she says.

Gail worries the beads of her rosary. Roman Catholics believe a god sent his only son to save the worthy. Adina relates. Only instead of her people sending their only daughter they clipped a part of their toenail and sent it wrapped in a skin suit presenting as a girl. Carl Sagan would say that Gail and Gina believe God is a flowing-bearded white man who sits on a cloud throne, "tallying the fall of every sparrow." There is no evidence for this kind of God and the evidence of science is everywhere: in the papers they rustle to note their annoyance, in the whirring motor of the floor cleaner down the hall that signals end of day.

Gail lifts the phone receiver and shows it to Adina. "You wanna call her?"

Her mother answers on the fourth ring, inexplicably angry. "Where are you?"

"You were supposed to pick me up?" Adina keeps her voice jovial so the secretaries think it's a ritual between them, for her to wait and her mother to forget, that proves how much they love each other, how great their family is.

Adina is a terrible swimmer. She always feels like she's drowning. What are they even practicing for? They never have meets or exhibitions. The secretaries wear sympathetic expressions. She hangs up, too deflated to smile. According to the laws of physics she cannot make it home in time to watch *Cosmos*. And since no one in the complex has a VCR, she has missed it forever.

✶

A neon display in the front of Beautyland proclaims the historic news: John Frieda has mixed together isopropyl myristate, linalool, and *Panax ginseng* root extract to create a serum for curly-headed girls. It is so powerful that even the normally unimpressed cashier, seeing them admiring the vials against the light, calls over, "That stuff is for real." Indeed, her hair, usually a spiral of ditzy half curls, has been managed into a polite shellac.

She says, "This is going to change everything."

✶

At the end of eighth grade, Adina receives an ivory envelope in the mail, her acceptance letter to the private high school where she and Toni will be scholarship kids.

Her mother pours sparkling cider into plastic cups. "I can't believe I have a high schooler," she says.

The high school is a long bus ride to a suburb with detached homes and backyards and pools. Another galaxy. That night under the Auto World neon Adina thinks of those rabbits in the Arctic. The pristine color waiting beneath their coats like secret royalty.

*

Mrs. Leafhalter will spend the summer in a Wildwood bungalow two blocks from the beach and owned by her niece who won't be there. Would Adina like to join Mrs. Leafhalter for the month of July to give her hardworking mother a break? Even though Adina can barely survive a night in that woman's cold apartment? The prospect of being near the beach is mildly interesting though she feels a scraping sensation when she imagines leaving Toni and her fax machine. Her mother's apparent glee at the prospect feels unfair.

"No thank you," Adina says.

The question had been a formality. She has already been promised to the house in Wildwood. Her mother offers a list of soothing details. Toni's brother Dominic will be there too, working in a Fotomat and living with a school friend's family. Adina will get to stay in a real-life bungalow like the detectives in her Nancy Drew books. She will get to experience a non-urban environment.

*

In July, she and her mother drive to the shore without stopping at McDonald's but when they reach the bungalow, they idle.

"I've never been without you," her mother says. "For even a night."

Adina is confused. Her mother forced her into the trip but is balking. "Are we going in?"

"Give me a minute." Her mother scans the immaculate garden border and quaint mailbox amid the street of run-down rentals. Layers of small patios dot the motels. On each one, an aproned man pokes meat on a grill. Vacation, Adina thinks.

✶

Adina and her mother sit at Mrs. Leafhalter's kitchen table, eating deli sandwiches. Bungalow has turned out to mean tiny house; a square family room attached to the kitchen, Mrs. Leafhalter's bedroom upstairs, a front porch where Adina will sleep on a pullout couch. Mrs. Leafhalter tells Adina she can do whatever she wants as long as she's not "loitering inside" all day. There's the boardwalk and beach and a township park a few streets away where she can rent a bike.

"Bikes!" her mother says.

Mrs. Leafhalter's sound is eck, one of disgusted incredulity, but it doesn't seem like she'll care what Adina does, which is promising.

"The parkway was trafficky, which is the reason we're late."

"Of course it was! You left at noon!"

"There was an accident, a real pileup."

"People behind the wheel are maniacs!"

Every pleasantry attacked, her mother comments on the surroundings. A butter dish lying on the windowsill. "You leave your butter out," she says.

Eck, Mrs. Leafhalter says, "Of course I do! Hard butter tears the bread!" It is a fact and an accusation that cues her mother to stand and remark on the traffic.

"You beach girls are going to have so much fun." Her optimistic tone is unconvincing. Adina walks her mother to the car. Ocean air has murdered whatever grass survived June.

"Hard butter tears the bread," her mother says to make Adina smile. "Read your books. I'll call every Monday and Friday."

"Are you going to stop at McDonald's?" Adina says. The idea of her mother stopping without her makes her throat feel leaden.

"No McDonald's until Adina comes home. You'll get a tan," her mother says. "You'll get some ocean in your hair," but Adina is no longer listening. She's watching a group of girls strut down the boardwalk ramp toward them, each of their matching jean jackets embroidered with an outlandish cursive *J*.

*

Adina is not allowed inside the bungalow during the day so she walks the boardwalk, bouncing a tennis ball. She pretends to be practicing for an important dance or she browses gag T-shirts in Wildwood Outfitters. Most involve feeling saddled by your wife, being over the hill, wanting to do nothing but golf. Every afternoon she walks to the Acme parking lot and waits for Dominic to finish his Fotomat shift.

He won't let her look at other people's photographs. "Privacy is sacred," he says. He's a rarity in the neighborhood, a sixteen-year-old boy who doesn't like cars. He wears giant syrup-colored sunglasses and has thick, curly hair he tries to iron straight like the boys who skateboard in the gas station parking lot. It never works, so the top is flat and the sides spring out like his head is sitting between two black clouds. Now that Adina has John Frieda's magic serum, her hair is shiny and lifeless. Not as well calibrated as the *J* girls', whose ponytails are full, bangs sprayed into sublime orbs.

Dominic chats with families picking up their vacation photos, saying things like, "You can take that to the bank," or "Keep your nose clean," things that don't mean anything except, here we are, having a day.

"You're like a sixty-five-year-old man," Adina says, and he says she's too young to know sixty-five isn't old. But she says she knows it's ancient because it's how old Mrs. Leafhalter is.

*

On days when she doesn't play cards at the airport Mrs. Leafhalter rocks on the front porch, commenting on passersby and flattening flies with a swatter. At night this porch becomes Adina's bedroom. There is a moss-green compact television she is allowed to watch if she keeps the volume low. She reads down a stack of library books, boys adventuring through the woods, girls supporting them, every so often interrupted by the sharp bleat against linoleum as another fly dies and Mrs. Leafhalter yells, "Got you!"

*

Every night Adina sleeps on a cot and except for the occasional trembling bass from the cars speeding toward a parkway shortcut, Adina sleeps well. She watches the moss-green television. She takes notes on the *J* girls' glimmering two-pieces to fax her superiors when she returns home. She imagines her mother circling coupons in her slip. She doesn't understand why she always has to be removed in order for her mother to breathe.

⁎

A wonder period of dream visits begins, unsettling and tender. Every morning, Adina wakes with the sensation of having fallen down a well that expanded to an infinite space where she moved within a canopy of souls. Every morning she is relieved to have only one body. She likes being the only her in the room. Her solo human body gives her enough to think about. Her hips slope. Her breasts arrive. B cups.

⁎

Every Monday and Friday afternoon, Adina leans against the kitchen doorframe and lists what she did that week to her mother over the phone. The niece is present in fridge photos. As far as Adina can tell, she is a smiling woman who wears sweater sets embroidered with decorative animals. Her mother is only an hour and a half up the parkway but feels as far away as Neptune. Her mother's voice makes Adina feel lonelier than when she doesn't hear it. She tries to be out when she calls.

*

Adina is in the back of Wildwood Outfitters reading a display of alcohol-related sweatshirts when the school of jacketed, ponytailed *J* girls approaches.

"You dance, right?"

Janae's ability to command respect is related to how high she's able to tease her bangs. She informs Adina that a local girl named Jessica had to drop out because her stepmother or real mother or father's girlfriend sprained her ankle doing aerobics so the whole family had to return to the city. Jen says it's a shame because Jessica could do an aerial, the worm, and the splits both ways. An aerial, the worm, and the splits both ways: No one has ever been as glamorous as Jessica inside Adina's imagination.

She says, "Yeah, I dance," and Janae says, "Do you know the song 'The Choice Is Yours'?"

If she says no, it will dispel the dream that is Jen, Jen, Janae, Joy, and Jiselle arranged like stars among the circular racks of T-shirts that proclaim *Heaven doesn't want me—Hell's afraid I'll take over,* waiting for her to answer.

"Listen to it tonight," Janae says. "And be at my house tomorrow."

Adina says, "I'm already there," and immediately regrets it.

Janae appears to be regretting it too, so Adina back walks out of the aggressively lit store. She does not have to ask where

Janae lives, she has memorized her awning, green with dark blue slats. Her admittance into grade-school royalty will be due to the puny ankles of someone who might be Jessica's stepmother.

*

Adina enjoys her first experience of being neglected. She leaves the house after dark and sits in the backyard. She can't see the stars or hear the ocean. But it is enough to be outside later than she has ever been. It is enough to sit on the damp lawn with her headphones plugged in, listening to "The Choice Is Yours" on repeat.

The bungalow's porch has flies and so-so ventilation but Adina loves the compact television set. Every night she watches Johnny Carson. One night, they show a rebroadcast of a Carl Sagan interview. Pinstripe suit, cornsilk hair, copper voice.

CARL SAGAN: Think of the arrogance of assuming that out of one hundred billion stars in the galaxy that ours is the only one that has an inhabited planet.

JOHNNY CARSON: Somebody said that if you were going to create a perfect living thing you wouldn't have two ears over here on either side, you'd have something coming out of the top of your head to hear sound all around.

CARL SAGAN: There's no question that we are the way we are because of the long evolutionary heritage. After all, our ancestors walked on four legs.

*

The following afternoon, Jen, Jen, Janae, Joy, and Jiselle show Adina the dance. Adina keeps her expression steady, points out where the formation is lopsided. Janae nods and sends Jiselle to the back of the formation.

The girls drink lemonade and Janae speaks professionally. They've agreed to allow Adina to dance with them for the Kaboom contest the following week. Winners get boardwalk passes that include all three piers and the Zorgons, the oversize plastic balls you can walk inside. Adina has watched them silently crossing the sand like exultations of wonder.

Kaboom is an all-ages club in the basement of the diner. On weekends it is only for adults but on Monday evenings they host a teen and preteen dance party.

"After the contest," Janae says, "who knows?" If Adina performs well, maybe their connection will continue when they return to where they actually live, near the sinking homes of Logan Triangle.

"What about Jessica?" Adina says.

"I'll figure it out," Janae says. Adina will hear this phrase's firm, nonchalant rhythm for the rest of her life. *I'll figure it out.*

The girls hit their first poses and Jen restarts "The Choice Is Yours." When they reach the last formation, timed to the talking part, *Engine, Engine, Number Nine / On the New York transit line / If my train goes off the track*—what Janae calls "the ruffle" begins—a thrill courses through their bodies that explodes on: *Pick it up! Pick it up! Pick it up!* When

Adina pumps her fist and figure-eights that's everyone's cue to leap into their final sequence, a heaving, pumping circle with Janae in front, beats around until she's in front again, hitting her pose, hand on knee, Joy and Jen flanking her, then Jiselle and the other Jen, then Adina. The final attitude. Adina thinks of the artist's rendering of the Big Bang in her biology textbook. She is made of stardust. Whatever scrap of Lower Township dance troupe tries to step will fail.

"Don't forget to wear a ponytail with a purple scrunchie," Janae says. "If we win, I hold the passes." She corrects herself, "When we win."

*

Adina's mother calls and she listens to Mrs. Leafhalter bark questions at her in the kitchen. In one week, the day after the dance contest, she will arrive to take Adina home to spend August in the hot, cramped city. *What time will you be here? Will you want lunch? You'd better leave early.* Adulthood seems like a yearslong equation to beat traffic.

Adina's mother tells her that her garden has produced string beans and she ran into Toni at the Shop & Save. "She's sad," she says. "She misses you. Her mother is sick again . . ."

Adina makes encouraging listening sounds though she is mentally running the final formation. During his interview with Carl Sagan, Johnny Carson says that every radio show ever recorded bounces into space forever. Adina wonders if the same is true for phone calls, if on a remote exoplanet an extraterrestrial culture is listening to her mother drone on about her planting. Carrots, pumpkins, watercress if it can grow in the city. *What is a carrot*, they might wonder. *Why is this human so concerned about it?*

Her mother's voice tumbles endlessly into space: You okay, little girl?

Adina hangs up, slips through the back door, and walks to the boardwalk to practice her steps. On Monday night Amadeo will see her dance, then they will climb into a Zorgon together and silently roll over packed sand. She'll laugh in slow motion, it will come out in bubbles, Ha (time passes) ha (time passes) ha . . . They will collide against each other again and again and it won't even hurt.

*

Saturday afternoon, hours before the dance contest, the boardwalk tests a new roller coaster. It is the white-spiraled steel inverted coaster pictured on the parkway billboards (*50 miles per hour of freedom!*) expected to open the following summer. Adina and Dominic watch them belt in six sandbags the exact heft and weight of a family: Mom, Dad, Grandmom, two kids, maybe the kid has brought a friend. No, Adina thinks, Grandmom would be waiting at the base holding everyone's coats.

The car jacks up the first ascension, an incline so steep it appears to go backward. Then an upside-down loop, then another, steeper ascension. Back-to-back spirals over the bank of barking stations and games of skill. Past the wide beige strip of sand, freckled with bright umbrellas and towels.

Dominic has delivered a letter from Toni that holds a redacted quality. Adina asks a series of clarifying questions as the sun dies in the giant frames of his sunglasses. His answers are variations of: She and Audrey had a fight. She doesn't want to talk about it.

The boys who skateboard in the gas station parking lot hang against the gate, watching the promo run. They point out where, if they were the ones riding, the one called Dollar Bill would drop to his death. They detail how his ears would explode, the color of his blood bursting over the metal then the crowd, the sound it would make when his skull collided against the concrete.

Dollar Bill's friends perceive him as weak, or maybe they just had to pick someone. Regardless, he's shaken. Adina can tell by the way he's constructing alternative outcomes. Okay, he'll fall but then he'll be like—he does a curlicue to kick himself off the ground. His friends aren't buying. The talk turns to dancing. When Kimberly wore that tight green dress. With those earrings. The tallest boy does her walk.

Adina shows Dominic the dance's final formation. He watches without smiling but claps at the end.

"If we win," she says, "I get to join their crew for good and they'll give me a *J* name."

He says, "You know those girls are phonies, right?"

Adina feels pain near her breastplate—loyalty for her dance crew. She tells him he doesn't know them and he says he knows them all right.

The sandbag family has cleared the first two inclines and are nearing the biggest loop. The possibility of danger brings the boys, Adina, and Dominic, back to the gate. The family makes it.

"Damn," says the tall boy, disappointed.

"*J* is for jealous," Adina says.

"*J* is for juvenile nonsense," Dominic says.

"*J* is for jerk wad," she says. A passing car drives across his sunglasses.

They walk back to Mrs. Leafhalter's house, trading what *J* is for.

*

Kaboom smells like cardboard and grilled cheese. The *J* girls and Adina smell like cardboard and grilled cheese. They clasp one each from a table of pinkish, nonalcoholic drinks and lean against the bar fronting as hard as they can. Jen, Jen, Janae, Joy, Jiselle, and Adina, who's having trouble getting her shoulders not to creep up toward her ears but other than that appears like a normal human girl.

Amadeo and his boys enter the club like princes and she is introduced as the new dancer.

"What's your *J* name?" Amadeo says.

"She'll get a *J* name later," Janae says. "If it works out."

Amadeo's gaze seems unaffected by the years of school they've spent together, years she spent quiet and scribbling at her desk. Adina experiences the clean slate of vacation. She can be popular here, she can fit in with an elegant crowd. His brother's car is parked near the boards out back, Amadeo says, does she want to see it?

"Contest starts in half an hour," Janae says, but signs off with a wave of her hand. The boys make siren sounds as they leave.

They're almost out of the club when Janae grabs her jacket cuff.

"Listen," she says. "Whatever he wants you to do, do it."

"We're only going to see his brother's car," Adina says.

"Don't be a dumb one. I'm looking out for you."

Adina is thrilled. This must mean she's in. Janae stiffens when Adina hugs her, waits it out.

*

Amadeo and Adina reach his brother's car parked in the alley, her heart in what feels like the final stages of arrest. He opens the door and says, what's up, to her.

The car is nothing special, but Adina intuits that she's supposed to be wowed. "Cool," she says.

"It's all right." He downplays. This is faux humility. He wants her to fawn, give him reasons to stay unaffected.

She hears the scream of rides in the distance, the metal chirp of diner noise. "Should we get in?"

"Whoa." He feigns protest. "Impatient?"

"I thought that's what we were doing."

"It's okay. You wanna see the upholstery. I get it."

Inside the car, he leans over and presses his lips against hers. She closes her eyes. He pushes his tongue into her mouth. The thought occurs to her as if lowered on strings: This is making out. But her interest is muted, more scientific than whatever passion compels him to pull a lever that makes his seat descend, startling both of them. His smoothness malfunctions.

"Climb on top of me," he says.

Adina has seen this position in a beauty magazine diagram. She swings her leg over his lap and positions herself on top of him. She has never been this close to a boy or anyone. His pocked cheeks, stained teeth, fish-green skin. He grinds his hips into her. Is this something? Adina waits for overwhelming feeling. For a moment, another boy's face is transposed onto his and she worries she has entered the car with a stranger. But he emits a manufactured, pained sound and his features resolve into the Amadeo she has spent years sitting beside in her imagination, who wants to hear about everything she's reading. His features become clear. She doesn't want to make out with him. She wants him to be her friend.

"Know what would be more fun?" He pushes her against the steering wheel, clearing a space to unzip his jeans. Adina is still processing the shove when his thing appears. Half erect. Flesh-colored mushroom with a dark cap. The first time she's seen one. It seems sentient. Definitely malevolent. She can tell because it's mapped with indigo veins that want out. Amadeo's eyes are expectant and bright. He wants her to do something with it.

"Look at this," he says, surprised. As if she didn't watch him fish it out of his underwear. "You want to give him a little kiss?"

The car fills with her laughter. "Him?"

His face registers shock, then changes to sinister. He pulls himself in, zips, throws the door open and lifts her out. He gets out after her, closes and locks the door. She trails him into the club where he abruptly does not know her. The club is his mood and displeasure. Her footing slips against the soda-slick stairs. Amadeo disappears into the crowd, then reappears near the stage, as if he's swum the entire room underwater. He leans into his friends and Janae, his posture jocular and teasing, relaying the story. Janae listens, tracing the line of her shoulder with a red-tipped nail. Her expression sharpens. Amadeo releases his grip on the group. Janae scans the crowd until her gaze lands on Adina. As if rehearsed, Jen, Joy, Jiselle, and the other Jen collect around her so by the time they reach Adina they are in formation.

Janae says they don't need her for the dance after all. "If I were you, I'd leave. This was a trial anyway." If the other *J* girls are confused, they don't show it. They must remain quiet to keep their status.

The Lower Township dance troupe stretches against the wall wearing yellow leg warmers that connect to Adina's falling heart. "But the contest," she says. "You need six." She can't remove the pleading tone from her voice.

"We'll figure it out," Janae says.

Adina senses a new person standing behind her and turns to find Dominic. "Are you okay?"

The prestige of his older age is canceled by his lichen of mustache and Michael Stipe T-shirt. The *J* girls huff and sigh, annoyed. Adina feels equal amounts of shame and relief. The *J* girls make devastating shapes with their postures as they turn away. The deejay announces the start of the contest. Dominic follows Adina out of the club amid a throng of cheering. The bass rattles the floorboards. Adina hopes to hear a voice or a clattering of heels, someone running after her.

How could she have known what a girl's laughter does to a boy?

If she believed the boardwalk T-shirts, a woman was a ball

or chain, someone stupid you're with, someone to lie to so a man can drink beer. If she believed television fathers, women were a constant pain, wanting red roses or a nice dinner out. If she learned how to be a girl from songs, it was worse. If she learned from other girls, worse still.

The bass notes of "The Choice Is Yours" begin, sounds that had until that moment filled her body with so much energy she thought she'd faint. She walks faster so she won't have to bear the entry of the tinny, female voices promising, *Here we go, yo, here we go*, the looping *This or that*, the *try* or *don't worry* or *you can't intervene*, divine statements that beat her around the circle in double time with something extra in her body, for once, abundance. The song has flipped on her—she's the one left without choices, *violated* and *decepticated*, no one running after her, no one calling her back.

*

Adina and Dominic reach the part of the boardwalk where everything is closed except a vendor selling watermelon slices and ice cream. The sun has set but throws light on the older girls with teased hair who sit on the railing like exotic birds. *Happy Birthday!* a man yells into a pay phone. A beach sprinkler shakes water onto the sand but there are no children.

Dominic has spoken with Toni and whatever went down between her and Audrey happened while swimming. "Toni was kicked out of Audrey's swim club or Audrey was? Or they got into a fight while swimming? Whatever it was made Audrey's father call my mom. She's furious. Toni is grounded. Nobody's talking. You'll have a lot of catching up to do."

They descend the stairs to the street. A family sits on a bench eating watermelon. Mom, Dad, son, and a baby in a stroller. Adina thinks of the roller coaster sandbags the exact shape and heft of a typical family. Even heartbroken, she takes notes.

The boy lifts his watermelon slice, pretending he will throw it into the dirt.

"Don't," his mother warns.

His father, chewing, looks over.

The warning endears the dirt to the boy even more. He tests the rind in his hand. Adina knows he wants to feel it leave his fingertips and see it course through space.

He hurls it, face neon with rapture. It thuds against the ground and sends a flower of sand into the air.

The father lunges behind the mother and knuckles the boy in the face. The boy yelps. The mother is thrown forward into the dirt, catching herself on her palms. The baby in the stroller gives its legs a shake.

"Go get it," the father tells the mother.

She rubs her knee where it collided against the ground.

"Pick it up."

She picks up the slice, half covered in dust. Don't even think about shaking off the extra. The father takes it and hands it to his son.

"Eat it."

The boy stares at his father from the surprised place before tears. The father turns a string of insults onto the mother before swiveling back to the boy who wants to be the most forgotten thing in the world.

The father presses the dirt-caked rind into the boy's face. "Go on."

The boy is crying.

The father says it again, louder. So anyone listening knows he is a good father. A block away, Adina and Dominic hear him.

Adina longs for her superiors to show up in their glorious spaceships and rescue her from shame. But the clouds remain unparted by celestial arrivals, and her mother is in the city, working.

✶

Three hundred forty miles above their sorry melons, the new Hubble telescope clicks and cruises in orbit, five miles a minute, the weight of two elephants, noticing, noticing, the birth and death of stars. Its bus-size eye can even observe the death of Adina's social life, an event that looks like a human girl walking "home," the salmon-colored fabric of her low-crotched pants dangling near the ground.

Maybe 3.7 billion miles into its own lonesome journey, her sibling Voyager 1 will turn its sympathy toward her.

The Golden Record does not contain an image of five ponytailed dancers hitting their starting pose. There is no image of a girl being walked home by her best friend's brother after seeing her first penis, or a mother, upset after another bad date, reheating that morning's coffee, or an older woman glaring at a freshly killed fly on her swatter like she's mad at it for dying.

Adina longs to do homework on the half-moon table while

the Flying Man rages outside. When she gets home, she will devote herself to her notes. No more dancing. No more wanting to be popular. She will fax twice a day. *Homework. Is Work. You Do at Home.* Her superiors will fax THESE OBSERVATIONS ARE SIMPLE BUT USEFUL. Better: She will fax that being physically present in one place while your mind is in another is loneliness. Loneliness can make you hang with phonies to distract yourself. Loneliness can make you send a ratty record into space. Her superiors will fax YOU HAVE CROSSED AN IMPORTANT THRESHOLD IN YOUR TRAINING. They will fax YOU ARE THE BEST HUMAN. SO MUCH BETTER THAN THOSE *J* GIRL SLUT-BAGS. They will fax WE ARE PROUD OF YOU.

This is the first time Adina has been away from the row home across from Auto World yet she knows exactly what her mother would say about the dance contest, the *J* girls, Amadeo, even this father pressing a filthy fruit rind into his son's cheek.

If he'll do that in public, what do you think he's like at home?

*

The only time Adina walks in a Zorgon that summer is with Dominic. He makes ghost noises as she tries to keep a serious face. It is more difficult to balance on the sand than she expected and not as much fun. She doesn't even take notes.

Dominic allows her to look through one set of developed prints. A family holds buckets of sand on the beach. A lopsided sandcastle. A family eats pancakes. A family holds a tiny fish and pretends to be awed. Their beaming faces upset Adina. She abandons the photos before she's halfway through.

"It's okay to be homesick," Dominic says.

*

Finally, the VW arrives, her mother inside, tan and cheerful. Adina runs across the lawn, throws her suitcase onto the back seat.

"You want to hit the beach one last time, little girl?"

Adina says, "Home."

Her mother drives north to the city. Adina chatters, relief unspooling her, until her mother says, "You've been storing up, huh?" When they cross the bridge into the city, Adina is surprised to see people in summer clothes holding wicker pocketbooks, carrying children, and eating water ice. Philadelphia had its own summer, even though her mother promised in more than one phone call that it was dead and dry and choking and nothing whatsoever was happening in her absence. A benevolent glow hovers over the pretzel vendors and the nothing space between the Kensington fields and the warehouses. Even Auto World shines. What is this heat in her throat, this urge to cry? It must be the opposite of homesickness, to return home to find it more beautiful, to return and still feel distance.

In the daughter's absence, the mother's garden has expanded past the second telephone pole. There is a bright square of basil, oregano, two kinds of mint—regular and lemon. Her mother points to each plant and explains how it could have done better—though, she hastens to add, each did the best it could. She is in a disciplinary relationship with the cherry tomatoes. Next year she will buy them a rolling planter so they can follow the sun.

"It was a mistake to keep them in shade. They love heat," she says. "They're like tiny Adinas."

*

Human beings, Adina faxes, *did not think their lives were challenging enough so they invented roller coasters. A roller coaster is a series of problems on a steel track. Upon encountering real problems, human beings compare their lives to riding a roller coaster, even though they invented roller coasters to be fun things to do on their days off.*

*

Television is off-limits at Adina's house so she spends most of August watching at Toni's. Toni is distant, says she doesn't like television, so Adina watches with Dominic. Dominic calls it their research and it has already produced several unshakable opinions. When the lawyer their mother is dating—a partner in the firm where she clerks—gifts them a VCR, they enter the kingdom of video rental stores.

Adina and Dominic arguing in the narrow aisles of Reel to Reel. Toni scowling on her bike before pedaling away to find someone who won't answer every question with a quote from *Elvira: Mistress of the Dark*, a film that is—Adina and Dominic agree—better than the original. Toni is not ready to talk about what happened with Audrey.

Adina and Dominic watch movie after movie. Adina sends fax after fax.

One afternoon they are watching their fourth movie when Matteo passes, throwing a ball to himself. "You should go outside like human beings and stop being weirdo vampires."

Dominic's gaze remains on the screen. "We don't have the same interests as you."

✶

Television Opinion #1: Shows should have memory.

In *Three's Company*, for example, a sitcom about a straight man pretending to be gay so he can skirt the rules against men living with women, Jack Tripper never references the other jobs he's had. Or that he and his best friend Larry woo girls at the Regal Beagle the same way every week. Jack Tripper's goldfish mind resets at the end of every half hour.

Adina prefers Columbo, the television detective who references cases he solved the year before, rewarding her time and loyalty.

✶

Television Opinion #2: Shows should have theme songs. On the long side, so Adina and Dominic have time to get psyched.

✶

Adina faxes her superiors who respond with replies that can generously be considered lukewarm.

LESS ABOUT HUMAN TELEVISION.

Her mother expresses similar sentiments, less subtly. "Christ, Adina, enough about *Three's* goddamned *Company.*"

✶

One holy, airless August afternoon, Adina and Dominic are stunned silent by the performance of Daniel Day-Lewis in *My Left Foot.* Dominic, tears basting his face, turns to Adina.

"There will never be a finer actor."

✶

Things I've learned about extraterrestrials from American movies:

They are small, separate, and alone.
They usually land in American suburbs and are found by a human going through a hard time.
Suburban Americans enjoy dressing them in ridiculous clothing.
At first, suburban Americans like the alien and enlist them in group activities.
If the alien exhibits their own desires, the suburban Americans feel betrayed.
Eventually, suburban Americans cause the alien pain.
Eventually, the alien ends up alone again.
Inevitably, the alien must go home.

*

Adina lies in bed trying to figure out a way she can know everyone on Planet Earth. America is easy, she can drive through it. She will send a letter to one person in every country and they can tell their friends and she can know everyone by association. But language is a problem and she doesn't know every country's name and she gets panicky and red-eyed about it. She wants to ask her superiors but her night lessons have stopped as if to echo summer vacation. She lies awake, longing for her people.

Carl Sagan's writings guarantee her longing is moot. Her people are likely so far advanced beyond human comprehension that they have tesseracted and reversed causality. Their time would not be points on a line but gestures containing past present future. To lie awake being sad was to mourn an event that perhaps had not happened yet or had happened eons before. Galactically speaking, Adina peers down an endless road for any sign of a car. Hoping for dust or an imperceptible disturbance in the gravel. There is no disturbance and, worse: She doesn't know how she relates to her people temporally. Her sadness thrown against the expanse cannot find purchase. Where are you? Pick me up. Get me out of here. She listens to every Philip Glass tape she owns, feeling futile and abject and dangerous and woeful and bratty.

Adina has become an American teenager.

MASSIVE STAR

(SCHOOL)

It is 1991 and the low-crotched-jeans craze has relented to a tighter, leaner cut that allows room for chunky boots. The first exoplanets are discovered orbiting PSR B1257 + 12 b, a pulsar in the constellation Virgo. A pulsar is a rapidly spinning corpse of an exploded star. Exoplanets are planets outside a solar system. In August, Adina, Toni, and Dominic park in front of a formidable suburban high school eating bagels from Adina's mother and watching gray-jumpered women read thick books. On regular days Adina and Toni will take the school-provided bus but since this is the first day of freshman year Dominic has driven them. The bagels are soggy from being wrapped in tinfoil too soon after toasting. The gray-jumpered women tilt their heads to the sky, so relaxed on the school's wide meadow it is as if they are in their own homes. They are replicas of those pictured on the orientation binder that insisted its students are no longer little girls but Young Women. Little girls carry plastic toys, gummed with their saliva. Young Women carry stacks of marginalia-filled notebooks. Dominic, Adina, and Toni eat soggy bagels and watch them in silence.

The high school is arranged on a collection of hills. On one, delicate steps lead to a phalanx of tennis courts. On another, a large steel statue in the shape of the school's mascot, an indecipherable twist of iron that is supposed to signify loyalty. The modern statue, an idea of wingspread, has a terrifying effect on Adina. This plus the unhurried nature of these young women makes eating her bagel impossible. The school sits on the third hill, ranch-style, its generous front doors thrown open to welcome the freshman class.

A bell rings. Adina and Toni exchange farewell shoulder punches with Dominic.

"Don't beep when you drive away," Toni warns.

The sound of his horn startles the young women streaming toward the front doors.

Adina at thirteen is an underweight, bucktoothed, nearsighted extraterrestrial with an aversion to mouth noises. Her democratic black hair contains every possibility: wavy, curly, straight. It hovers in, over, and around her small face. She had hoped one of the exoplanets was hers, so she could finally point to her hometown on a map. But the planets, bombarded by the dead star's radiation, cannot support life. She hopes this school will be a kind of home, that it will welcome her opinions on film and television, and reward close questioning. The way that during the "lost lecture" Carl Sagan answered the student who asked, "Do you believe in God?" by saying, "What do you mean when you use the word God?"

*

Most of the freshmen have alumnae mothers and aunts so they arrive already knowing the school's customs. One of them, a squat blonde with a dyed-blue ponytail, sings "Castle on a Cloud" from *Les Misérables* during the morning welcome assembly. Later, she stands in front of the first-year lockers and explains the balloon ritual to Adina, Toni, and a few other newbies. The school store sells items like mini staplers, pens, and helium balloons. When it's a young woman's birthday, their friends buy them balloons. "Isn't it great?" she says.

Her name is Dakota and she refers to the ritual as if it is about camaraderie but Adina intuits it is a way to deduce popularity. Adina's Earth birthday is September. There won't be enough time to make friends. She's not like Toni who impresses everyone with a quick comeback. Toni has joined the school newspaper where she already manages two other freshmen. They've told her about this girl with the dyed-blue hair. How her mother donated a piano to the school's theater department, how she's destined for Broadway. Adina loves balloons, alone or in aggregate. She will save money to avoid the humiliation of no balloons or, worse, only a few. She will buy herself a respectable, pride-saving amount. She imagines holding a fistful of strings. It is impossible to be unhappy while holding a bouquet of balloons.

✶

That evening, Adina goes to sleep and "wakes" inside the Night Classroom, surrounded by mirthful light. It has been months since her superiors have visited and she is happy to see the Shimmering Area, a relief she associates with family.

The Night Classroom has changed. She is seated at the end of a long sharp table whose edges reach into the distance to a place she cannot see. She is surprised when a figure emerges from within the shimmering. A part meant to represent the whole, she intuits they will be her new mentor. It is a focused pairing based on her particular needs. As she attends high school on Earth during the day, she will be in immersive study with this mentor at night.

The figure flashes, the human equivalent of hello. She intuits the name Solomon, a king's name from her Earth lessons. She likes its three *o*'s and sturdy consonants. This sound is as good as any to refer to them. Solomon becomes more defined amid the shimmering, until it stops somewhere between a person and an entity. Not fully dispersed from the group, not fully group.

They want to "discuss" sound. Most humans believe that space is silent. Because there is no air, sound can't travel. But sound is produced in space at too low a frequency for human ears. For everyone else, space makes a racket.

Planet Cricket Rice is silent. They don't "speak" or "yell" or produce radio waves. Even the equivalent of music is intuited. A concert in the park on Planet Cricket Rice would look like people sitting quietly on a stage. Only there would be no people, chairs, or stage. The intention would not involve hearing. Everything on Earth: rain, construction; and some things not on Earth: the sun and clouds, is an alchemy of sound and feeling, a hum, more akin to thought. This "hearing" can extend into an object's interior, to very far away, to intent, to objects that don't produce what humans believe to be sound. Every year she is alive, Adina cultivates the ability. Ideally it will become distinguished and act as if independently, an ability she can cast and reel like fly fishermen do a line.

*

Adina's Italian class drags crude understandings of declensions through the enigmatic lessons of *The Little Prince* while Professoressa Gillespie taps on her desk with a ruler. Professoressa Gillespie is an unimposing woman with a distinctive collection of handbags, the reveal of which every afternoon is the class's only joy. In the book, a royal boy from a planet the size of a house travels the universe seeking assistance for his vulnerable rose. Along the way he meets characters named for their chief characteristics: the king, the lamplighter, the geographer. He finally finds help in the character of the pilot, who has crash-landed in the middle of the desert.

Adina struggles to remember each noun's gender and that the double consonant requires what Professoressa calls "molti muscoli."

"Why is the situation dire for the pilot?" Professoressa says in Italian.

Adina raises her hand. "No agua."

"Aqua?" Professoressa says, pretending to drink a glass of it.

"Water," Adina says in English.

Professoressa says, "Wooder?"

The other students titter.

Adina corrects herself. "Water."

*

Adina and Toni spend two hours a day on the bus. They do their homework, sleep, stare out the window at the suburbs dashing by. During study period, the Young Women spread their books around the large library tables. Since the bus is their homework time, Adina and Toni draw and chat. The library's windows overlook the tennis courts and they study amid the pleasant thwock of volleys and returns.

Dakota asks to join their table. "Do you hear ambulances a lot where you live?"

"All the time," Toni says. "Nothing but ambulances." Toni does not share Adina's desire to belong. Her accent has deepened. She's told everyone their neighborhood is filled with mafia.

"How did you learn to sing like that?" Adina says.

Dakota fidgets. "I've been taking lessons forever."

"You're good," Toni says. "I like the way your voice goes . . ." She mimics Dakota's vibrato. The girls laugh.

"I don't have the range of an opera singer." Dakota's voice is sober. "So I won't get a scholarship to college." She sounds as if she is reading from an index card. Someone has told her this more than once. The librarian calls from behind her desk. "Save the talking for the discotheque."

Dakota says, "Was that the dumbest question in the world? About the ambulances?" at the same time Toni says, "What is a discotheque?"

"Kind of," Adina says to Dakota. Then, to Toni, "That's what old people call a dance club."

"I'm sorry," Dakota says. "I only drive through the city when my mother takes me to dinner theater auditions."

Toni nods. "It would be like us asking if you hear sheep."

"Sheep!" Dakota nods. "I sleep with one."

"Bah," Adina says.

Toni makes a siren sound. Reer. Reer.

"Girls," the librarian warns.

"But do you?" Toni says.

"That's a farm," Dakota says. "Not a suburb."

*

In the English language, adding "be" to a word makes it mean "adorned by." Belilaced. Bedaisied. Bescented. Bediamonded. Befeathered.

*

Most of the Young Women live within walking distance of the school. Every morning they arrive, many joined by their mothers—unhurried blondes in sensible beige pants. They accompany their daughters not for safety reasons but for pleasure. Mothers throw casual goodbyes over their shoulders. Mothers help print the school newspaper. Mothers appear at lunchtime holding trays of honeyed croissants. Mothers keep score, run the school shop, load the lip of a flaccid balloon onto the helium tank while making conversation. Mothers wearing goggles in the science lab caution against impatience when mixing solvents.

*

Adina's mother is promoted from time card typist to administrative assistant in the Human Resources Department. She and Adina spend less time in the row home across from Auto World, yet their relationship, instead of deepening with rarity, is fraught.

Adina's hearing has become anticipatory. She knows her mother will make a round, wet padunk sound when swallowing coffee. She braces against hearing the business move down her throat and pre-fills with rage.

"Will you please please stop doing that?" she yells.

Her mother pauses, the cup halfway to her mouth. "Doing what?"

✶

Kristin, a fellow Italian student who escapes critique by being molto gradevole, has a birthday. Young Women give her balloons over the course of the day and by Italian class, she has a respectable bundle. She walks reverently down the hall, popularity trailing her like silent, bulbous cysts. Yet Kristin is upset and distracted. No matter how many times Professoressa Gillespie calls on her she answers, "No lo so." Finally, she is sent to the nurse's office.

"For sadness," Professoressa says.

Kristin struggles to collect her books and balloons. Professoressa pushes her and the balloons through the door.

At the end of the day, Adina and Toni pass her, sulking in the nurse's office. Above her float the balloons, uncollected. Some lie sideways against the ceiling like the heads of giants too tall to fit. Even though she has a respectable number, Kristin wants more. She believes the balloons were given to her out of pity. She gazes at Adina and Toni through the office windows, flattened by grief.

Toni says, "I'm so glad my birthday's in the summer."

✶

Adina misses the bus on purpose. She assumes her mother won't drive her; however on this day she insists. She's always a little glitzy on Adina's birthday, a little tipsy.

On the way, her mother gets lost, pulls over, and asks directions from an older man walking a concerned-looking poodle. She uses what Adina recognizes as her work voice. It's the one she answers the phone with when Adina calls to be reminded what temperature she needs to bake a cake. She knows the temperature but wants to hear her mother say, "Three hundred fifty degrees, then take a fork and stick it in the middle. If it comes out clean, it's finished."

The morning is see-your-breath cold in the heatless car. The man chuckles at the women, bundled in hats and scarves. His poodle jumps against the door as he speaks. They follow his directions through neighborhoods of wide lawns and Value Stores. A street of mini castles. Turrets.

"How do people live like this?" her mother says.

Adina is surprised to not share her mother's opinion. She likes her high school, the open, questioning faces of her teachers. "Some of my classmates have their licenses already."

"Don't start."

"It would be easier. I'm looking out for you."

"How does a freshman have a license? Aren't they all like fourteen? Have they been serving time?" Adina's laugh encourages her. "Riding the rails? Oh no," she says when they reach the last hill before the school. "Pray."

Reaching the top, they high-five.

"I'm glad you had to drive me today. You're fun sometimes."

"Sometimes," her mother says.

They pull into the school where her mother idles in the long oval driveway. She gives a low whistle toward the entrance where Young Women with mannered backpacks file in. She hasn't asked about the school's history of educating strong women, or any of Adina's teachers' names.

"Do you know," she says, "there are people who when they ride in cars, only ride in cars? They don't point things out to make the other person laugh, they don't joke around or say anything interesting. They sit there. If they say anything it's like, 'Make a left at that Burger King.' They don't even joke about things like the Flying Man. It wouldn't occur to them. They sit there, driving in cars. Throughout every area of their lives. They work a job, have dinner. No humor. It's called being a literalist and most people are one. I'm glad you're not."

"I can't believe there are people who wouldn't joke about—"

"Most people, Adina. Just ride in cars." Unease flips the edge of her voice. Adina senses her mother is talking to someone else. "The day you were born," she says. "I was so scared. Everybody was talking about some woman on *The Price Is Right* whose top fell off when she was running down the aisle. Even the doctors. I was like, I'm having a baby! Help! I went under and there was a light. A beautiful, amazing. My pain went away. I only wanted to reach that light. Then, I woke up and there you were. So tiny, like a sparrow. I watched you through the window. The nurses told me I almost died." Students chatter past the car. "I don't know why I remember that contestant. She was so . . . exposed."

Adina is disappointed, this does not match the idea she has of her birth. A senior she recognizes from the theater department holds the building's door open for a teacher, making what appears to be a self-deprecating comment.

"Look at these girls," her mother says. "I bet they've never been scared of anything in their lives. But you like it here? It's okay?"

Adina wants to be honest yet uphold a daughterly loyalty she does not understand. "It's okay."

"It better be more than okay. Don't let them treat you like a scholarship kid."

"What was it like?" Adina says. "To almost die?"

"Honestly?" Her mother's expression means she's deciding whether she can handle hearing something. "It was no big deal." She backhands tears from her cheeks. "Hey, birthday girl. What's the matter with you?"

Adina decides to err on the side of honesty. She explains that the school has a balloon ritual and she is worried she will not receive any balloons.

Her mother cradles the bridge of her nose with a gloved hand. "Balloons." She reaches over Adina and opens the door on her side. "Go get balloons. Get more than anyone. Thanks for the fun. Go learn. I love you. I'm late."

*

Toni waits at Adina's locker, holding three green balloons. A few girls from the school paper stand with her, smiling shyly, pink and purple balloons hovering over their shoulders. Over the course of the day, Adina receives more and more. Even a few of the mothers add to the bouquet. No other student has received balloons from mothers. Adina rouges with embarrassment, stuttering thanks.

"Guarda tutti i palloncini di Adina!" says Professoressa Gillespie.

"Wow," Kristin says. "You're so popular!"

Adina remembers her morose gaze in the nurse's office. Her mother's words an awning in her mind. "Balloons." She spit the word. The admiring glances she passes are hurtful. What a spectacle she is.

At the end of the day, she must ask Toni's help to haul the balloons onto the bus. When the bus driver congratulates her haul, she says, "Thanks. They're not really mine."

She feels straddled by them. Toni turns saucer-wide eyes toward her. "You are the most unhappy person I've ever seen hold a bunch of balloons."

The bus clatters down the long driveway. The balloons sway with every bump, unfailingly charming. But Toni wears her excavation expression that means she can't hide. "You know why everyone wanted to give you a balloon?" she says.

The bus carangs over a pothole.

Here it is, Adina thinks, the needle. If she doesn't answer, maybe Toni will refrain from sharing the humiliating reason she's currently umbrellaed in shame. That the women feel sorry about her face, or that she contains an unsettling weirdness that can't be made cool, or because her mother can't buy her the silken socks that accent a well-formed calf and instead buys the two-dollar ten-pack from House of Bargains (not even the main warehouse but the clearance rack—practically in the back alley for as far as they have to walk to reach it, its random assortment of returned, remaindered, discolored, and malfunctioning clothing hanging off cracked hangers, pooled on the floor so that if they find one sock they have to search another hour for the other), socks that are too stiff to even slouch so stay unfolded up the whole length of her oddly angled calves, her calves, for that matter, that jut to each side with no understanding of what kind of muscle they are or the responsibility they have to be load-bearing, though Adina spends hours trying to push those socks down, they remain like wearing dry sponges.

Her socks, her calves, her mom? So many reasons to pity her. Toni will say everyone wanted to give her a balloon because she's ugly, oddly hipped, puny.

Toni says, "It's because you're funny."

*

Adina, Toni, and the balloons get off at Toni's bus stop. Toni lives in a chasm-like house separated from the street by an assortment of cars that Matteo and Christopher work on in perpetuity. Toni makes sandwiches in the kitchen while Adina waits outside, watching them move from car to car. They spend every afternoon like this, knowing without asking where the other brother has left off. They don't need language to sense it's the axle on the Mustang, rust on the Ford. Matteo, head under the Mustang's wheel, holds out his hand for the correct wrench. Their mother in her second-floor room where they deliver grilled cheeses or school notes.

Adina has only met her once: a tiny, wincing woman. Toni doesn't speak about her mother's illnesses and because of the unspoken property of best friends, Adina doesn't ask. They are years away from experiencing how illness dissects a spirit.

After a few minutes, Dominic scrapes through the front door. He wears all black, flannel shirt tied around his waist. A metal chain connects his jeans to his wallet. He has a new walk, a wincing-cowing movement, as if he's always waking to blinding sun. He swears the only good music is coming out of Seattle.

"You got a good bunch," he says.

"Thank you," she says. "I hate them."

He nods. This is what he expected. He removes a butterfly knife from his pocket. "Let's kill them."

What balloons escape his knife Adina murders against their busted gate. Matteo and Christopher watch, wiping oil from their wrists. "Missed the red one," Christopher says. Soon, the deflated balloons surround them on the lawn. They spare one, a yellow.

"So, how's school?" Dominic laughs.

Adina says, "None of those girls have ever been scared of anything."

"That might be true," he says. "But don't let it make you jaded."

Toni emerges from the house carrying sandwiches. "What the hell," she says about the balloons.

✶

Adina's mother is doing taxes at the half-moon table when she arrives home. Adina hands her the wide, yellow balloon.

"Don't tell me," she says. "You only got one?"

"I got a bunch," Adina says. "But I killed them."

Her mother's expression changes from sad to impressed. She ties the balloon to the chair back. "Good girl."

*

That Saturday morning, wrapped in coats and scarves, Adina and her mother climb into the VW.

Her mother loves the long, flat ribbon of sand and the predawn car ride so much she allows a stop at the McDonald's drive-through where they order two hash browns and a box of chocolate chip cookies they share during the ride.

At the giant golf ball, her mother turns to her. "Almost there."

They find parking at a public beach and when they've settled on a blanket her mother pulls two plastic cups and a bottle from her bag. "It's time for you to try wine." She fills her cup to the brim and Adina's halfway.

"It smells like pee and flowers."

"That's chardonnay," her mother says. "Before you drink, make a toast."

"To Earth," Adina says.

"To you."

Adina drinks the thin, pungent liquid. Her mother enjoys the moment more than she does, which pleases her even as it tags her with a sense of underperforming. Her mother's cartoonishly large dark sunglasses make her appear conspicuously ethnic. Her black-and-gray tweed coat reaches the floor like a cape. Adina wishes she would wear more fashionable light-color coats, belted in the middle like the mothers from her school. She wishes her mother would straighten her hair. She wishes she would walk around the block a couple times to lose the pouches that have bloomed around her middle. She wishes she would stop wearing control-top pantyhose since they've gone out of fashion. She even wears them with sandals, thick seams zigzagging over her toes.

At least the surf's ruckus covers the sound of her mother's swallowing the last of her wine. "Mothers are allowed a second cup," she says, refilling.

Families arrive with blankets. Adina walks the shoreline searching for an uneaten shell. Seagulls careen overhead. She returns and sits next to her napping mother until she jolts awake and says they should get back before traffic.

On the ride home, her mother says it's okay if Adina wants to plug her headphones into her cassette deck so she can listen to *Organ Works*. "We don't always have to talk."

Adina stares into the warm windows of passing houses. Every so often, she glimpses a stranger's life. A woman holding a pot, crossing to a table. A man watering a plant. Every one of them has a mother. At the end of a long birthday week, salt air weary, the simple thought feels miraculous.

✶

Toni writes a critical exposé for the school newspaper about the birthday balloon ritual that is met with bored dismissal except for a group of elegant juniors who invite her to join an unsanctioned writers club. Adina admires their keen gazes and sharp jeans. They wouldn't be out of place in a French noir film, filling out the background, evoking editorial cool.

*

In the spring, Il Piccolo Principe finally meets il volpe. After a Young sweating Woman fumbles a particularly hard jumble, Professoressa Gillespie yells, "Silenzio!" places her hands over her ears, and stares out the window. That afternoon's handbag had been an eggplant-colored Coach knockoff that Adina incorrectly predicted would mean an easier class.

Professoressa Gillespie asks Adina to read the rest of the page out loud. Adina's ears fill with the thwocking of tennis balls. No matter where she is in the building, someone is always playing a match.

She sounds out the first few sentences. Sono una volpe. Non sono addomesticato. When she reaches a snarl of consonants, her mouth will not obey. Professoressa Gillespie mutters.

Adina notes the sympathetic expressions from her classmates. The untamed fox waits in the meadow.

"I don't understand why you're so bad in Italian," her mother says that evening over chicken and rice. "You're so good at English!"

"They don't write the tests in English, Mom." Adina says. Being a poor Italian student burns her stomach. This burning is a wish that without her knowledge signals to somewhere far beyond her.

*

That night, Adina wakes in the Night Classroom.

Solomon spreads an array of colored stones on the table in front of her. One by one, they illuminate. Each produces a shift in her understanding of the Italian language, as if striking a hammer connected to a string inside her. She is a harpsichord. A yellow stone illuminates, and Adina knows the gender of every noun. A green, and the fourth and fifth definitions of more obscure words become known to her. The last rock, salmon-colored, glows, and Adina understands, as if a scrim has vanished, the philosophy behind the language. The force and shape of Italian. Her doubt (masculine) recedes. She is filled with happiness (feminine).

*

Adina wakes fluent in her bed. Solomon has not taught her new information, only how to access what she has. This spreads beyond the language into the metaphorical. *Il Piccolo Principe*, she realizes, is not only a story about a pilot in the desert coming across a little boy. It is a parable about purpose. This recasts her understanding of the *J* girls, the Beautyland clerk, Mrs. Leafhalter. She closes the book at dawn, jittery with affection she longs to share. She faxes her superiors.

What is essential is invisible to the eye.

GOOD, reads the reply.

✶

"*Il Piccolo Principe.*" Professoressa's voice is needled with exhaustion. "Does anyone want to read their response paper?" The class chuckles when Adina raises her hand.

Adina reads aloud, trills, pauses for dramatic effect, chuckles at her own droll humor. When she finishes, she anticipates praise.

Instead, Il Professoressa is furious. "How did you do that?"

"I studied," Adina says.

"You cheated."

No teacher in this school has ever accused a student of cheating. The wide clock above the door ticks. Students as surprised as Adina jostle in their seats. Il Professoressa picks up Adina's book, turns it over, and lets it land gracelessly on the desk. "Yesterday you knew nothing and today you're fluent?"

The sentence grows in volume until the sharp, shrill "fluent?" It conjures the class bell. Everyone jumps. "Go." Students fleeing shameful situations collide in the unhappy hallway. Clogged with tears, Adina finds Toni at her locker. She won't tell her what happened as they walk outside to the line of moaning buses, or during the quiet ride back to the city, or at Toni's stop when she says, "Okay then, see you tomorrow, Adina," and with a final, questioning look, leaves her alone.

✶

Beauty magazines insist: Trace your lips with a liner three shades darker than the color that fills them. Beauty magazines help Adina distinguish her human shape among other Young Women. At best, she could be described as triangular. She is not the girl leaping into midair to spike a volleyball. She is the girl freeing her boxer shorts from the cinch they make between her legs when she hopes no one's looking.

One night, she announces to her bedroom mirror, "This season, I will cover all my fashion bases."

Beauty magazines insist she become acquainted with how rouge is spread on what's referred to as the "cheek's apples." Rouge color is based on your season, which can be deduced by consulting pie charts. The first pie chart contains shades of ivory, eggshell, champagne. The second is made up of pinks titled cotton candy, flamingo. The third pie ventures into beige. Adina turns the page, hoping for a darker pie.

She brings the magazine to the kitchen, where her mother scribbles onto a tax form. A chicken boils on the stove.

"What color rouge do I use?"

Her mother consults the three pies. She turns the page and sighs.

"Use the darkest slice of the beige pie," she says, returning to her work.

"Oatmeal?" Adina tests.

"Sure."

Adina is an oatmeal summer, which means she should dust her cheeks with coral colors, and wear bold, saturated hues. A hue is a shade of a shade.

*

Human beings, she faxes, *use makeup to feel great about themselves*.

After dinner, a slip of paper is waiting in the fax machine's tray.

ACTIVATE IRONY.

✶

"Good theater," says the Acting teacher, "is about what an actor doesn't do."

It is a late Friday afternoon in the beginning of junior year. The Acting teacher, a flannelled woman of indeterminate age, with a long, purposeful nose and a head of tight gray curls, drags a television and VCR into their classroom and urges them to notice what they don't see. She presses play on a scene from the movie *Young Frankenstein*. In it, the ingenue played by Madeline Kahn pretends to be sorry to see Gene Wilder's batty-scientist character leave town. She resists his hug, fearing it will ruin her hair. The train puffs next to them. Everything is black and white. Madeline Kahn is not in love.

"What is she not doing?" the Acting teacher asks. Sometimes she smokes cigarettes with seniors on the fire escape behind the gym. She rewinds and replays the scene, leaning close to the screen. The image of the train is reflected on her nose and cheeks. "What is she leaving out?"

The students pair up to act out the train scene. Adina is matched with Dakota, whose hair is newly dyed purple. Dakota plays the scene as if she is truly in love. It is not what the teacher asked for but Adina compliments her and she blushes, proud. When it's Adina's turn, she cannot make her lip quiver the way Dakota can, or smile as straight and wide, so she plays it for laughs.

The Acting teacher pauses to watch. "Adina knows what to leave out."

The open windows let in ripe, washed air. The school's hills are striped by sun through clouds. For the rest of her life Adina will connect this image with the first time she was praised in front of others.

*

In spring, the school theater group announces auditions for the play *Our Town*. It will be directed by the Acting teacher and interested Young Women are encouraged to apply.

Adina reads the play during a study period, then reshelves it, breath skippering. She loves the monologues from the narrator that detail the geography and demographics of the New England town. She understands his careful, focused reporting. She does not tell Toni when she signs up for a slot after dismissal, early enough so she can catch the bus.

*

A sweet-sixteen season.

Banquet halls, United Skates of America, family rooms. Photo albums, party bags, quick slips of vodka. A series of crossover episodes: seemingly none of Adina's sitcoms are safe from a random drop-in from a character who couldn't possibly live in the same universe.

*

Her mother's favorite sitcom, *Cheers*, airs its final episode. It is such an important event that Adina is allowed to watch. They turn the television's knob to channel 3 at the appropriate time, chicken over rice steaming on their television trays.

A group of barflies in assorted shades of brown reminisce and reach final, humane conclusions. When it's over, Adina's heart pounds.

"I don't think I want to watch a last episode of a television series again," she says.

Her mother's cheeks are bright with tears. "Okay?"

Adina attempts to fax the experience to her superiors. She mentions Woody, the winsome bartender from the Midwest who replaced the craggy but gentle Coach. She describes the pressure sitting on her breastplate: loneliness, nostalgia, nausea, something else she can't articulate that makes her eyes hurt.

It is, she faxes, *the Worst Feeling*.

After a few moments, the reply squeaks through:

ENDINGS ARE HARD.

Adina resents this cursory, offhanded remark that dismisses the depth of pain she's in. For the first time, Adina feels that no one on Earth or even beyond understands her.

*

Adina does not choose an audition monologue from *Our Town*, though every role will be played by a Young Woman.

Instead, she will recite the penultimate monologue given by Gerry Conlon, Daniel Day-Lewis's low-level crook who is mistaken for an IRA operative in the movie *In the Name of the Father.*

She rehearses his way of barreling down a sentence as if it will end with an emphatic period then at the last moment launching into air. She builds to the last two lines when Gerry demands to know why his father's cruel coaching was necessary. He had been a good athlete. He'd won the football game.

She delivers it to Dominic over the phone.

"Really nail that final line," he says. "That's what makes his dad's face crumple."

Adina makes a note.

"Hey," he says. "I got into Brooklyn College. I'm moving to New York. I found a place through a buddy. It's only about two hours if there's no traffic. It's a place where I can be myself."

"You can't be yourself here? I know," she says when he doesn't reply. "You can't."

In the hallway, Adina's mother says, "The tissues I buy keep disappearing. This house has some kind of tissue vortex."

Adina can't tell whether Dominic's voice sounds strained because he is ambivalent about moving or because he detects she is upset.

"I'll miss you, Adina," he says. "You don't have to say it back. I know these things are hard for you but I'll miss you, I will."

*

The day of the audition, Adina walks the slanted, carpeted auditorium aisle to the stage. Dakota sits along the stage's edge, drinking a cup of tea. She auditioned earlier to spirited applause. Adina's feet are two pounding hearts that deliver her up the stairs and turn her toward the sea of expectant faces. The Acting teacher sits in the middle of the theater, surrounded by students who seem to know her implicitly.

"Begin when ready," she says.

"Why do you always follow me?" Adina begins, and realizes her voice is too small to fill the space. She attempts to summon the desire that prompted her to sign up for an audition slot. She understands she must match it to the voice delivering this monologue. The shame of fouling the ball. She finds herself on the opposite side of the stage, compelled by an urge she does not recall. Moments later she is on the other side of the stage. Her forearms tingle. Underneath lines about paternal neglect, Dominic moves to Brooklyn. The fox waits in the meadow. Even as she details the events of the disappointing football game, she walks up to Toni's house where Dominic no longer lives. How will she continue her film studies without him? Where is Brooklyn? Why must he leave to find himself if it means moving so far away? Her voice arrives. Though she is projecting words about a tender, aggravating father into the hushed auditorium, she is talking about Dominic. She says football: she means Brooklyn. The Acting teacher leans forward in her chair. Her lips move as if performing the monologue with Adina. "And that's when I started to rob! To prove that I was no good!" Gerry Conlon's pitiful tirade concludes. Adina awakens in the auditorium with no memory. The Acting teacher wears an unreadable expression. Shock?

Her entourage wordlessly consults her for clarification on what they've experienced.

The Acting teacher scribbles a note, rethinks it, crosses it out. "*Moonstruck*," she says finally, ". . . was one of the monologues offered as an audition option. Did you read it?"

"I read all of the suggested monologues," Adina says.

"*Moonstruck* is the story of an Italian woman from a city who doesn't want to marry the man she's marrying."

Adina and her mother have memorized every word to *Moonstruck*. It is the only movie that has ever made her mother jolt from her recliner with laughter. But playing Loretta had seemed too easy and would expose Adina too much in a school where she has already trained herself out of city pronunciations. At home, she pronounces *water* like Loretta does, *wooder*. In the halls of this school, she widens her mouth to make the more ambitious, suburban *a*.

"Was *In the Name of the Father* one of the suggested monologues?"

The hypothetical question prompts the students to turn widened eyes toward the auditorium's carpet, but the teacher's tone has landed more abruptly than she intended. Her voice softens.

"You're Italian, yes? Last name Giorno?" Normally when people mention her last name, they deliver it in an outsized accent that indicts the final vowel. But this woman is merely checking a fact. "You have this in common with Loretta?"

Adina nods. She can't get her voice to work.

"But instead you performed a monologue from the perspective of an incarcerated drug dealer falsely imprisoned in

Northern Ireland?" An Event feeling sharpens the auditorium's air. Something Is Happening That Defies Easy Explanation. Even the piano that Dakota's mother donated seems death silent. Adina longs to be dismissed so she can catch her bus and spend the hour-long ride home pressing her forehead against the dirty seat. She understands as clearly as if it has been embroidered on the stage's father red curtain: When the cast list is posted, Dakota will receive the role of Emily and Adina's name will not appear.

"I've never seen anything like that," the Acting teacher says. "I've never seen anything like that at all."

*

Dominic hurls his duffel bag and suitcase into the car of a friend who will drive him to New York. It is a crisp, chilly morning. Adina and his family stand on the curb wearing sweaters and coats. Daffodils have shown up in her mother's garden like cheerful ancient telephones. New York City is only two hours up the turnpike but it might as well be Neptune. Adina doesn't know anyone who lives there. The Statue of Liberty is a key chain, not an actual place where people work and raise families. She studies Dominic's face for signs that he is already growing distant, becoming less dear. But he punches Matteo's shoulder, smiles behind his giant sunglasses, and wears a Martin's Aquarium T-shirt; he lists the movies he wants to see with Adina the first time she and Toni visit him in what he calls "the big city."

"Visit soon," he says. Toni will look after his Mustang

while he's gone. Adina will no longer have to take the bus. They can leave a whole fifteen minutes later.

Dominic hands Adina a cassette tape. "I know you love hip-hop and the Glass Man, but it's time for you to listen to R.E.M. Write me and tell me what you think."

He hangs out of the car and waves as they drive away. His kind, serious eyes. It feels impossible to return the gesture. Adina sticks out her tongue. The car is one of many chugging toward the boulevard, but it contains one of the only humans Adina loves. It is a family moment. She wonders if Hubble can see them with its powerful eye. Five people waving toward a retreating car.

✶

The *Our Town* cast list preens on a pushpin outside the theater office. To no one's surprise, Dakota will play the role of Emily. But to everyone's, Adina receives the role of the Narrator, the character who reports on the town's comings and goings. It is the largest part in the play.

Adina's human body is too small to hold her joy.

✶

In the movie *Boomerang*, a narcissist hotshot advertising executive discovers that his new boss is a female version of himself. After a series of romantic ups and downs, the advertising executive realizes he loves Angela, played by newcomer Halle Berry. Beauty magazines' skin-color pie charts expand. Products for braids, extensions, coarse and curly hair appear along with instructions: Scrunch then let dry unassisted. Blow-dry with round brush then flatten with a straight iron. Moisturize edges. Use calamine lotion to avoid midwinter ashiness.

*

Adina's *Our Town* costume is a simple black suit. She must do her own makeup. Toni comes over and they practice contouring. Adina walks out to the family room where her mother is doing taxes.

"You look like you've been in a car accident." She gets up, wets a paper towel under the kitchen faucet, and drags it across Adina's face. When she's finished, Adina is red-faced and makeup free. Her mother applies a light powder to her cheeks and nose, dusts her eyelids with a shade called Foliage, and rouges her cheeks.

"You're supposed to put a complementary color in the creases of my lids," she informs her mother.

"You're too young to have anything in your creases," she says. "This is makeup for a girl your age." Her mother's beauty routine is the same as the other women in the neighborhood: fingertipping Vaseline over her face before bed then covering it with thin plastic sheets she bought at Beautyland. "You have your whole life to be a slave to the cosmetic industry."

When she returns to her room, Toni sits on her bed, surrounded by her observations. Adina has carelessly left out the folder where she stores her faxes.

Toni looks up from a page, eyes wide. "What are these?" Adina gathers them from around her until the only one left is in Toni's hand.

Adina's superiors haven't implicitly told her to hide her identity, but she has seen what humans do to extraterrestrials in film and television. *E.T.*, *Close Encounters of the Third Kind*, *Small Wonder*, *ALF*. It begins with good intent: to get the extraterrestrial medical aid or take them trick-or-treating. But then society intrudes. Relationships ultimately lead to exposure and exploitation. Confide in someone during a vulnerable moment and end up strapped to a gurney being probed by scientists. Most times, pain. Sometimes, death. Americans, especially those who live in suburbs, cannot be trusted. Distance from humans equals safety, no matter how lonely, no matter how much Adina longs to connect. She must keep herself a secret.

Still, Toni has never judged her, not for having a small apartment or a weird mother or for chasing status through balloons. Adina longs to solidify their friendship against the influence of new activities and other friends and the everyday slings and arrows of high school. Is that a valid reason to share her secret? To shore up what's between them?

Toni senses the measurements being performed. "I feel the same way about the Seafood Shanty lobsters."

"I can't talk about it," Adina says.

Toni senses she is on friend math's losing end. "Guess I should get home and see what the boys are up to," she says. It's not like Toni to use her family as an excuse. This is unfair. Toni has secrets too. She still hasn't shared whatever happened with Audrey at the pool, big enough that the mention of Audrey's name makes Toni's posture change and make a hasty exit, like this one.

"Don't forget your makeup," Adina says.

"Keep it."

She follows her friend down the hall and through the family room. "You leaving, kid?" her mother says.

"Yeah, I gotta get back."

"Drive safely. Ring once when you get there."

"All right, Mrs. G., I will."

Shuffling at the door, slam shut, goodbye. Over her mother's questions, Adina strains to hear the engine of the Mustang before her friend drives away. Their words had remained pleasant, kind even, but a knot in Adina's chest makes it hard to sleep.

*

Adina finds Toni in the parking lot after school the next day, riffling through cassettes in the Mustang. When she smiles, Adina realizes: Toni is hot. It must have happened while she was distracted by theater: Toni has stopped trying to tame her thick, screaming hair and it has repaid her by arcing around her face in a way that gives her chin narrative. Her nose has reached an agreement with her black eyes creating a loving, piercing gaze that Adina avoids whenever it forms, as if dodging a searchlight.

Toni wants to drive to the 7-Eleven and buy Chipwiches. A Chipwich is a slab of ice cream between two thick cookies. Adina has written several faxes about them. They eat them driving home to Adina's house, which she has begun referring to as "my mother's."

"Do you know that when most people drive in cars they just drive in cars? They don't say anything funny? They just sit?"

"This is why I hate most people," Toni says. She asks how Adina's notes are going and Adina says, What notes? Toni frowns, throws the car into a higher gear.

They reach the house where Adina's mother is rolling the tomato carts toward the sun. She waves for them to come over.

"Have you ever seen such healthy ones, Toni? They have their own transport! I'll send some home for your mother. We'd have to make gallons of pesto to use all this basil. Here are Adina's rosebushes. I said I'd be happy if I got one snap pea and I got a handful." Her mother guides them through the stalks and bushes, pointing out successes and failures, places she hopes to do better. The garden extends past the third telephone pole. The current crop of row-home kids help her haul dirt on the weekends. The complex's handyman, a ruddy man charmed by her garden, has recently gifted her two industrial-size sprinklers with timers. Every late afternoon they switch themselves on and arc and pump across the sky.

*

Distance grows between Adina and Toni. Should friends know everything about each other? If they pocket formative experiences, will they begin to pocket their time too? Adina resents having to be the braver friend. Resentment and love collide into the desire to tell her friend who she really is. She will say, *Toni, you know how people are from Earth? I'm not.* And Toni will say . . .

*

On a Friday afternoon toward the end of senior year, the cast and crew of *Our Town* sit on the gymnasium's hard floor eating pizza. Some of the actors are already costumed, some still wear their school clothes, Adina wears her suit pants with a V-necked T-shirt she's propped her napkin into to catch errant sauce. Her classmates' faces are powdered and lined making them look like themselves but brighter. Everyone is speaking more loudly than normal. Soon they will finish getting ready then warm up and stretch, exchange good wishes, go over last-minute notes.

Adina worries her mother will get lost in the chilly night. She has only been to her high school on her birthday in freshman year. She hopes she will sit with Toni and her brothers and not alone. She will have to guide her mother home through the dark and not go to the ice cream shop to celebrate with the cast.

At 6:00 p.m., a crew member says, "Adina, I think your mom is outside."

They peek through the front windows to see the VW lit by a sputtering lamplight. Her mother has allowed too much time and is an hour early. Adina walks out to the car where her mother is listening to talk radio. She startles when Adina raps on the window.

"At least come into the vestibule. There are benches. You can sit."

"I'm listening to my program." She waves her off. "Go rehearse."

Adina runs lines with the cast but is thinking about her mother in the cold car.

*

Our Town is Emily's story but the narrator is the story's vertebrae. Over three months of rehearsal the cast has grown into their roles so that Adina no longer considers them high school students but Mrs. Gibbs, Mrs. Webb, George Webb. They know how to help someone struggling to remember a line without venturing off script, how to counter one another's bodies, making certain the audience keeps the best view. For three months Adina hasn't done anything alone except sleep. So unlike her solitary writing. This must be what it's like to have a big family, she thinks, kissing every actor on the cheek before entering the stage's bright grasp.

Onstage, she shelves herself and becomes the town's reporter. She lists statistics as if she's lived there her whole life, as if she feels its sun against her neck. When the audience laughs, a thrill buzzes her veins. In the last act's funeral scene, she detects a quality of sustained abeyance in the theater's hushed quiet—the precipice of tears. Under a solo light bulb, Adina delivers the final lines. The light bulb burns out on cue. Silence fills the auditorium. Adina, standing in the dark, fears they've performed the play incorrectly. Had they not been audible or authentic? But it is only the audience realizing the play is over. When they do, applause shakes the stage. Her mother and Toni stand in the front row. She is relieved to see

Toni, smiling and shouting her name. Professoressa Gillespie. Her other teachers. The mothers she recognizes from around the school who she's never spoken to but fill the chorus of her high school life. The lighting, costume, and prop girls, backlit and clapping in the rafters. By speaking another person's words onstage, Adina has connected to so many humans. They hold programs and flowers, jackets hanging from their forearms, clapping against their wrists, shaking their heads in disbelief, beaming toward the cast returning to stage. The cast raises their clasped hands, then brings them down as they bow. The applause bears them back. Houselights turn on. Everyone stands. But Adina can also feel the bodies of those not present. Mrs. Leafhalter, the *J* girls, her grade-school teachers. A familiar silhouette suddenly reflects against the crowd—a set of strong brown hands, an intimate, sloping stance. Why would her father stand in the doorway of this beaming, leaping moment? Why would it be him who occurs to her here? But there he is, alongside a hope that wherever he is he's as happy as this.

*

A reknowned city college for theater is offering a scholarship. The Acting teacher tells anyone interested to write a three-page essay detailing what acting means to them.

"Is anyone interested?"

Dakota and Adina raise their hands.

Adina begins her essay that evening. She writes it like an end-of-year summary for her superiors but instead of reporting on humans she's describing the ways a stage feels both private and like a connection. She can run lights and sound, can sew a simple dress pattern. Her mother has said they won't have money for anything but the local college but won't be able to argue with a scholarship. An acting college. She repeats it and stares at the night sky for any trace of affirmation.

*

The class of 1995's prom theme will be What a Long, Strange Trip It's Been.

On a Sunday of stock-still skies, Toni drives them to the farther, less crappy mall that has two floors and a fountain that ejects water into a reservoir shaped like a clam. Joining them is her middle older brother, Matteo, whose car is broken and who is already annoyed he has to be in public with his sister and her friend.

Matteo is Adina's least favorite of Toni's brothers, having inherited his family's tendency to present ideas cruelly in list form. Still, she's thrilled to be venturing outside of their neighborhood on a Sunday. In the last weeks of school, Toni has spent more time with the newspaper girls and hasn't been responding to Adina's jokes. She hopes this mall trip means the simmering between them is over.

On the second-floor promenade Matteo gathers them into a huddle and informs them that he (a) no longer knows them, (b) will continue to not know them until they meet back in front of the Earring Pagoda in an hour and fifteen minutes, sharp, so they can go to Spencer's and find their mother a card, and (c) SHARP.

Every outing with Toni and her brothers includes buying a card for their mother, always coming out of the hospital or trying some new treatment. Adina misses Dominic who would have stayed with them and made respectful comments about the dresses they tried on. His postcards describe New York City movie theaters as charming. Thinking about him seeing movies in charming theaters makes her eyes hurt.

The woman behind the department store jewelry counter works a smile onto her face when she sees them admiring the posts. Toni tells her they want earrings that don't suck.

The woman leaves to pull options and Toni turns to Adina. "I want to talk about your notes."

"I write them as fun."

"But there are responses. Do you write those too?"

The woman returns with a few sets of earrings. Toni tries on a pair of long hoops and shows them to Adina. They make her seem older, professional. "I like them," she says. "How much?"

The woman tells her they are forty-five dollars. "That's insane." Toni motions to the sale sign. "Aren't they on sale like the others?"

"Afraid not."

"When will they go on sale?"

"I couldn't say. Perhaps you'd be interested in one of the other pairs?"

The department store's air feels stilted. Adina doesn't understand why this woman's cheerful words feel mean. She can't look at the woman's knife-sharp collar or salon-lightened hair.

Toni turns to Adina. "Let's walk to Hot Topic."

On the walk, Toni's eyes are trained on Adina as if she is a bird she worries will fly away. She halts. Audrey and two other girls lean against the second-floor railing, huddled over a small item that is making them laugh. Feeling Toni's gaze, they look up. A trio of confused female faces offset by feathered bangs and green eyeliner.

"Hey," Toni says. Audrey says, "Hey."

The two girls consult each other, then Toni, who has made their friend's smile fade. Toni straightens, a soldiering of strength. Around them, families eat ice cream and stare into middle distance.

They say hey to each other again. Toni's sneaker squeals against the tile of the mall's floor as she turns and walks, fast, veering to miss a family of pretzel eaters. A little boy drops his, Adina picks it up then double walks to catch up. Toni is already inside the store, trying on plastic earrings shaped like forms of weather: lightning bolts, clouds, moons. She pretends to be unaffected but Adina sees the sorrow stiffening her shoulders. Adina doesn't know which part of her friend to address.

"Those are rad," the person working the counter says.

Toni agrees. She buys two pairs. As the clerk rings her up, she says, "Tell me about the notes, Adina. Why are you keeping this from me?"

Adina is tired of chasing her friend and confused by this double standard of sharing. "I'm not keeping anything. I told you about Amadeo's penis. You haven't told me what happened with Audrey."

Toni's face purples. Adina has violated the code of not bringing it up. Instead of apologizing, Adina doubles down.

"If we're keeping things from each other, maybe we're not even friends."

"Oh my god." Matteo is in the doorway, yelling. "You're late." The two denim-clad girls waving goodbye to him go unremarked upon, as does the fact he is wearing a new sweater. This one is covered in geometric shapes on a dark gray galaxy of knit. "What are those in your ears? That's not what Mom meant! You're going to get in trouble and I don't care!"

"I don't care if you care!" Toni says. "Worry about your pathetic life and leave me alone."

"Mom's going to punish you and this is going to be me: laughing and laughing." He holds his stomach and pantomimes.

They walk to the card store, trading insults. Adina notices how their eyes flit to the other after landing one to make sure it hit but not too hard. They list what they don't care about, which is everything the other mentions. Both parties agree: Their mother will kill Toni, Matteo won't care, Toni won't care about either the killing or the fact that Matteo won't care.

The card is for something good this time: their mother's latest surgery has gone well and after a period of bed rest she will be allowed to drive. Matteo says her mother and the law firm partner will get married and Toni says, whatever, she'll be at college.

They read get well cards out loud to each other. Adina finds a card where a wife chicken wearing an apron tends to a husband chicken sick in bed. A bowl of soup sits on his lap.

"Quit complaining and eat it!" the wife chicken says.

"Number one, chicken soup is good for the flu, and number two, it's nobody we know."

"I don't get it," Matteo says.

Toni studies it. "This guy is good."

"Oh yeah," Matteo says, pretending to reconsider. "He is good. Let's buy it."

At the food court they buy egg rolls that by the time they reach the car have made an oily grimace on the bottom of the paper bag.

*

They drive to the Willows and sit on the Mustang's hood, eating. The trees are in bud. Across the meadow, Matteo throws a stick toward a flock of turkeys. He yells, "Look how stupid these birds are."

"Those turkeys are going to get angry," Adina says. "And kill your brother." She hopes the joke will make Toni laugh so she knows their fight isn't causing permanent damage.

"I hope so." Toni stabs her egg roll with a fork to mark the middle. Her ritual: Tear at the fork's perforation. Scoop the slawed innards onto a plate. Eat the crispy exoskeleton then the slaw.

Matteo gets bored with the turkeys and kicks at the ground.

"I can't believe I'm related to that person," Toni says. "The thing about an egg roll is . . ." On the other side of the meadow, a bird squawks. Matteo pauses. The turkeys lift their heads and reveal their trembling throats. A movement of branches.

"Did you forget you were in the middle of a sentence?" Adina says.

"You can eat it any way you want, is what I was going to say. I got distracted by the thought of that department store woman." She mimics the woman's haughty pose. "I really couldn't say."

Adina hadn't realized her friend had even registered the woman, so smoothly did she reject the earrings and walk away. "She's lonely."

"You always think the best of people, Adina," Toni says. "Even terrible people." In billions of years the sun will be a distended red giant star that reduces Earth to a cinder. But on this night it underlines the horizon in a magnanimous pink, throwing pale squares onto Toni's face as she gathers her hair into a bun.

"All right," she says. "I'll tell you about Audrey."

*

In the beginning of that summer, Audrey invites Toni to her family's swim club.

Toni's mother takes her to the mall and buys her a one-piece, a cover-up, and a wicker open-mouthed pocketbook.

Toni enjoys her first afternoon at the swim club. They invite her again. And again. Until she is, to her mother's delight, joining them every weekend. To avoid the embarrassment of wearing the same bathing suit every week, Toni switches out with her older one, and her mother charges a third.

The swim club's pool operates like a communal garden:

Everyone has a patch. Audrey's family sits under the same umbrella every week. The southeast corner is prime real estate. It belongs to the Snow family. Mother and Father Snow ("That's how they refer to each other," Toni says. "Mother, will you pass the tanning lotion?") and their two high school–age children sit in their bank of chairs and entertain other families. They rarely do the visiting. Toni says that being called over by the Snows was tantamount to getting a high-five from God.

Pool politics aside, Toni enjoys working on her tan and reading without her brother's constant interruption. "That's when the trouble started," Toni says.

Adina's family is Sicilian which means she's dark brown all year but Toni's family is from Northern Italy. During the winter, her skin is pale olive but in the summer it deepens to Adina dark.

"Audrey and I started to get close. Not like you and I close. Different. We would sit next to each other. Once in a while her hand would be next to my thigh. This is where the Snow Family comes in. By the way, their real name is Polnecheck but they changed it. To Snow."

Toni does not have to clarify why this is a mark against them. In the language of their neighborhood, you do not replace your lawn with Astroturf, you do not put on airs, which means anything from pronouncing French words correctly to sending your child to private school, and you bear your ethnicity, regardless of the anguish it brings you.

"One day the Snow family visited Audrey's. You would have thought it was the president. They introduced me. I said hi and kept reading my book. By that time, I was very dark.

Audrey was swimming. And Mr. Snow said it was nice they let me join them. Audrey's mom was like nodding and making it sound like I lived with them. And Mr. Snow said, be careful with that tan, you'll have to start carrying the clubs."

"What clubs?" Adina says.

"Golf clubs."

"Why would you have to—"

"Because nonwhite people carry the clubs. This shit isn't logical. When I told Audrey she got defensive. I told her to forget about it because I didn't want it to keep us from hanging out. Because I liked her. I told her, I really liked her. She said she didn't know what I was talking about. She only saw me as a pal from school."

"You like girls," Adina says.

Toni says, "You knew that, right?"

Adina thinks about it. "I did but didn't know I did."

Toni nods as if that's what she expected.

"So she told her father you were gay and you got uninvited to the swim club?"

"The opposite," Toni says.

Across the meadow, Matteo goose-steps toward the turkeys in the advancing dark. Toni yells at him to stop bothering the turkeys. "One of the pool boys taught me what a hand job is. I was so mad at Audrey I gave him one behind the snack bar. Someone saw and told her father. That's why I got uninvited to the swim club."

Clouds gather over the Mustang. Hand jobs and fathers and boys throwing sticks at wild animals. Adina remembers something Mrs. Leafhalter said. Hard butter tears the bread.

"Sometimes I don't understand anything," Toni says.

Matteo vanishes into a pocket of darkness the trees make with the hillside.

"Toni," Adina says. "I'm not from here. I'm from very far away." She explains the activation, the fax machine, the Night Classroom, roller coasters. She feels every cold molecule between them as she waits for her friend to answer.

Toni says, "No one around here thinks like you, Adina. You don't fit and you don't lie. I mean both as compliments. There is something about your notes that I think everyone can relate to. If you stay here, I think it will die." She stabs the last egg roll with a fork, unaware of how profoundly she's affirmed Adina. Adina understands that every day the sky will darken and lighten until there is no more field or duck or dark. Until whatever happens to them happens.

"What is a hand job?" Adina says.

Toni cups her hand and moves it back and forth. "You go like this until he ejaculates. It's like thick salt water. It gets all over your hand."

Matteo is yelping. Legs pumping, he half runs, half falls across the meadow. Yards behind him, the gaggle of turkeys gives chase. Wobbling, chattering, fast. "Start the car!" Matteo screams. "Start the car!"

✶

The next morning, results of the acting scholarship are announced over the PA. Dakota has won. She will attend Philadelphia's premier school for acting. Adina will live at home, work shifts at the Red Lion Diner, and attend night classes at community college. Adina wonders at Dakota's expression when the results are announced. She appears genuinely sheepish amid the shoulder claps from the students surrounding her. Adina is a leaf falling from a high building. But she gives her friend a thumbs-up from across the room.

*

That evening, Adina is visited by Solomon. She is relieved to see them, to be sitting at the endless table. Inside the center of Solomon's shape a keyboard of ribs shine. They are happy to see her too. Yet Solomon brings sorrowful news. This will be their last lesson. She has learned well and they are their equivalent of proud, which exhibits and manifests like everything else. They allow space for her pleas for the lessons to continue. They remind her: She is not meant to have a regular childhood or adulthood. She must do her job—collect data and have experiences and report back and leave when they say. She does not have free will like her classmates who are spending this week scouring the aisles of home stores for lamps and chairs that will make their dorm rooms feel like satellite locations of their family homes.

But her friends are leaving and because of her Earth circumstances she can't follow. She feels constricted. Left behind. Solomon listens. Colors bloom within them as they register her feelings. When she is finished, they reverberate in mauves. There are benefits of not being from this world, she understands. There is good news. Though their lessons are concluded, Adina is ready to hear the sound that comes with reaching this developmental threshold. Solomon will tell Adina her real name.

Asleep in her bed in Northeast Philadelphia, she makes two fists.

Solomon makes a sound comprised of three tones, or syllables. The first is a glass bottle dropping onto grass. The second is a vinyl scratch. The third is oceanic, the rush of waves. This confirms Adina's private suspicion that she is in some way of the sea.

Solomon sounds out her name again. Glass bottle, scratch, rush of waves. She wants to hear it over and over. But then they make a more human sound, a crowd expressing delight at the first few explosions in a fireworks display. It means goodbye. Before she can protest, Adina wakes in her bed, cheeks covered in tears, devastated to find herself on Earth.

*

Adina and Toni sit in the hallway outside the prom wearing plastic weather earrings. Adina wears storm clouds, Toni wears lightning bolts. Their backs are pressed against the lockers, bass massaging their spines. They rap every word of "Bust a Move" to each other.

Dakota emerges from the gym. Since the scholarship results were announced she's been aloof, but she walks over, resolute. "Adina." She sits next to them. "I'm so sorry about the scholarship."

"It's not your fault," Adina says. "I'm sure my essay wasn't as good as yours. Probably too personal or dumb."

Dakota fidgets, opens her mouth to speak, shuts it.

"What's going on with you?" Toni says.

"I don't want to go to acting school! My mother forced me to apply!"

Adina assumes this is a gesture of generosity, underplaying the honor she feels. "It will be so cool," she says. "So many Shakespeare in the Park performers came from that program." It must be human empathy that compels her to cheer her friend who received the scholarship she wanted, though she didn't learn that on Earth.

"You don't understand," Dakota says. "I didn't write my essay. I didn't even fill out the application. My mom paid some college professor like five hundred dollars."

Young MC says that after several disappointing romantic experiences he agrees to be the best man at his friend's wedding. There, he accidentally hits on a bridesmaid. She is ready for a different life. He wants it. He gets it. He wants it. He gets it. Adina has heard this song a hundred times. Young MC raps the story as if it is happening in the present moment He wants her to experience love's arrows alongside him.

"That's great," Toni says. "You can tell the scholarship people and withdraw. They can give it to Adina."

"I've already accepted," Dakota says.

"But you didn't earn it," Toni says. "They'll find out, won't they?"

"It's the only school I got into. I have to go. I'm sure there will be great opportunities for you too, Adina. Life is not a pie."

Adina realizes Dakota's intent. "You don't want to unaccept," she says. "So why even tell me?"

Dakota crumples in front of them, her dress's lace collar making a grimace on her chest.

"Get away from us," Toni says. Adina has never seen her too upset to curse.

Dakota stands, turns, changes her mind. "You're mean," she says to Toni. She disappears into the gymnasium. The music switches to another song.

Adina and Toni walk outside to where the Mustang is parked in the navy, moonless night. Toni raises the volume on "Excursions" because she knows Adina loves Q-Tip's voice when he says, *Don't be phony and expect me not to flex.* As they drive away, Adina memorizes the hills, the tennis courts, the wide doors, and the indecipherable statue. These structures had been in place the first day they idled out front eating damp bagels, on the precipice of a new galaxy that appeared impenetrable but had turned out to be more impenetrable than even that.

✶

Toni's mother marries the partner in the law firm. He is willing to send his stepdaughter to any school she chooses. In July of 1995, Mustang packed to the roof, Toni moves to New York City. Adina wears her waitressing uniform: white button-down tucked into formless black pants. She wants to hold Toni in place the way she does the ribbon when her mother ties a bow on a present. Instead, she stands on the curb, again waving to a retreating car that holds a friend. Fulfilling the promise to bear witness to every departure so the person leaving doesn't feel their time has been wasted.

*

It is a cruel crescent of a summer. Adina lies in bed anxious about college and waitressing. How will it work? Every so often a certain carbonation emerges amid whatever interaction she is having, a sense that the day has taken form and is looking around. She feels watched, as if an important membrane has unpeeled to reveal the bald futility of whoever she is with and whatever they are saying. How unlikely it is that any of it will add up to anything. A serrated pain collects behind her eyes, her neck. Something Else. It arrives containing a quality of ongoingness; a dream that tricks the dreamer into thinking it is recurring. At first, the Something Else rummages in her mind for short periods; the time it takes her mother to move from one page of coupons to the next. After a while its visits lengthen to an afternoon. Whether it feels malevolent and how closely it cuts varies by day. It connects to the feeling of that night at Kaboom, the image of cars driving away.

*

Toni sends luxurious monologues in letter form about the person she is becoming at college. Adina writes about Auto World's Flying Man or the Sunday she waited on a popular local band until, after Christmas of her first year, she can't think of anything to write. She stops replying to Toni's letters. Instead, she writes to her superiors. One afternoon, adjusting her mascara in the diner's bathroom, she realizes she hasn't spoken with Toni in months. There was a time when she couldn't imagine spending one day without speaking to her friend. But after a shift, reeking of ranch dressing, picking up the phone to call into her friend's New York life feels similarly impossible.

*

There's a reason it's called alien-ated. Because I am an alien, I am alone. When you are alone, there is no one to tell: There is a bird whose call sounds like hoo-where-la-hoo! Or, there's a spider landing on your head. So you tell yourself. There's a spider landing on my head. I should move.

When you're alone, you are in the right place to watch sadness approach like storm clouds over an open field. You can sit in a chair and get ready for it. As it moves through you, you can reach out your hands and feel every edge. When it passes and you can drink coffee again you even miss it because it has been loyal to you like a boyfriend.

BETTER.

RED SUPERGIANT

(WORK)

On an unknowable day in the 1990s, Voyager 1 spacecraft surpasses the distance of Pioneer 10 to become the farthest human-made object in space. Even from this distant vantage, Adina thinks, it would still be able to see the Red Lion Diner, an enormous neon-accented construction that glows twenty-four hours a day alongside the Roosevelt Boulevard. Adina works the Early Bird shift, which begins at 4:00 p.m. and ditches at midnight when the goth girls arrive to work the drunks. Every afternoon at five till, octogenarians empty out from the retirement homes that border the diner. The Early Bird Special is a four-course meal for $7.99 designed around one of three choices of protein: chicken, steak, or scrod. The scrod, by far the most popular option, requires many follow-up questions. Broiled, baked, or fried? Wet (with sauce) or dry (no sauce)? If wet, cream sauce, butter sauce, or tartar? Tartar is the popular choice. During prep, tiny cups of the sour, herbaceous cream constellate on the back counter.

Adina remembers every early bird's strict preference. When she pretends to mix up dry and cream sauce they gaze on her with kind, shining eyes. Adina's favorite early bird is Lottie. Every afternoon she arrives in a matching pantsuit, removes a linen napkin from her pocketbook, tucks it into her shirt, and announces in a sharp voice: "Scrod, broiled, side of mashed and spinach. Piping hot! Dry as a bone!"

"No tartar? No lemon?" Adina protests.

"You know I like it dry!" Lottie says.

"I'm required to confirm. Lukewarm, right, Lottie?"

"Kid, I said piping hot!"

Adina likes that she can see the results of waitressing. If the counter that runs like a spine throughout the four large dining rooms is grimy with the last shift's crusted ends, she runs a damp washcloth over it until it shines. This is a welcome change from her studies and anxieties that spiral endlessly into the sky.

When Adina delivers scrod to Lottie the woman says, "Bless your heart," every time.

The Early Bird shift is run by veteran waitresses who can count their tips, eat rice pudding, and smoke at the same time. Heather's second husband is much better than the first and she has only heaven to thank. Phyllis can devote an hour every weekend to her watercolors if her husband handles the kids' breakfast. Melissa doesn't understand how Adina got mixed in with them—waitresses are supposed to have worked a year before getting this choice shift. Adina doesn't interrupt, brag, judge, complain, overtalk about herself, or ask questions they'd find dumb, which she intuits is almost every question.

"When is my dessert going to be ready?" says an early bird.

Melissa balances a tray of five specials. "Whenever."

"When is whenever?" the early bird says.

Melissa, baffled, says, "It's whenever."

Soon, the veteran waitresses are warning her about irritable regulars and filling her dressing stations though she hasn't asked. They give her a nickname: Little One.

*

On Tuesdays and Thursdays, Adina attends classes on a satellite campus two short bus rides away. Four brick buildings surrounded by ambitious trees. English Composition, Ancient Medieval Renaissance Thought, Sociology. She learns about the hunting routines of early humans but never what jokes made them laugh, whether they liked sex, if they sang to their children.

Humans are inherently social, she faxes. *Even so-called hermits who live in the wilderness are connected to other human beings by their minds. Early humans lived in groups, creating huts to gather in.*

The incoming fax reads:

WE HAVE OTHERS REPORTING ON THAT.

STICK TO YOUR OWN LIFE.

The fax is at once a rebuke, a relief, and, most important, a revelation, because it introduces Adina to the most beautiful word she's ever heard: *others*.

Where are these others? she faxes. Reasoning it is more likely to receive an answer if she attaches her curiosity to practicality, she adds, *It would be useful at this stage to compare notes, combine efforts.*

NO NEED TO COMBINE.

The tone is typically dismissive. But Adina longs to combine. At the end of her shift, stiff with cleaning bleaches, she counts her tips and goes home to her childhood bedroom.

Sometimes she eats a quick dinner with her mother but more often her mother is at work. Her mother is more of a colleague now: available for consult but just as happy to be kept abreast of only the highlights. She's been told that her promotion to assistant to the HR director will be the last because she does not have a high school degree. Adina does sit-ups, showers, faxes her superiors, tracks the night sky, watches late-night television, files her notes in orderly folders. She is nineteen Earth years old with the life of a middle-aged divorcée. Is this all there is?

*

After a two-year battle with cancer and three marrow transplants, Carl Sagan dies.

His name becomes a unit of measurement that means at least four billion. The news report shows footage of him sliding into a black hole, the image as intense and intimate for Adina as a childhood toy.

When you're little, she faxes, *sadness is a kid you can kick out of your game. A simple, fast-food feeling that leaves as soon as the bully is gone. Deeper sadnesses get buried into one's coastal shelf, accessible only by your adult version.*

She is unable to complete her nightly set of sit-ups. She sits against her bed, cheeks covered with water. *One of her fathers is gone.* Carl Sagan never stopped searching for her. He will continue forever, into the past.

*

As long as there are budgets and finite human life spans, human opportunity is a pie. This is unlike a father or friend pie because you cannot control it and there are only a certain number of slices. Humans who insist opportunity is not a pie have usually enjoyed the majority of slices.

*

One night, an older man comes in during Adina's shift, sits in her station, and asks if the special is really that special. Across the room of mint-colored booths, Heather overhears, raises her eyebrows.

"Four courses," Adina says. "Tea, coffee, or orange juice, soup or salad, entrée, and dessert, $7.99."

"That's only three," he says.

"Juice is a course."

"Juice is a course, eh? Well, well, juice is a course."

He likes to hear himself speak, Adina notes. This is common. Many of the early birds consider their advanced age a guarantee to a constant stage. She makes a good audience to their performances about the failings of their hips and children.

The man orders decaf, steak, rice pudding. "You're a cute brunette," he says.

She wonders why some men make even quotidian statements with authority, as if she's been waiting for their verdict. "I'll put that order in."

In the kitchen, Phyllis finishes a dirty joke. The cooks pause, holding their dangerous tools. "You okay out there, Little One?"

Adina delivers the man's steak then returns to refill his decaf. He hums a tuneless song Adina doesn't recognize. A few mumbled words. A singer, she thinks. Sometimes they get musicians visiting from New York. He asks in the sing-song voice what she'll do when his dick is in her mouth.

She senses Melissa, Phyllis, and Heather behind her.

"What was that?" Heather says.

He holds up his fork in protest. "I'm just eating my steak."

Heather shoves her order pad into her waistband to free up her hands. "Say it again."

The man apologizes, insists it was a joke. He eats the rest of his meal alone and when he is finished, Heather gives him the check.

"As soon as he sat down," she says after he leaves, "I called it."

The tune remains in Adina's head. When she drags a rag over the tables at the end of the night. When she takes the bus home. Even the next morning when she does everything again.

*

Keith Nguyen is a boy from her Sociology class who runs the student newspaper. He is a firsty-lasty: someone consistently referred to by their full name. One day in sophomore year he announces to the class that he needs a reporter for that weekend's lacrosse match. On a late-autumn day when the city appears rusted, Adina takes the bus to the suburbs where athletic girls bend and sway. She enjoys the flashing of limbs against the grass, the slap of ball against oak. She types her report in the college's computer lab, prints it, and leaves it in Keith Nguyen's mailbox. It feels like only light-minutes pass before he is chasing her down a hall, face flushed in confusion.

"You were supposed to report on the lacrosse match," he says.

Adina worries she has given him the wrong set of papers. "I did."

Keith Nguyen reads from the article. "'The girls pretend not to notice the other team when they take the field but it's clear they are awash in jealousy'? 'The late season sunlight makes the grass glow like milk'? 'One of the coaches says, "You've got a lot of nerve" in a mean way but the girls smile'? 'She seems like the kind of woman who would not fill you in on a conversation you've just joined'?" He pronounces every sentence as if it is a question, to ask Adina, *What is this?* "There are no scores," he says. "You don't even say the teams' names!"

"Wouldn't everyone there know them?"

"People want to read what they already know."

"Why would they want to read what they already know?"

"Comfort! Stability!"

"I can add more about the grass?"

Keith Nguyen appears stupefied by the circumstance in which he finds himself. "I don't have time to get anyone else to write this. I have to print this. In the newspaper." He wants her to fix a problem but Adina is proud of her write-up. Hearing it read aloud made her like it even more. He walks away, every so often hitting his hip with his fist still clenched around her article.

*

That afternoon, Adina fills coffees and chats with the regulars. Lottie hasn't come in for a week and she is trying to shuttle anxiety. An older woman who said, "Surprise me" about the scrod's wetness places her hand on top of Adina's.

"I remember a girl who looked like you who loved Nancy Drew books."

It is Mrs. Goldman, the woman who sold paperbacks out of her van at the Roosevelt flea market. She tells Adina she sells books in a brick-and-mortar store in the city. No more van. "I remember your intensity," she says. "I thought you'd become a writer."

Adina remembers the hush of anticipation as the woman slid the van door open every Sunday. The book that taught her the term making out. All the metal things being sold on blankets at dawn.

"Nope," she says. "Just a waitress."

"A waitress can be very literary too."

"I guess so." Adina hears the chef call her on the kitchen's microphone: "Little One, your scrod is ready." Little One. Scrod. "I gotta go," she says. "It was nice to see you, Mrs. Goldman."

The hope in her eyes, waiting to hear what wonderful news Adina will share, dims. "It was so nice to see you, Adina."

Adina delivers the scrod and returns to the kitchen. She leans against the doorframe, wads of checks and tips fattening her pockets. She is relieved when the woman gathers her coat and pocketbook, stands and looks toward the kitchen, a pause that creates a chance for Adina to emerge and say something better.

✶

One Saturday morning, Adina works the morning shift, a solar system of new customs and concerns involving eggs. Returning home, a familiar car is parked in front of the complex.

Across the lawn, her mother shows Dominic the future sites of plants. "Look who it is!" her mother calls. "Home visiting his family."

"Thought we could go for a ride." He gestures to the Mustang.

"I'm in my uniform."

"Well? Change."

On the ride, Dominic pulls a bong, a toilet paper roll, and two tinfoil hats from his back seat. The toilet paper roll is stuffed with fabric softener. "This takes away the smell," he says. "And the hat protects you from mind control from other planets." He's been reading about UFOs and tells her that New Mexico is a hotbed for sightings.

"Those are fake." Adina arranges the hat on her head.

"That's what they want us to think!"

They park and sit on the Mustang's trunk. The Willows are articulated in snow. It is cold but there is sun. Dominic teaches her how to pull smoke into the chamber.

"Pretend you're about to get caught stealing," he says. "Gasp to pull it into your lungs."

She does it but the smoke doesn't retract.

"Try again," he says. "Again," when it's still not working.

She wants to hear every movie he has seen in New York. "We might be here for a while." Does he have a favorite movie theater? "Of course. New York is nice," he says. "New York is lonely."

"How can you be lonely in a city of ten million people?"

During his time away Dominic has figured out his hair. Its waves are arranged to create a shelf under which his dark eyes shine.

"Hard to imagine," she says. "I've never been lonely."

"That's great," he says.

"I'm not sure if it's great or not because I've never been anything else." Dominic's smile fades. Adina is bragging.

"I think I'm lonely all the time," he says. "Like all the all the time."

Adina realizes that her human body is comprised of correspondingly named spaghetti. Spaghettis. Orecchiette, the Italian word for ear. Each of her knuckles, gnocchi. Linguine, little tongues. Elbow macaroni. She points each out to Dominic.

He says, "You're making me hungry."

They take the way home that leads to the Terwood Road Hill and the wide meadow where on most nights deer stand pearled in moonlight. This night, no deer. But there is a moon, so surprising and wide it quiets them.

Adina asks if he's dating anyone in New York and he tells her no one special. A boy he liked in his Life Drawing class turned out to be too in love with drugs. This is Dominic coming out to her. He says a boy in his class loves drugs and Adina says, "That's too bad."

There are deer after all. Two, identical in size and features, standing close to each other like repeated thought. They watch the car, one works something over in its mouth in what Adina intuits to be a judgmental way. "Do they know we're high?"

"They know you are."

At the end of the field, Terwood Road ascends into a sharp stomach-dropping cliff.

"Oh no," Adina says.

Dominic accelerates. "Oh no is right."

The hill, the gut pull of weightlessness, the gravity of fear. Dominic plays a song on the Mustang's new CD player, chucks it onto a mountain of them in the back seat, tries another. Adina is grateful to have a friend in New York who visits her. She is grateful for the car's heat though it smells like mud and ink. She wishes it was possible to drive forever. They return to Adina's house.

Though relying on rides is a hassle, Adina likes the moment before getting dropped off. The reserved people she grew up with only seemed comfortable sharing after they pulled to a halt and before she got out. The space's brevity allowed candor, the rare remark that contradicted the phoniness that comprised the everyday behavior of whoever was driving—the friend's parent, older brother, or sister, the teacher—could even contradict whole ways of living. Maybe the certain end point furnished a deniability both parties could use if anyone dared call the other out in other, more visible places like family rooms and kitchen tables. The confiding party could say that Adina hadn't heard correctly or that they never said it—The Thing. Having kids is not as great as I thought. There was a man before my husband. She didn't mind if they attempted to shelve it as soon as they said it or pretended it had been her keeping them, her hand poised on the door handle, listening as she usually did, with all of her heart. Adina is well-suited to the secrecy that facilitated these vestibules. She lives for them—the only time adults appear in focus, aware of themselves as humans. This comforts her as if they've said, *It's okay, Adina, we are alive, we are here with you, walking around*. Sometimes when she thinks a ride won't include one of these vestibules, she lingers, to encourage it.

"You can keep the hat," Dominic says, and she says, "What hat?" She has forgotten the tinfoil circling her head.

She gets out, turns around, and speaks through the open window. "I'll give it to you when you come back? A loaner."

He says he'll stay in New York for the holidays, eat Chinese food, and listen to Dolly Parton.

"How is your mom with that?"

Dominic says, "Our mom is our mom."

It's the closest they come to mentioning Toni. The unnecessary, telltale first-person plural.

*

Adina, high, faxes late into the night.

Plants are the earth's hair. Genius *and* ingenious *mean the same thing! Same goes for* thaw *and* dethaw! *Why are there two words for what you do to a frozen chicken and only one for missing your best friend or the look Pat Sajak gives to Vanna White when they walk to their separate stations at the beginning of every* Wheel of Fortune *episode? Why is there only one word for* waiting*? And not even one word for when you discover only after pouring your cereal that there is no milk?*

She is woken up by an incoming reply squeaking through the machine:

THESE OBSERVATIONS ARE UNSURPRISING AND MEDIOCRE.

ARE YOU ILL?

*

Keith Nguyen visits her in the diner, looking stupefied.

"Everyone loves your article," he says. "I've never gotten so many compliments."

"Glad it worked out," Adina says. "You seemed really aggravated."

"It's the most popular thing the paper has ever done. I misjudged how many people would be interested in a lacrosse write-up that isn't about lacrosse."

"People are weird," Adina says.

"There's a swim meet this weekend. Will you write about it?"

Adina considers water lapping against the stone sides of a pool. Cascading off a swimmer's hands as they pound down the lanes. Even standing in the diner's loud glade, she can see the arc of elbows, the shapes of the swimmers' mouths sucking air. The snap of goggles. The brightly colored caps.

*

Adina's mother's garden grows beyond the third electric pole. There are rosebushes in red, pink, and yellow, a hank of daffodils and three kinds of mint, daylilies and moon lilies to trumpet every hour, snap peas, radishes. Every week her mother fills boxes of whatever's abundant for the residents of the complex. She doesn't charge. It gives her an opportunity to check in, she says, to linger in the doorways exalting over a well-formed basil leaf. Benches face the garden's center and every afternoon there's someone sitting on one gazing at a bud or a bee as if dreaming. So close to Auto World.

One hot August afternoon, Mrs. Leafhalter calls Adina's mother to remind her she doesn't want snap peas in that week's box and mentions her heart has been doing funny things. When Adina's mother presses for information she tells her to quit the fourth degree and hangs up. Adina's mother walks to the woman's apartment and finds her sprawled on the kitchen floor.

Mrs. Leafhalter's will specifies her desire to be cremated and scattered into the Atlantic Ocean. Family members who'd never visited arrive to box up her things. They are unsmiling variations on Mrs. Leafhalter. One of them walks over to Adina's apartment holding the moss-green television set.

"My aunt wanted you to have this."

Adina recognizes her from the bungalow's pictures. She wears a sweater with a smiling owl. Adina thanks her, says she will cherish it. The woman nods and rejoins her family.

Though it's the middle of summer, Adina's mother draws a bath and closes the door.

*

The television set gets three channels well and five poorly. Adina watches a nature documentary about a colony of genetically identical aspen trees named Pando. It is a forest but is, genetically, only one tree that grew from a flea-size seed. The singular plural. The parent tree is male so to sit in this grove would mean to sit among acres and acres of the same man. Adina thinks of Toni's brothers, her stepfather, the boys they went to school with. Men and men and men. Adina spends a week reading about him/them. The books describe the sound of the wind blowing through this aspen grove as water rushing, but the cacophony is really the multi-stranded voice of a single organism, the biggest on Earth. Quaking men. Comprised of many but solo as a star. Adina knows what it's like to be one consciousness in an intergalactic stew. She longs to hear him/them. By the time she reads about Pando, it is like many beautiful things on Earth, in danger of dying. Human pressure has created wildfire conditions, overgrazing, bark disease.

Adina stays awake all night, aware of every passing moment.

What even is an individual? Where even is Utah?

She misses Solomon and her people, deeply rooted in each other, many sounds beating as one.

*

Humans express mundane concern and sympathy using expressions like Oh Nelly, uh-oh, dang. *There are no direct translations for what are called idiomatic expressions.*

WHY NELLY? WHY NOT *OH FIRE HYDRANT*?

Names are often used to avoid cursing. Saint Peter, What the Sam Hill? *They fill a space. Other humans realize the sentiment is not quite right, but not filling the space would be worse. Remaining silent or motionless when someone has shared that their insurance won't cover a routine gynecological visit would be construed as remote and rude. These valueless expressions are acts of kindness and participation.*

OH GARAGE? OH LAUREN?

Whoever is operating their communiqué possesses the literalism of a seven-year-old. *Human* is the word that normally answers their questions, but human is what she's on Earth to define, and she can't define the word by using the word.

If when I explain human behavior you insist on logic, we won't get far.

*

In January of Adina's junior year, the Red Lion Diner loses power in the middle of the Early Bird shift. Regulars sit at the counter with the veteran waitresses, playing cards and telling jokes. Lottie explains a dance they used to do in the city and holds Adina to demonstrate. When humans enjoy themselves they no longer feel the passage of time. They forget the constraints or failures of their physical bodies. When the electricity returns with a shuddering pop they are disappointed because they've been enjoying a stolen season.

Adina likes the satisfaction of completing a waitressing shift. Checks filed, dressings refilled, apron folded, people who need to be told she's leaving told. This reliable unzip of freedom arrives every time, an end-of-day relaxation. Yards better than a day in college.

*

Adina sits in the college library accessing her new email account, meant to evoke the feel of a mailbox. In her "mailbox" next to glowing envelope icons she finds chain letters that threaten death if she does not pass them on. Why would anyone want to do this? She feels far away from other humans and far away in the general, galactic sense.

Adina types Toni's full name and *nyu.edu*.

Hello, she types. *Is this thing on?*

She presses send.

When there is no answer after ten minutes, she leaves and drives home. She wishes she could see a movie with Dominic. She misses the companionable silence, the previews, even people eating popcorn loudly in the dark.

*

Two women around Adina's age are seated in her section. One has a familiar way of considering the menu like it better impress her. Janae. Heather is in the weeds and Melissa is in the back, arranging school pickup with her husband, so no one can cover for her. Adina approaches the table as if it contains strangers and not the orchestrator of her greatest humiliation.

"Adina," Janae says. "Girl, oh my god!"

She introduces the woman across from her as a coworker. They drove down to the city from Syracuse, where they go to college. "Adina and I went to school together back in the day," Janae says. "Do you still live here? How was high school?"

"Good," Adina says. "You?"

"You know how it is. So good. Wow. We used to have so much fun."

"We didn't," Adina says.

Janae's smile slips. "Okay. It was only the best time of my life."

"We did not have the same experience."

"Really?" Janae tells her friend. "I only remember great times."

"At the dance. With Amadeo?"

Janae lets the menu drop to the table. She shifts in her seat. Her friend asks a question without words and Janae blinks prettily, no trace of joke in their endless black.

"I don't remember," she says. "It's wild you still live here. I thought everyone left as fast as they could. Even that weird girl Toni lives in New York now, I hear. Adina! I can't believe it. After all these years."

In the kitchen, the waitresses collect around the dressing station. Seeing her, Melissa clears tears from her cheeks. "It's Lottie," she says.

She had been on dialysis for a little over a year ("That's

why we wouldn't see her for long stretches," Phyllis says) but her prognosis was looking up until she took a turn the week before ("Cha cha cha," Lottie had said the day the power went out, gripping Adina's waist and leading her across the floor. "Not cha cha bleh,") and went downhill fast ("It was peaceful," Heather says. "A blessing," Melissa adds). Her son stopped in earlier to tell them.

Adina sits, dumb with shock. She says she's sorry, and Phyllis says there's no sorry. There's just it sucks. Heather rips a check from her pad. "Ever since I turned fifty, people have been dying."

Phyllis says Lottie was much older than fifty and Heather says, "You know what I mean. At fifty, people start to leave the room."

✶

Human beings fetishize no organ more than the heart. This manifests in language, the heart has its own vocabulary. When they like someone they say: There's a girl after my own heart. They will stand or sit very close to the person they love with their heart. Bless your heart. Cross my heart. When they are sad they say: My heart is broken. They will tell large groups of people things they don't believe. But the heart is just a muscle with an important job. Only an area in the body.

Eyes are another commonly fetishized part of the human body. The seeing parts. But once they were only pockets of sensitive atoms on the foreheads of primordial fish. Sightless skin that yearned to make something fantastic out of light. It had to invent looking to look. First, it turned itself inside out. Then it developed permeable parts that allowed the light to change it, articulate its sensors, manipulate and clarify, until it was no longer skin, but grasping, blinking membrane, able to look and look and look. Light is the only artist. It created the tools to see.

Arms are also a fetishized part of the human body. The holding parts.

✶

Adina's mother digs at a stubborn rhododendron root. "Salt Lake where?"

Adina will be gone four days. Heather will cover her shifts. She will land in Utah with enough time to catch the bus to a hostel outside of Pando. The hostel runs shuttles to the aspen grove. She leaves her itinerary with her mother in a folder the color of aspen leaves, including the names and phone numbers of the airport, hostel, and shuttle companies. She has read the FAA's annual report and an aeronautics textbook.

✶

Adina's mother drives her to the airport. Adina is twenty-two Earth years old and it is her first flight. It is a low slung, late-spring day, winds of less than five miles per hour coming from the west. Low ceilings in Salt Lake City.

The airport carpet is teal with tan palm trees. A family of thin, tan people with overlarge sunglasses stand in line at the airport's coffee shop. Mother, father, daughter, daughter. Father stands at the glass counter yelling options to the daughters. Do they want croissants? A muffin? "What kind are those?" he asks the clerk. "No, those. Those. Lemon what?" He shouts to his daughters, "Lemon poppy." The father wants the daughters to participate, play, not in a game way but theater. Gate 12 in Terminal D is their stage. The daughters perform paging through a magazine. The mother performs a conceptual piece with the items in her pocketbook. She removes each one, places it on the café table, frowns as if it has disappointed her then with a weary headshake returns it to the bag. Amid the more relaxed postures and bodies of the other travelers this family (celebrities, Adina is certain, though she doesn't know who or from where) seem placed by a director, like they're something other than human. Exotic, emphatically groomed insects, not kind or at ease. Underneath their smooth performance lies a restlessness, as if they are distracted by their potential effect. "Are you sure you don't need anything?" The father checks to see whether they are being watched. Insulated by layers of cream and wealth his family ends up appearing discomfited and separate. What a terrible feeling.

The realization begins simultaneously at the top of Adina's head and the base of her stomach. If she boards this plane, she will die. She should leave, take an hour-long bus ride back to her neighborhood. When her mother asks, she will say the airport's carpet was teal with tan palm trees. Something about it connects to this feeling of doom. Maybe because palm trees don't belong in Philadelphia. Instead, she walks the gangway. When she reaches the lip of the plane she halts, allows those behind her to pass. A flight attendant makes an announcement on a manilla, spiral-cord phone like theirs. Seeing Adina, he covers the receiver. "You okay?"

Adina finds her seat and secures the buckle across her waist. Checks and tightens it. The plane ignites, burns a few things up inside itself. It reverses smoothly, out of proportion with a clanking that's coming from the rear. The plane hurtles down the runway. They can't possibly make it into the sky. But then the plane shivers and retracts parts of itself into itself and they are flying. Humans with window seats point to cloud formations. Adina closes her eyes. They climb into the sky. She counts to one hundred, a tip she read in one of the beauty magazines she allowed herself to buy in the airport's newsstand. It's been years since she's read them, but their frivolity is the only thing that will keep her attention through the agony of takeoff until they breach the clouds where it is always a sunny day.

During turbulence, Adina locks herself in the bathroom and counts to five hundred. Her powers of observation are malfunctioning. She hears every part of the engine. Turbulence tumbles her back to her seat where the flight attendant offers drinks, unaware of their doom.

Adina's voice is calm. "Are we going to crash?"

He smiles. Would she like water? Coffee?

"Chardonnay," she says.

She sips it, belted aggressively to the seat. They clear the sill of turbulence.

The flight attendant's voice startles her. He has returned to crouch beside her.

"After reaching cruising altitude," he says, "nothing can force a plane out of the sky. So what are you afraid of? Wind or engine failure?"

"Staying the same forever," she says. "And wind."

*

When they reach Salt Lake City, Adina straps her bag to her back, clears the receiving line of captains and flight attendants (thank you for keeping us safe, she tells the flight attendant, staring until he, registering discomfort, turns to the next passenger), walks into the airport's hub, bright with sound and travelers, follows signs for ground transportation to the basement where candy-colored counters offer different ways to take a train. Adina chooses the clerk she guesses least likely to ask questions. She requests a one-way ticket to New York City, opens the envelope of cash meant for the hostel and slides over the correct amount.

Adina does not breathe in the center of the noble grove of aspens. She does not hear their ethereal sigh. She buys a lemon poppy muffin and descends an escalator to a galley of heaving trains where she boards the California Zephyr. The train travels through Utah as she eats cake from a napkin, proud of herself for venturing this far and ashamed of allowing fear to retract her like a dog on a chain. But the cake is good. Sweet, with a fair distribution of seeds. That afternoon a mountain range overtakes the Colorado horizon, announcing itself so boldly it feels like sound. They move through daises of gentle trees that diminish toward the mountaintop. She's never seen so many, green like cooked broccoli, straight as sentinels. She takes notes, trying to describe their color in the sunset. Instead of only Utah, Adina will see Utah, Colorado, Nebraska, Missouri, Illinois, Ohio, and the other side of Pennsylvania. Fear has enabled a broader adventure.

The train squeals to a halt in Omaha. Passengers announce they will go outside to stretch their legs. Adina calls her mother on a pay phone. The receiver is a cold bar in the night. She has seen goats perched on the top of a cliff, a horizon filled with smoke, pale wheat making language with the wind. Travel has already sharpened her intuition. She senses something enormous and anticipatory in the dark surrounding her.

Her mother answers, halfway through a laugh, knowing it's her.

"Guess where I am?" Adina says.

"Well, Utah. I hope?"

Adina holds the phone out so her mother can hear the train, an anxious creature huffing in the night. She says, "Guess again."

*

Adina returns home and has barely dropped her things before faxing her superiors. She is mirthful, giddy.

Dear Everyone, I'm dropping out and going to New York City.

She wonders over the urge to use a salutation. She has never addressed them before, has always gotten to the point.

The incoming fax reads: OH NELLY.

*

Adina takes the bus to Jenkintown where a Toyota Tercel sits in front of a suburban house. An older man emerges with his son who seems annoyed they are selling his car. In exchange for an envelope of cash, he places a key into her palm. Light, nickel. Adina can't believe she owns this car, that she can hang whatever she wants on the rearview mirror. This is money: With enough of it, you can get what you want. She has planned the first song she will play on the cassette deck, A Tribe Called Quest's "Excursions." It is a warm day. She removes her jacket and places it on the passenger seat like a friend. She accelerates, enjoying the pressure of movement. The certain brakes. She rides home past Terwood Hill to feel fear leap into her throat.

*

Keith Nguyen visits during her last day at the diner. Her writing has become so popular people stop him on campus to ask about her. It must be the honesty, simplicity. He says she can keep reporting from New York, though she won't be a student. He maintains a bemused stance but is disappointed when she declines.

"I'll miss your voice, Adina. You're not like anyone else I've met."

"That is an auspicious distinction."

He insists he doesn't want the chicken fingers she's wrapped up for him but looks pleased as he pushes out the door.

*

The veteran waitresses stick a candle in a dish of rice pudding and sing "New York, New York."

Three aproned women, paused in work, hair dyed outlandishly, arms around one another's waists where their order pads are shoved, singing a classic medley off-key

"Don't forget us when you move to the Big Apple," Heather says.

"Forget us, Little One," Melissa says. "Forget us as soon as you leave."

*

The move to the city creates a vestibule, a one-last-thing-before-I-go impulse that Adina decides to act on.

Mom, she will say, *I have something to tell you.*

It will be like the movies her mother loves to watch on their new, thin television. Ash-blond women sharing revelations at oversize kitchen counters. Your husband is not your husband. Your father is your brother. Only this will be her daughter, clearer.

*

Adina and her mother spend her last Saturday in Northeast Philadelphia organizing and boxing her belongings. Skee-Ball tickets, never enough to win the spider ring, photo booth shots, her collection of books and tapes.

They order square pizza and sit at the half-moon table.

"I have a daughter who's going to New York," her mother says. As if she is trying to understand having a daughter, daughters themselves, New York City, and the act of going somewhere other than where you've grown up.

"What did you think I'd do?"

"Have a kid?" she says. "Get married? But you've never even had a boyfriend."

Adina shakes her head. "Not interested."

"No one?" her mother says, and Adina understands that her mother has been waiting to ask. "Even . . . girls?"

"Not interested. I'm sorry if that's disappointing."

"Hey," her mother says. "You are not a disappointment."

"Mom," Adina says. "I have something to tell you."

She places the piece of pizza down and takes a long sip of water. "Here it comes."

"I am not really from here."

"From where?" her mother says. "Philadelphia?" She sits in the cross-legged way that makes her look like a teenager. Adina gestures to their plates, slick with oil, the table strewn with house keys, hair bands, the tool that collapses the air mattress, her car keys buckled to a key chain reading DON'T CALL IT A COMEBACK. Small, easy-to-lose, integral objects. "Here."

Adina explains the activation, the fax machine, the Night Classroom, roller coasters. Her mother takes absent-minded bites of her pizza, expression deepening into confusion. Some words are harder to say. Father. Mission. She uses the word extraterrestrial hoping it will sound less scary to her mother and because she has never understood what she is allegedly alien to. The word is derogatory and overly general. At least extraterrestrial provides a frame of reference and a location for prejudice. Extra—in addition to. Terre—Earth. And yet. She is wholly of and not of Earth. Relief grows as she confides in her mother, as if each word removes an obstructive item of clothing that hindered her ability to feel weather. By the time she is finished, she no longer fears her mother's reaction. She is lighter and more herself. A shell-less snail.

"The day you were born," her mother says, "I was with my girlfriends getting my nails done. They were going to a club. It started with a pulling." She motions to her abdomen. "They said it was indigestion, but I knew. You were early, but I knew."

A passing car's 808 drum vibrates through the house.

"I was born here," Adina says.

"Is what I'm saying. Two miles away. Someone went to find your father but I had no support. No family. You came from me. I almost died. There was a light and everything. I was there."

"I know," Adina says. "But what I'm telling you is also true."

"That you think you're an alien?" Her tone makes it clear: This is a theory Adina has about herself.

Adina doesn't want to believe that her mother aligns with the *J* girls and the man at Beautyland and Toni's older brothers and everyone else who ignores human suffering to maintain the status quo. "That I am one." Hurt stiffens her words.

"This is a hard one to follow," her mother says. Outside, her garden is closing itself up for the fall. "New York, I understand. Dropping out, even, though I don't love it. But this makes it sound like you don't want to be in the world. What did I do wrong to make you not want to be in the world?"

Adina realizes her naivete. Coming from a background where everything is work, of course her mother categorizes her news as within the realm of her own mental failing.

"You didn't do anything wrong," she says.

"Whatever it is"—her mother stands, places Adina's dish on top of hers, swings the cardboard box, the conversation, shut—"it's probably best to keep it to yourself."

*

The next morning, so early the garden is cinched in frost, so early Auto World is closed.

Books, copybooks, television set, fax machine. The trip will be three cassettes long: Tribe, De La Soul, R.E.M. Business is being conducted online and phones are shrinking but the Flying Man remains unchanged. As Adina loads the last of her boxes into the car, he performs an exaggerated goodbye across the street from her mother's more subdued one. *Where?* it says. *Over there? All the way to New York City? Goodbye, Adina. Goodbye.*

Her mother stands on the curb and gives instructions. Don't speed, don't turn right on red, call when you get there. "How would you feel about me going back to school? I'm considering. At night. GED first, then college, maybe."

Adina imagines her mother sitting at a desk in a classroom. Making funny comments. Sharpening a pencil. It's another crisscross. Her dropping out of college as her mother enrolls. She waits for Adina to answer, looking nervous.

"You'll be great," Adina says.

Her mother appears noticeably relieved. Adina starts the car, whisks away anger, having granted the validation she had hoped to receive. Through the passenger window, her mother hands her a toasted bagel wrapped in foil that Adina knows is already soggy and an adolescent aloe plant from her garden. "For burns." She wraps the arms of her robe tighter and walks back into the house, stooping to throw the neighbor's paper over to their landing. Adina drives away.

Mother heating Lipton tea in the microwave. Mother taking swipes at the back stairs with the broom, old bristles crackling and ineffective. Mother holding chives like pom-poms cheering in the garden. No more daughter, yelling from the kitchen: What's my social security number? What's the Fibonacci sequence? How big is Canada? No more daughter doing homework in the back room, launching at the sound of her name.

Adina takes the boulevard to the Pennsylvania Turnpike to the New Jersey Turnpike to Exit 13, Verrazzano Bridge. At the tollbooth she holds a fistful of coins out the open window, in love with the smell of exhaust. She's never lived anywhere except her mother's house. There is no traffic. The trip is only two hours north, but as she navigates the nebulae of lanes on the Brooklyn-Queens Expressway, honking and merging and driving offensively like Dominic told her, Statue of Liberty dodging her between the unfamiliar buildings, she feels light-hours away from her landmarks. It is her third and final lost home. Comets and her mother's lilies. Auto World and the stars.

Whatever it is, she thinks, *best keep it to yourself.*

SUPERNOVA

(NEW YORK CITY)

Astronomers discover an ultra-cool red dwarf star in the constellation Aquarius orbited by seven Earth-size planets the same month Adina moves into a junior one-bedroom under the flight patterns of JFK and LaGuardia airports. The chief characteristic of her new neighborhood is sound.

Adina's apartment building is bordered by the elevated 7 train and a halal meat-cart-vendor warehouse. Every morning when the sun peeks over the 7 train's silver flanks the halal vendors drag their metal carts, ancient and unwilling as dinosaurs, down the alley past her bedroom to the street and load them into large trucks. The trucks drive into the city and drop each cart off at a location designated by seniority, veteran vendors getting corners near Wall Street, newbies taking the outer avenues where fewer people walk. Adina knows this because she has spent a few early mornings in conversation with a vendor named Lionel who drives a later truck. The vendors spend the day fulfilling the lunch requests of the city's workers. Then, at 7:30 p.m., when the sun sinks beneath the pigeon-dirt-speckled awning of Caress Hair Braiding, the vendors drag their carts back down the alley past Adina's bedroom. Planes, subways, carts. Every few minutes her apartment shudders from whatever mode of transport hustles by. These sounds don't bother her because they are not dainty eating noises and because they are signals of movement that make her feel successful. She has become a sort of hub.

Lionel is a native New Yorker. Adina asks if he has any advice for a human who has just arrived.

He says, "Trust the group."

*

Adina builds two bookcases and slides her fax machine onto the lowest shelf, next to a tidy stack of paper. She arranges her books by author and her folders of notes chronologically, hangs the string lights her mother packed. The apartment is the shape of an uppercase L, her bed shoved into the smaller part. Everything else is living room. A nonworking fireplace takes up so much space in the larger part of the L that it seems conspicuously unlit, like a friend who's not speaking to her. But this might be a projection in this city where humans walk and yell and eat and pay single-mother quick, so quick Adina doubts whether her own single mother could keep up. She stands on her bed and without leaning too far can touch both walls.

*

Adina works as a receptionist for Landry Business Solutions. She has no idea what the company does. When people ask, she says, when businesses have problems, they have solutions. If they press her, she says it involves outsourcing. There are no fax machines at Landry Business Solutions because everyone uses email. She answers the phone, keeps the candy jar filled, and monitors the bathroom key. Ten minutes out of her twenty-minute training was candy-jar related. The other ten consisted of bathroom-key shakedown tactics. People are always losing the bathroom key and the receptionist before her must have gotten frustrated, because she hot-glued it to a New York license plate. Adina has no friends at Landry Business Solutions. She assumes they are too busy outsourcing and thinking of solutions. They don't bother her and, unless they receive a FedEx package, she doesn't bother them.

Adina likes her hour-long commute on the 7 train, which is both an express and a local. The express's number 7 is bordered by a diamond, the local's by a circle: This is the only way for commuters to distinguish which will bring them to their station and which will go singing by. Adina likes when at a stop a commuter leaps on and, balancing as if on a wire, yells, "Express or local?" because they are tourists or because the number's shape has been obscured by time or city sludge. Adina likes yelling "Express!" and watching the commuter stumble delighted to a seat or "Local!" and watching the commuter bat against oncoming people like a moth before leaping out.

*

Adina goes to work, comes home, steams broccoli alongside an uninspired chicken breast, and does not call Dominic or attempt to make friends. Like Italian, learning New York requires constant listening, discipline, and translation.

Thankfully, the city contains eight million teachers, eager to correct her. "Can't use that here," a New Yorker says about her golf-size umbrella. "Step aside if you don't have it," another says when it takes her too long to make change at the token machine. Her Philadelphia pace, accessories, and attitude do not translate. The full-price boots she bought with her mother aren't built for the city's walking and within a month lay heelless and crumpled by the door. Cheap sneakers work best. She walks miles a day, gaining fluency, the city's parks unrolling in front of her, big as boroughs, its caves and beaches, its terrifying and helpful denizens.

*

The seven Earth-size planets orbiting the red star dubbed TRAPPIST-1 are debuted at a news conference in Washington, D.C. Adina watches on the television that hangs in the Landry Business Solutions lobby, where a woman in a sharp pantsuit waits for solutions.

The planets are temperate enough to make water possible, which means they have the potential to support life. They may even have oceans. Researchers believe the planets closest to TRAPPIST-1 are tidally locked, one side always facing the sun, the other in perpetual night.

The phone rings as the lead astronomer says, "Answering the question 'Are we alone?' is a top science priority. We've made a crucial step towards finding if life is out there."

"I'm here," Adina says to her boss Santino, who has called to ask if the woman is still waiting for solutions.

"She is," Adina assures him.

Adina longs to call into the universe and have someone answer. But when the astronomer says "Life," he means creatures who look like him. Adina changes the channel to a rerun of *Friends*. It is 1999 and Americans are obsessed with the situational comedy about six rich white people living in this city. Adina doesn't understand why the show is funny; the characters struggle so baldly underneath their meaninglessness, desperate to preserve the cordoned-off theater of their absurd lives. She has spent many faxes describing their bad Christmases, blind dates gone awry, irritable fathers. Chandler, meant to be the funniest character, delivers his lines with black-hole eyes. No human can thrive. In this episode, Phoebe advises Monica not to date a wrestler, citing a parable from her own sad childhood.

"You're a real bummer," Rachel says.

*

Between phone calls at Landry Business Solutions, Adina types her faxes into a Word document. When she finishes a page she moves it to a folder labeled, *Finished*. Over the course of several months, Adina revisits her past selves who loved betta fish, the Flying Man, Amadeo, and dancing. She had detailed every moment of the *J* girl dance, from the pumping opening sequence to the final, threatening stance. Occasionally, she pauses in the Landry Business Solutions waiting room, halted by the memory of a subject she'd detailed with meticulous patience but no longer cares about. Was there ever a time when she thought retail stores had sales because they loved their customers? When she thought it was impossible to be unhappy while holding balloons? Blue bettas, red glasses, the moon. Her past passions sound tinny when clinking against the jar of time. But they add up to a stack next to her elbow, a growing collection of desire and insight that might acquire significance if she trusts that it will. When the completion of a folder coincides with a Friday afternoon, she buys an oversize cookie from one of the bodegas that cluster beneath the train platform like cave flowers. Grapefruits shiver as the train roars by.

*

Adina's neighbor dresses three ceramic geese on her stoop in seasonally appropriate attire. Papa, Mama, gosling. Fourth of July American flag jumpsuits, back-to-school plaid. Every season their fresh costumes are an unexpected note of whimsy in the rattling neighborhood. On Thanksgiving, the parent geese are dressed as pilgrims and the gosling as a turkey. Adina is transfixed by the mind of a human who would dress a ceramic gosling as its cousin bird. It turns out to be a practical woman who commutes to an accounting job in Manhattan. She finds the outfits online.

"It's big in the Midwest," she says.

Adina looks forward to the costume changes that arrive without warning. She likens them to launching a new season of her own life. She's not alone. One spring afternoon she walks home to encounter other neighbors collected at the stoop, marveling over picnic blanket attire, the gosling holding a miniature basket of plastic daffodils.

One neighbor turns to Adina, beaming. "She's outdone herself."

✶

Adina's boss Santino paces the nondescript hallways of Landry Business Solutions positing hypothetical questions.

"Why would there be an order for paper when I see boxes of it stacked in the hall?"

"Is there a reason I don't have the Preston case on my desk?"

Santino has expressed through several hypothetical self-inquiries that he does not believe in "excess communiqué." When they dare ask a question he offers an anecdote about his daughter, Kendra. Perhaps he's read a management book whose #1 rule is: *Use a family member as an example for everything*. He is unable to process a thought without funneling it through some mundane thing Kendra has said or done. No Landry Business Solutions worker has met Kendra, but based on Santino's anecdotes, they can assume she files reports days before they are due, doesn't bombard him with questions when he walks in the door, and bemoans the thought of people reheating fish.

Taped to the kitchen microwave is a computer-generated image of a smiling salmon bearing a thick X. It was placed there by Santino. Yet for weeks he insists it was posted anonymously by an employee who must share his hatred of fish stink. At every stilted break room meet-up, Santino contemplates the identity of his anonymous fish-stink-hating compadre.

"I wouldn't want to run the risk of making that guy angry," he says. "He might put up a poster of me."

This amuses Adina where she sits at her desk typing her most private thoughts into her work computer. She imagines a sign with an overweight man clinging to the wallet chain craze of the 1990s, under a wide, generous X.

*

The ego of the human male is by far the most dangerous aspect of human society.

THIS HAS BEEN WELL-DOCUMENTED.

*

One year passes. Then, two. Computers get smaller, car phones get bigger, the internet broadens into a galaxy she can hold in her hand. TRAPPIST-1 turns out to not be as exciting as the astronomers hoped. No aqua. Boot-cut jeans that had replaced low-crotch jeans give way to skinny jeans that allow no space for boots so are worn with slimmer Chelseas or demure white sneakers. Adina's mother passes her GED and attends night classes at a local college. Online shopping is invented.

One particular model on Anthropologie's website appears to be in perpetual agony. She startles Adina as she scrolls the store's wares: a smile, a beatific glance, then her: devastated. In a hip-length top, a flowy jumpsuit, a drop-waisted wrap dress, she is inconsolable. So different from the other models, pleasant and isolated in their editorial panels. She hooks her thumbs into the loops of relaxed denim and stares out in horror. Why isn't anyone helping her as she pretends to bend over to pick up an invisible desired object? How can anyone think about après-ski wear amid this woman's nightmare?

*

Old rituals in new cities: Every week, Adina stops into her neighborhood animal shelter to see the fish. One evening, a tiny dog sits in a small cage with his paws folded in an aggravated stance as if she's late.

The shelter employee unlatches the cage and the dog springs out, the size and color of a butternut squash. The 7 parps by, rattling the beds and toys. The shelter employee scoops him into one palm and hands him to Adina. The dog perches in the crook of her elbow, heaves a sigh, and closes his eyes. He's a papillon, the French word for butterfly, and was brought in that day by a nurse moving to an apartment that won't allow pets.

"Butterfly," the shelter employee says. "Because of his giant ears."

Adina has never been the only thing separating a living creature from death. But he is obviously hers because they have the same shade of brown eyes and because he also seems annoyed by the shelter employee's slowness.

She pays the adoption fee but leaves him overnight so she can spend the evening gathering the softest things in the city. She buys tender treats in the shape of bacon strips. A child's blanket for his bed. A sweater with an embroidered deer.

"For winter," she tells the store clerk.

The next morning, she returns to the shelter where the little dog glares in his cage.

"He made a racket after you left," the shelter employee says. "A barking problem you'll have to train out of him."

Adina cannot match the placid little dog with the idea of making a racket. "Probably because his hopes were up."

The employee shrugs. A black kitten appears over his shoulder like a manager.

At home, the winter sweater fits. The little dog circles himself a few times, trying to bite the deer on his back. He sits, glances at the nonworking fireplace, the books, her box of notes.

She says, "This is your home."

That night when Adina goes to bed, the little dog goes to his bed. He curls into himself and falls asleep. Adina watches his furred chest rise and fall.

*

Adina teaches the little dog to sit, turn around, and offer his paw. The stack of finished papers by her elbow grows. She develops relationships with the bodega clerks. Her favorite is Emilio, who sells round rolls two for a dollar, has a daughter who is dating a boy he doesn't like, and said the second time she bought an apple juice, "Ah. Your regular."

She meets a fashion student who encourages her to find what he calls "your signature jean jacket." Everything in his apartment is vintage. Gumball machines, coatrack, milk glass. What's old is always better, he tells her. They scour the cramped aisles of the city's vintage stores, holding up options and dismissing them. He knew they'd get along, he says, because he's a Cancer and she's a Libra. Libras appreciate beauty. They drink beers on a rooftop where an old movie plays. It is about Sam Shepard wearing a leather coat. Sam Shepard wears that leather coat to the grave.

*

Every so often the Something Else runs its system through her, but nothing that can't be dispersed by a bagel from the place she likes.

*

The fashion student peels a hard-boiled egg in a familiar way and Adina realizes friendships are reincarnations. Everyone reminds her of someone she knew. *Was the world on a twenty-year loop or did the human mind only have the capacity to make a finite amount of correspondences?* Delilah from work is a third reincarnation of Janae. The fashion student is a reincarnation of Dominic. He has the same party spirit. His effect on her is the same. She tells him things she's told Dominic. They are not new friends; they have a whole history.

*

One day at a downtown vintage store Adina and the fashion student find the perfect jean jacket. Cropped high enough to show her delicate waist, sleeves short enough for her stumpy arms. The fashion student holds it over his head like a religious relic and walks to the cashier. Adina intuits by the oversize way he pulls the bills from his wallet that he is already abandoning his idea of them. They've lasted a sexless month, and most of those days were spent planning their handful of outings. She was never sure if they were friends or dating. She'd at least never felt comfortable enough to correct his astrology. She's a Virgo. But she gets the jean jacket out of it, the one she wears all the time. The one her mother compliments when she goes home for Christmas. Over dresses, over turtlenecks, under scarves, over pajamas. The one she'd draw if the assignment was: *Draw Adina.*

*

The employees of Landry Business Solutions are arranged around the conference table in the gray, featureless meeting room. An array of halved bagels wilt under fluorescent lights. Adina sits in the corner taking meeting notes and struggling to stay awake.

Santino uses an anecdote about Kendra's boyfriend to explain why Landry Business Solutions employees don't get the week between Christmas and New Year's off. The story requires him to mention that he and Kendra are what he calls "Snoopy enthusiasts."

Every Landry Business Solutions attention span snaps into focus.

"Did you say Snoopy?" Soren, the office manager who in his spare time presents one-man shows on global warming, means, *Why would anyone do that?* But Santino answers the literal question. "Charlie Brown's dog."

"Enthusiast?" Delilah says. "Is travel involved?"

Santino is buoyed by the first appearance of interest from his employees. "You can go all over the place," he says. "Last year we went to Tokyo. That was for Kendra's high school graduation. It's a big deal to go to Snoopy Town."

Delilah falls back against her rolling chair and Soren says, "Please tell us everything about Snoopy Town."

No employee has ever encouraged Santino to elaborate. This is the Landry Business Solutions equivalent of a table bursting into flame. Adina remembers the day her grade-school classmates tried to imagine an Arctic hare.

Santino explains, joyful saliva collecting in the corners of his mouth. He rolls the cuff of his cargo pants to reveal a tattoo of Snoopy sitting astride his doghouse and says the former Mrs. Santino left because "she failed to see the appeal."

The sound of the conference room door opening startles them. Lou, who eats lunch at his desk everyday, can-size headphones blocking out the sound of his fellow employees, hurries in.

"What's up, Lou?" Santino's calf is still exposed. Snoopy winks like a star.

Lou stands on a chair and turns on the corner television. He flips until reaching a news channel. Someone has flown a commercial aircraft into the One World Trade Center building in Lower Manhattan.

"Around ten minutes ago," Lou says.

"An accident?" says Soren. "Is this going to affect us?"

"I doubt it," Santino says. "That's over sixty streets away."

The lights above them dim as if reconsidering. The employees of Landry Business Solutions look at one another then up at the television.

"I should get back to work," says Delilah.

"It's okay." Santino throws a worried glance toward the front where the elevator has dinged to signify someone arriving. "We can watch."

The reporter's face goes slack. There is a flurry of commotion behind him.

"Oh my god," Soren says.

Santino says, "Everyone get their things."

The employees of Landry Business Solutions run to their desks then to the lobby.

Santino leads them to the stairwell. "Take your time," he says. "Stay calm." Snoopy enthusiast, Adina thinks, Snoopy. Is there some kind of emergency training that accompanies loving a comic strip character? Santino has never been this direct or in charge. At every floor, employees from other offices join them. People with jobs in tech and solutions and outsourcing who she sees in the morning and on lunch breaks eating sandwiches wrapped in paper. A parade joining a parade joining a parade. They reach the ground floor. Santino announces to the lobby security guard that his people are out.

"Don't take the subway," Santino says. "Everyone walk."

Adina and Delilah turn east toward the Fifty-Ninth Street Bridge.

"Oh my god." Delilah points. A cloud of debris has bloomed over the lower part of the city. Adina cannot control the thundering in her head. She doesn't know if Toni and Dominic are okay and whether Philadelphia has been hit. No one's phone is working. They join a sea of walkers heading to the bridge. Some people from the lower streets are floured in soot and debris.

On the bridge, drivers stand next to their cars and stare toward downtown. A campfire smell.

One woman turns to Adina and Delilah, blank with shock. "Where are they?"

"Did you lose someone?" Delilah says. "Ma'am? Who did you lose?"

"The Towers," the woman says. "Where'd they go?"

With every step, Adina worries the bridge will explode. A receiving line of people hand out bottles of water when they reach Queens. Restaurant owners yell, free food, drinks. Hours later, Adina arrives at her apartment where the little dog raises himself onto his back legs and pumps his front paws, cheering for her. There is a message from Dominic, her mother, and, remarkably, Toni. Call me. Adina walks outside, takes the stairs up to the empty train platform. She holds the little dog against her heart and watches the smoking sky. No subways run. No commercial planes fly overhead. Even the halal meat carts are stalled outside, vendorless. Her crowded, perpetually rattling neighborhood is silent.

*

Her superiors intuit the massiveness of the event. Weeks of steady communication with Planet Cricket Rice follow. Responses are friendlier. Adina's human bias muddies her perspective and she imagines the faxes being sent by a chattier operator. There are no differentiated beings on Planet Cricket Rice. The closest human equivalent would be that the responses are initiated from a different side of the plural. She experiences an era of well-being and connection. This emboldens Adina to make the mistake countless writers before her have made. She attempts to write about New York City.

New York City is . . .

Hours pass and she cannot think of a word to end the sentence. Everything she tries reduces or exaggerates. An epic sea, a wagon wheel, a nutritious carrot. She ends up documenting the aggravating city ordinance that takes up most of her time.

*

By far the most complicated conjugation in New York City, she faxes, *is Alternate Side Parking regulations, or ASP.*

ASP are two- or three-hour windows during which time it is illegal to park on a street. This enables cleaning trucks to drag massive rotating brushes along each curb. Each side of the street has a different ASP window, some weekly, some biweekly. To observe ASP, New Yorkers move their cars to the other side of the street, temporarily blocking the cars parked there. This is called double parking. Sometimes the double-parked cars get tickets and sometimes they don't. Some drivers stay in their cars for the ASP window, making work phone calls, reading, listening to the radio. My apartment is on a biweekly street—the east side requires me to move my car between the hours of noon and two on Mondays and Wednesdays, the opposite side between the hours of two and four on Tuesdays and Thursdays. Every

Monday and Wednesday at five minutes before noon, the buildings in my neighborhood empty as drivers hurry to their cars. They exchange jokes, casseroles, gossip. The cleaning trucks roll by, kicking up dust. There is no contiguous day except for Sunday, my favorite. I have tried to avoid ASP by driving into work, however Manhattan drivers deal not only with ASP but also with loading zones, commercial districts, and Law & Order *filming. I leave work early, set my alarm for dawn, and note every street's ASP window, even when I'm nowhere near my neighborhood. Move the car, wait a few hours, move the car back. Next day, do it again. A dance. So far I've received a ticket for moving my car five minutes early, moving it ten minutes late, and parking in front of a garage I swear was built after I parked.*

HOW IS NEW YORK DIFFERENT THAN PHILADELPHIA?

Adina thinks about it. Writes: *Narrower streets.*

✶

Post 9/11: American flags, public anger, excessive *I love you*s. Adina suspects all three of being in place of other, more authentic expressions. What would these people say instead of *I love you? I'm scared. I worry I will never recover. I love you* is a can of soda that comes free with every meal. Yet every day humans suffer from lack of hearing it.

✶

Both early, both wearing denim jackets. They shuffle through a hug, find a table, order water.

"What's the most popular pizza?" Toni asks the waiter.

"Mushroom," he says.

"Is mushroom the same as portabella?"

"Portabella is portabella."

"Let's have the special," Adina says. "Pizza, salad, bottle of wine."

The waiter takes their menus. As if some important business distraction has been removed, discomfort grows. Adina cannot return Toni's solid gaze.

"I emailed you," she says. "Like a hundred times."

"You did?" Adina had opened her email only once, that time in the college's computer lab. "I'm sorry. I wrote to you then never thought to check again."

"What email address did you use?"

"Your name plus your school plus edu."

Toni closes her eyes to allow what looks like bemused frustration to pass. "That's not how email works. That is very . . . Adina. Dominic told me you have a dog? Squirreled away, writing, always thinking." The waiter brings wine. "It's not okay," she says. "To hide from everyone."

"I'm sorry," Adina says, her sound of the night.

"I'm sorry," Toni says. "I should have made the invisible conversation visible. I'm trying to get better at that."

"I'm trying to get better at saying 'I love you,'" Adina says. It is the first time she's thought of it but it is not a lie. It clears the discomfort. Toni's face opens into a smile.

"You should be trying to get better at email."

"I think I'll have more luck with *I love you*. I may even say it tonight."

"Don't try to make me laugh. I'm mad. There were many

things I went through without you. I've been promoted. I'm assistant to the editor now. I'm dating Audrey."

"Toni, no!"

"You are not allowed to say a damn thing," she says.

Adina tells Toni how every night Butternut crawls underneath the covers to sleep, heart beating steadily against her side. Toni says she hopes one day she'll be able to acquire her own books. She was dating a few women along the L train when Audrey got in touch.

Adina says, "I don't have to tell you why that's a bad idea. You already know."

"You don't and I do."

At the end of the meal, they linger on the sidewalk.

"I'm going to say it now," Adina says. However, Toni's nearness makes the words impossible. "This is a lot of pressure."

Toni says, "I'll turn around and count to three and on three I'll turn back around and you'll say it."

Adina agrees. Toni turns around.

There had never been bitter, upsetting words between them, only a glacial expanse that had frozen every experience without her. Here she is, her friend, familiar face making its famous expressions. Adina's shoulders tingle. She experiences a feeling of return. Toni is counting, overloud and slow: One, two . . . A father and son walk by carrying a giant balloon. The lamps turn on in the park. Electricity is the existence of power in a terrain of charged particles. Adina knows how they feel.

*

Post 9/11: If you've been putting something off, do it. Adina joins a gym and buys a granite-colored flip phone. It sits on her desk like a stone that's good for skipping.

Adina's mother's voice on her voicemail: "Someone must have been asleep at the wheel because I was accepted into a program. I'm going to study education, at night, after work. No big deal, I just wanted to let you know in case you called and I wasn't here. I know how you worry. I'm not dead. I'm learning."

✶

The trainers at Pulverize gym go by their first names and the first letter of their last names. A new member, Adina tries every terrifying-sounding class. Mince, Shred 2002, Annihilate.

Adina arrives at the gentle-sounding Beach Body to find an instructor dressed as Wonder Woman, plugging in a '90s boom box at the front of the room. LL Cool J's "Mama Said Knock You Out" bursts from the overhead speakers. "My name is Yolanda K.," she yells, swiping off the lights, plunging the windowless room into darkness. "I'm a double Cancer and I'm here to help you love yourself."

✶

Humans believe that where a star is positioned when they are born dictates qualities like whether they like books, crave order, or want everyone around them to be doing their best. However Western astronomy relies on a tropical year, which is based on a fixed picture of the sky as astrologers saw it millennia ago. A sidereal year accounts for the sky as it has shifted over time. What most people think is their astrological sign is wrong.

If it hangs around long enough, humans will assign significance to anything. What finite softies!

✶

Adina seats clients who have problems and are waiting for solutions. Sometimes the person with solutions is late. Human beings don't like when other people are late. They get frowny-faced and huffy. So Adina entertains them. She makes the candy jar talk or she tells them she has a friend who owns vintage ice cube trays. You pull a silver crank to release the cubes. She says, "Would you like to own vintage ice cube trays?" Normally they say yes because when they are waiting human beings can be very participatory. Then she says, "Not me! I don't need getting ice to be a charming experience!" She pretends to be very anti–vintage ice cube tray. In this way she yanks the tablecloth out from under the bottle of wine and candle of the conversation. Sometimes, the person waiting for solutions realizes they are sitting in a nondescript waiting room being told a joke by a smiling, attentive, usually thoughtfully dressed receptionist whose sweater is tagged with the fur of what appears to be an orange dog. This upends the expectation the person had of what the experience of visiting the Landry Business Solutions office would be. When Santino or whatever sales associate comes to fetch them, their face has normally taken on a cast of wonder, not unlike those admiring a fireworks display.

*

Even fear cannot halt New York City forever. ASP regulations return. Emilio piles a family's worth of turkey on one roll. These quotidian things exist alongside the profound and grave, as America's knowledge expands to include facts like the World Trade fires burned hotter than cremation fires. Soren, the only Landry Business Solutions employee with a sense of humor, begins to refer to himself as post-9/11. Post-9/11 Soren will pay for bottle service and will not continue friendships with people who always expect him to travel to them. Meet in the middle once in a while, he says, or no Soren.

*

On top of Adina's yearly review, under the heading OVERALL COMMENTS, Santino writes: *Good with people.*

This bothers her.

She calls her mother who says, "Would you have preferred 'Bad with people'?"

*

Things Yolanda K. yells:

You are a human being! What is happening to you is real, don't go into autopilot! Every movement has an intention and every intention has a purpose! Biceps all day! Seek out ways to say yes to your body! Start with the yes and work backward! Yes to green tea! Yes to ten more! If it doesn't feel right, use that No button! You all have one. Your button is a Hell No button, Marlene, I know. The only word we don't use is almost! Never almost do it! Almost Village is close to Nowhere Land!

*

Adina has held her job for long enough that a miracle occurs: She accrues savings. She opens a savings account and receives a slim book to keep track. The account is linked to her checking account like a bracelet. To transfer money from one to the other she fills out a lunar-blue deposit slip at the bank. She likes to recheck her math on the ledger, though she's always correct.

*

One morning, the Landry Business Solutions bathroom key goes missing. Adina makes an announcement over the never-used PA system. Why they have a PA system is a mystery since only twelve people work there and they sit in one room. She could easily walk into that room and make a medium-volumed inquiry but she is not allowed to leave her desk. Her announcement over the PA is: *Will whoever has the bathroom key please return it!* Three hours later Delilah slams the license plate key on her desk. The door had gotten stuck, and she had been trapped in the bathroom for hours. No one heard her yelling. She missed a meeting, and still no one thought to search for her. She heard Adina's announcement in the bathroom where she sat, hating her. Someone from another office finally heard her and climbed through a heating duct to free her.

*

Delilah left early. It's a bad day when you realize how unimportant you are.

Human beings who are squeaky wheels get everything they want. Quiet humans who don't complain get nothing. A squeaky wheel will complain when they have an obstructed view of a movie screen until they get a better seat. In the better seat, they will find another thing to complain about. The floor is sticky. The cup holder isn't big enough for my deluxe soda. I have to believe quiet humans who don't complain see half the screen but are happier. But maybe they're not. Maybe they spend their lives sad they can't participate in conversations about movies. Harrison Ford was in that movie? they say. I had no idea.

The reply arrives immediately:

HUMANS IN THEIR OWN BODIES WALKING THEMSELVES AROUND.

Adina doesn't know whether it's meant to be consolatory or a simple restating of her thought. It's been years since she's tried for answers but on this day the poetic nature of the indifference emboldens her.

Am I doing okay?

OH YES.

The words are comforting. The halal meat carts rumble past her bedroom window and the room fills with the tang of spice. It must be seven thirty.

Are you doing okay?

She makes tea and waits for the response. The rumbling stops. One of the vendors whistles the theme song to a popular television show she can't place.

The fax squeaks through:

WE ARE ATTEMPTING NOT TO DIE.

Adina tries to extend her intuition into the words but cannot.

Literally?

OH YES.

What's happening? Is the planet at risk? Please tell me more.

She stares at the words on the page: ATTEMPTING NOT TO DIE. She finishes her tea, paces the apartment, falls asleep on the floor, the little dog curled beside her like a comma.

*

Within a few hours of Adina returning home to her mother's house, Butternut is wearing a new, floral bandanna.

"For summer," her mother says. She gives Adina a tour of her garden, pointing out her successes, failures, and hopes, holding Butternut against her chest like a furred brooch. The garden is wider than the previous year's by a foot. A tiger lily path, a district of rosebushes, a neighborhood of herbs containing several plants each of what her mother calls, "essential Italian spices." Portulacas still make up the colorful border. The complex's teenagers weed: She pays them in herbs.

An older woman emerges from her apartment to thank her for that week's box, which included a satisfying radish.

"Was it you who got the giant one?" Her mother's cheeks brighten. "That one had its own zip code!"

"And who is this?" The woman closes her eyes and leans into the little dog as if expecting a kiss.

"This is my grand dog. And you remember my daughter? She lives in New York."

"New York? I was a dancer there many years ago."

"Show us some moves," her mother says.

The woman pretends to push her mother away. The joking compels her back into the apartment. Adina tells her mother that in New York there are community gardens where people pay dues to keep a patch then give boxes like her mother's to subscribers.

"This is more like helping out neighbors." Her mother tilts her gaze toward the sky. "I'm doing well in school," she says. "Someday I might graduate with honors." Then, to quell whatever emotion Adina is revving for, says, "Let's not make a big fuss."

*

At the end of the weekend, she kisses her mother goodbye. "I love you."

"Are we saying that now?" Her mother looks panicked. "A few years in New York, she starts saying 'I love you.'"

"Almost five," Adina says.

"Almost five," her mother says. "At what point does one become a New Yorker?"

"Never."

Adina honks as she drives away.

✶

When Adina reaches five years living in New York, she returns home from work to find her door ajar, lock hanging from its busted innards. The little dog dances in the middle of the rug. Her superiors still haven't written to explain their situation, if it is dire or if it's a joke, though she faxes questions every morning.

She owns nothing another human would deem valuable, so the thieves steal only a pillowcase, to transport what they will steal from someone else's house. Her faxes and folders are untouched. She feels judged and vulnerable. The locksmith can't fix the door until the following day.

"Like I was a filling station," Adina tells Toni, arriving at her apartment to spend the night. "A supply store."

✶

The more money you make, the more items you can add to your life. Most of these items are obvious, televisions, cars, but there are also activities you are suddenly able to participate in. Gyms! Training sessions! Tanning!

The transmission doesn't quite get to the thorniness that

hovers between the thought of her mother wearing the same dress every day to work and her yoga-specific bra.

*

What time you eat dinner is a sign of class, she faxes.

Whether you can eat dinner is a sign of class. Whether you can stay in a hotel room is a sign of class. Which hotel you stay in is a sign of class. Your name is a sign of class. At what age you began to drink coffee and how you take it. Tea is a sign of class. Clothes are a sign of class. Whether you have children and how many children you have is a sign of class. At what age you took your first plane ride is a sign of class. Schools are a sign of class. Where you live is a sign of class: mansion, apartment, shack, house. How many homes you have, including no homes. How many and which races live where you live. Whether there are landscaped highways where you live is a sign of class. How you hold your fork and knife is a sign of class. How long you linger. If you are willing to let the waitress wait. Who you think is attractive. Your haircut. Your partner. Whether your house is cluttered. Whether you drink soda. What you know by memory is a sign of class. Whether you can control your anger. Crime is a sign of class. Whether you've been to prison and for how long. How you handle domestic abuse. Having been to certain cities is a sign of class. Whether you travel. Why you travel. What kind of boats you've been on. Whether you have friends in groups or solitary friends like lighthouses by the sea. Whether you pad on the bare floor or use slippers. Your dog. Hue is a shade of a color is a sign of class. The amount of time between realizing you have a hospital-worthy illness and how long it takes you to see a doctor is a sign of class. Where you feel comfortable: A *large ballroom set for a wedding, a hair salon, a supermarket. How you feel around horses. Whether you have glasses. If your teeth have been straightened. How many pillows you use. The shape of your nose. Whether you have a wheelchair. What kind of wheelchair. Your corrective lenses. If you sit in the front, middle, or back of a plane. The amount of time it takes you to decide is a sign of class. How much space you take up. The trees in your neighborhood. Your underwear. Whether you wear a watch. How much time you spend helping your kid with their homework, including no time. Optimism is a sign of class. Kindness. What kind of high heels you wear. Exhaustion. If you gyrate your hips when you dance, how well. How well you understand music. On what occasion you dance and hear music. How many artists you know. How many scientists you can name. Whether you "see" money. If you know how to pronounce the word behemoth. Whether you know it's more accurate to say* indicator of class. *Whether you have a winter coat, an offer, another option, a cane, pajamas, sleep aids, hearing aids, lovers, retirement, a checking account, a credit report, a social security card, your nails done and how: clean and clear or colors or with the acrylic long nails that make typing impossible. During the long night, upon hearing a sound on the other side of the house between where you sleep and where the babies sleep: whether you can imagine the noise sharpening into a malevolent force or assume it's a soft-shouldered deer hushed in the moonlight.*

WE GET IT.

*

Her superiors never clarify the survival faxes so, like any upsetting event, eventually she must file it into a folder and continue.

*

A wedding season.

Smiling people wagging their asses in formal clothes. A series of technological advances; musicians double-loop and auto-tune vocals so it sounds like you are being dumped simultaneously by ten people. Adina acquires the ability to hear around larger sounds to hear subtler ones; a woman talking in a middle car as the 7 glides by.

*

Adina and Toni meet for sesame seed pizza almost every Thursday.

"Audrey is moving to the city."

"Oh no," says Adina.

Toni sighs. "Oh no is right."

*

At the Bleecker Street train station, Adina leans against a steel column, heart leaping, as a train arrives. The brakes of this train combined with this particular station's acoustics—gliding and fading—create a three-syllable word from her mother tongue. It is a binding principle from Planet Cricket Rice that means the deepest way to match, either in ideas—as in, two sentiments, or in affection. One of its other meanings is the unseen collective agreement to strive toward a fortuitous outcome.

Only the track at the Bleecker Street station expresses the sentiment. It halts Adina on the transfer between gym and home. She carries her notes and half-eaten lunch in one bag and in another, her sports bra, gym shorts, and sneakers. She is damp with sweat, having, as Yolanda K. demanded, "lunged herself clean." Loved, exhausted, holding what she cares about, Adina listens to the word from her language, until its conscious meaning recedes and is replaced by the sound of an arriving train. Even though she is alone, she feels surrounded by family.

*

Others. Throughout her life, the word has been a yellow thread, showing through the fabric whenever she meets someone who glimmers in a particular way. Who are they? Are they reporters on motherhood, medicine, war correspondents working dangerous beats? Why hasn't she met any? Why is it necessary for her to work, always, alone? She and human beings share a profound desire: To find other extraterrestrials and feel less alone. Is she alone? Are there others? Where are they? Where are they?

*

Every human is affected by gravity. No human can fly. No human can destroy or create matter. The laws of physics are agnostic.

NOT ALWAYS TRUE, reads the reply. THOUGH WE UNDERSTAND WHY YOU WOULD THINK THAT.

*

A man on the train tells Adina to go back to wherever she's from.

"That's Northeast Philadelphia," she says.

"Then go there," he says.

She arrives shaky to meet Toni for coffee. They are on their lunch breaks from their offices on either side of the city. They have met at a coffee shop in the middle.

"When I'm in New York," Toni says, "I feel like Philadelphia is home. When I'm there, I miss here."

"I should have explained that to the dude on the train," Adina says.

"Don't look now," Toni says. "But there's a man in the corner who is the spitting image of Gabriel García Márquez."

Adina scans the room. "You're saying that because you're rereading *Love in the Time of Cholera.*"

"He invented magic realism, Adina. This corner dude is a dead ringer."

Toni returns to work and Adina stays to buy a croissant. Yolanda K. advises her students to eat within an hour after working out so their bodies don't revolt.

She thinks about what Toni said about home. Is it okay to have an idea of home that is nebulous? To know there is a planet that is hers but not its location? If she could somehow find Planet Cricket Rice, would she be homesick for Earth? Earthsick?

"One day when you feel as beautiful as you are," a voice says, "I'm going to take your picture." Adina turns. The Gabriel García Márquez dude is speaking to her. He wears a serious expression and an old-timey camera around his neck. "Do you know who I am?"

Adina says, "You invented magic realism."

He says, "I'm your father."

*

Adina calls her mother from the gym. "How do I even know it's him?"

"Did he seem charming, a little off?" She says. "Did he look really, like really, Italian?"

"He's a dead ringer for Gabriel García Márquez."

"Who?"

"I always forget I have one. A father, I mean."

"Everyone has a father, Adina." Her mother's voice is quiet, calm. "The question is, do you want a relationship with him?"

"I don't know!" Adina's volume startles a woman stretching on a yoga mat. "I have to think about it! I'm late for class!"

*

Things Yolanda K. yells:

Keep pulsing while I tell you a story. Once I dated a woman who never said anything other than no! Keep pulsing. I'd say, "Do you like this movie? Do you like frogs?" Always no! Keep pulsing. I asked her, "Can you please find opportunities to say yes?" Not half the way down, Justine, all the way! One guess—what do you think she said? Keep pulsing. She had a very can't-do attitude! She was a can't-do! Like a honeydew, that's right, Marlene, but not as sweet!

*

They drink glasses of water at a Chinese restaurant.

He smiles when she orders sesame chicken. "Your mother's favorite."

He says, "I'm in town for a temporary job, then back to Philly."

He says, "Your mother was always a pushover."

Adina memorizes the deep creases around his eyes and mouth. The way he considers the waitress as he pretends to think about his order. The objects of him: faded denim button-down tucked into sharply pressed jeans, thick black wallet flipped open for cash, no pictures, signet rings. The scents: evergreen, olives, a sharp knife.

He says, "Do you need any money? You sure?"

*

When Toni picks Adina up to drive them home for Christmas, Dominic is sitting in the back. He wears thin black jeans and a Strokes T-shirt. "What's up, kid?"

"To no one's surprise," Toni says, "Dominic has become a hipster."

The Mustang still holds the same earthen smell, the same playing-cards-in-spokes sound when it accelerates. The Mustang had always been a reflection of them as brother and sister: bratty, irreplaceable.

Dominic asks if he can hold Butternut on his lap and the little dog falls asleep, chin tucked against his elbow.

*

Her mother is at work when Adina arrives. String lights, tins of cookies, textbooks stacked on the half-moon table. Adina washes and dries her mother's dishes, folds her laundry, and reads from a stack of her *National Enquirer*s. Intergalactic creatures have kidnapped the members of a retirement home in Rancho Cucamonga and their children are taking the aliens to court over back rent. Home, two ways: back in a room with her mother's pleasures and reading inaccurate theories about an intimate part of her identity. After eight, her mother lurches through the door, carrying a bag of groceries. Butternut throws himself against her calves. She no longer drives the VW bug powered by prayer but has upgraded to a reliable Camry.

Adina takes the grocery bag out of her mother's hands. "I do not want a relationship with him."

Her mother pulls a bouquet of carrots from the bag, red

and orange peppers, a box of penne, a roll of toilet paper. She uses a carrot for a mustache. "That's that, then."

They chop peppers. "Let them be big enough so each one is its own mouthful," her mother says. Adina doesn't like when she says words like mouthful, words that cannot be divorced from sex. Other words like that are suck, fingerhole, and cock. She asks her not to say mouthful anymore, but her mother hops up and down with the knife in her hand singing: *mouthful!* The little dog stands on his hind legs and pumps his front paws.

They add string lights to the living room. Her mother wants to attend Midnight Mass despite what she calls "the whole hypocrisy thing. It cuts deep, Catholicism. It's hard to unlearn."

They set the table for two and play music so Adina can't hear her mother's mouth sounds. Butternut snoozes in his grandmother's lap, wearing a sweater she bought for him that reads *Elf in Training.* Adina thought they'd agreed the Beatles were awful but here is her mother pulsing her shoulders to *Revolver.* The Catholic Church, music while eating, sweaters. Blankets cover every surface, their fibers beam underneath the string lights. Age is softening her like butter that's been left out. To others it might seem like a mess. But Adina likes this new mother who, free from the pressure of keeping her safe, sings "Taxman" in a flat tone and asks questions from a list she's compiled on a legal pad. "What's going on with Toni and Audrey? What's lighting you up?"

"You have 'What's lighting you up' written down?"

She tips the pad so Adina can see: What's lighting her up?

Adina tells her mother that the most significant relationships in her life are with the little dog and the SETI institute and Yolanda K. because she values her no matter how few lunges she completes and wants good things for her thighs.

"You don't want to talk about love." Her mother sighs. "I get it. Well. I like someone. His name is Charles. He's an electrician. He's in my Philosophy of Math class. I don't know his whole thing yet. Early days."

"Charlie?" Adina pronounces the name as if it has committed a crime.

"Charles." She pronounces it as if it is load-bearing, redeeming it and signaling its significance. "Family name. Irish, I think."

Adina remembers her mother on the front couch, waiting for Mark. Her kicked-off heels. The seams of her pantyhose lying unevenly on her toes. She says, "How can appliances be programmed to turn themselves on? If an appliance can turn itself on, doesn't that mean it is never truly off?"

"I'm not sure." Her mother does not understand this is meant to be a segue out of and not a deepening of the topic. "I'll ask Charles."

Recent observations attain searing focus. Music, blankets, string lights. Not age softening her mother, but romance.

*

Human beings, Adina faxes, *spend their lives pretending their parents are people with no needs. They do not want their moms to talk about sex or die.*

*

On everything possible, human beings place a sunny-side-up egg. Most humans think this is great, these are the same kind of humans who rejoice when biting into a doughnut to discover jelly (terrible) or a chocolate truffle to find cherry syrup (terrible).

If you request no sunny-side-up egg on your croque madame (married) or croque mademoiselle (not married), the human you are with will invariably say, But that's the best part! If they forget your request and the sandwich arrives avec egg, you must gently relocate the egg with your knife to the side of the plate where it will sulk over the edge, the person you're with chastising you. When you say, Well, would you like my egg, they will say no, as if offended by the question.

*

It is Halloween. Yolanda K. wears a foliage-inspired jumpsuit. The halal meat vendors hang pumpkin cutouts on their awnings. Toni's publishing company hosts a lecture where a Famous Writer speaks about sympathy and fails to mention the event has a costume requirement. When Adina arrives without one, Toni says no problem, she has brought one for her. She wears a blue dress and devil horns and appears pleased with herself as she pulls a Martian antennae headband from her tote bag. Adina puts it on. Toni claps and dances around her. Audrey is on her way. Excitement makes her optimistic.

The Famous Writer has recently published a book of poems about vegetarianism. In line, she announces she will not sign books. "Instead," she says, "you will sign mine."

Everyone in line murmurs meaningfully. A vested man tells her they studied her work at Yale.

"Don't be a slave to this Ivy League world," she tells him.

"Didn't you go to an Ivy League school?" he says.

"Yes, but I was on scholarship."

"Scholarship," he says.

"A grant, really. From my grandmother."

When it's Adina's turn she tells the Famous Writer she is a friend of Toni's and that she read an article that describes sympathy as a flowering effect in one's body.

"I like your antennae," the Famous Writer says.

"Thank you. I'm an alien."

"We all are," the Famous Writer says. "Did you read the article about the new findings from outer space? Surprisingly good for that garbage magazine."

"Didn't you have a poem published there?" someone in line says.

The Famous Writer says, "Two poems."

*

The party is in a converted train car. Literary types dressed as movie killers and political figures eat tortellini from one another's plates and hover around the Famous Writer. A bookseller who at another party asked if Adina knew where to get "decent cocaine" sits in the corner selling copies of the Famous Writer's poems.

Toni pulls a boy wearing a *Sgt. Pepper* jacket over to Adina. "Have you met my friend? She's an alien!"

"I want to believe," he says.

"I'll tell the others," Adina says. "Which Beatle are you?"

"The Mexican one!"

"I don't like the Beatles."

"Everyone likes the Beatles!" he says.

"I guess I'm not everyone."

"Obviously. You're from another planet."

His name is Miguel. A curved line with a sharp cliff face. The swallowing sounds he makes while drinking his beer don't annoy her. He asks if she's going to the after-party and Adina says, no, she's already gone to the pre-party and here she is at the party party and that's a hundred too many parties for her. He asks if she'll go to the after-after party and she says maybe. The thin joke extends across the night of two subsidiary parties and a sugary glass of chardonnay. This is flirting.

A drunk person shoves into him, convinced Miguel will have a lighter and when he doesn't, turns inconsolable and leaves. The bartender turns the music's volume louder. The room takes a stifling step toward Adina.

Miguel says he plays piano and has synesthesia. "I can see sound and feel color. Would you like to know what your voice looks like?"

"I hate sound!"

"Who hates sound?"

"I have an aversion to certain sounds! Such as noises people make when they eat! Throat clearing! A chair scraping against the floor! They fill me with a murderous rage!"

He gestures around them.

"Ambient noises are fine! It's the quieter noises I can't handle!"

"Is that why you hate the Beatles?"

"They are everything that's wrong in the world!"

He goes silent, blinking. Adina recognizes this reaction from other times her opinions have trespassed beyond societally acceptable.

"They're the reason I'm a musician," he says.

"Well, it was nice meeting you. I hope you enjoy this mean girl's book of broccoli poems!"

He laughs. The drunk person returns, begging him to admit he has a lighter. "I should take him outside and get him some help."

That's the end of that, Adina thinks. She finds Toni and says goodbye. Out front, the Famous Writer announces to a group of rapt students that she is related to no living person on earth.

"There's no possible way that's true," Miguel says.

"It's painfully, utterly true," she says.

Adina attempts to sneak by, to walk home in her antennae, dignity intact.

"Alien girl! Wait!" Miguel catches up. "Are you leaving?"

"I'm walking home to the final party," she says. "The party of me going to bed."

"I want to go to that party," he says. Then, reddening, "I mean, I also want to go to bed. Not with you. At my own . . . I have an early dentist appointment. Can I walk you home? I find your candor refreshing."

"Let's talk in a year and we'll see how refreshing you think it is."

The remark lands too rigidly and Adina wants to retract it. "Do dentists want you to close your eyes?" she says. "In an exam? I feel like I'm creeping them out if I stare but if I close my eyes I don't want them to think I'm asleep. I want them to know I'm alert and with them all the way."

"I always close my eyes," he says. "Like kissing."

The Famous Writer is losing her grip on her followers. She says, loudly, "I grew up poor. I didn't have a car or a smart phone or anything."

Adina knows this means she grew up with money. People with money list what they did without. Poor people list what they had.

The moment of turning away arrives when humans are most likely to make mistakes. Adina has observed it countless times on the street: they reference earlier, irrelevant conversations, offer warnings about traffic, make false promises or, worse, force each other into unwanted hugs. Miguel doesn't warn or request or make promises. He shakes her hand then walks away at a medium rate. It's professional, not unkind. His jacket is well-tailored. He is short and carries himself rhythmically as if hearing a song. He halts, returns, leans toward her to create a conspiratorial space. "In all seriousness," he says, "I'm an alien, too."

The bar's sound wobbles. Before she can reply, he says, "Goodbye, Adina," and walks away. Above him hangs the wide moon, full or almost full she's never sure.

*

Her arrival at home is met with fanfare. Butternut cheers and cheers.

I think I met an Other! A pianist with synesthesia! Is he one of us? Miguel! she faxes.

Miguel, she thinks.

*

Yolanda K. says that while they do one last set of windmills she is going to play a special song.

Tina Turner's "(Simply) The Best" fills the room. Yolanda K. delivers a monologue, walking and correcting through the rows of spiraling arms.

"You know so and so?" She names an actress who is famous for a movie in which she played a plucky cat. "So and so has always made fun of fitness. But then she went to a group class at our other location and guess what happened? She loved it. Working out helped her depression and attitude and self-awareness and outlook and anxiety and life in general. It's not about your body, it's about your brain and, I'd add, your beauty. You leave here and take care of everyone else, but this is the thing you do for yourself. You can never look bad when you're doing something for yourself."

Adina immediately thinks of exceptions. Murder. Incest. Murdering someone on your way to commit incest.

Better than anyone, Tina Turner sings. *Anyone I ever met.*

Yolanda K. says, "Let's lunge for twenty and head into the weekend like champions."

They lunge for twenty, thirty. Yolanda K. asks, Do they

have twenty more for her? They do. Adina could lunge for days. But Yolanda K. says, "Class is over," and tells them to scoot because the man who leads the next class is a real bitch.

✶

There are Snoopy enthusiasts, Adina faxes, *who travel the world, collecting memorabilia. They dress like Snoopy, name their children after Snoopy characters, and engage in debates with Charlie Brown enthusiasts (a different gang and vicious, according to Santino), who believe that the appearance of the mute dog was arrogant and ruined the comic strip.*

This report doesn't get to the marrow of her intent, so she tries again:

There is nothing a human can't craft an opinion about.

That doesn't do it, either.

A hobby is a pleasant way to pass time and distract oneself. Stamp collecting, baking. A way for the mind to say: Look over here. *But it can't stop the inevitable. Hobbies are a way of staying present so humans do not have to think about death. Yet the inevitable looms and grows.*

✶

Miguel invites Adina to a performance and on the appropriate day, she walks through a labyrinth of practice studios to find him. Musics emerge from each one she passes: a violinist in the final swells of a concerto, a quartet, a shamrock of heads bowed over cellos, a flute! An unincorporated orchestra of sound. At the end of the hallway, she pauses to hear them converge.

In a black box theater, a group of humans mill on a riser around a piano. Miguel, seated at the piano, waves when Adina enters. The lights dim. Everyone finds their seat except for a tall woman in a floor-length black dress, who offers a welcome into the microphone, and says she will sing a song called "My Day Will Come." She and Miguel smile at each other which means: begin.

As the woman sings, Adina knows she is hearing something that has been kept private for a long time. It is raw and ugly and wobbles at the edges. The singer must not be stable in any normal way or perhaps she is more stable than all of them. Miguel plays blousy riffs that grow stronger and become choruses that repeat like Philip Glass's, but each time he alters their rhythm and intention. Adina feels pinned in place by this singer's unique way of making sound. Miguel must know the captivating effect she has on the crowd because at the end of the song he takes her into a hug and says, Sarah Glide, everyone, into the microphone so the audience can applaud. His eyes are warm with admiration. This endears him to Adina, clapping in the crowd.

✶

To express appreciation, human beings hit their hands together. The more they appreciate it, the harder and longer they hit.

*

Yolanda K.:

"Whenever you are reaching out with true spirit, someone reaches back. Catch eyes with someone else in class. Anyone. This is not a suggestion. Do it now."

Everyone's eyes are caught so Adina looks at herself in the mirror, expecting to see a goddess emanating a buttery glow. Instead, she sees a petite woman in a half-top lunging politely. Hair frizzed above her head like a disoriented halo. Unattractive redness blooms through her cheeks and neck.

"Smile," Yolanda K. says. "Each of us is on the same team, and we're all coming in first."

Adina smiles at the girl in the mirror. The girl in the mirror, bound by physics, returns her smile.

*

Toni's boss informs her that she may begin to acquire projects that speak to their readership's new, weirder demographic. Adina and Toni order what they call their date meal, Cobb salad and sesame seed pizza.

"Humor is moving toward the weird," Toni tells Adina, who sips her wine with interest.

"Your notes," Toni says, "are what the world needs."

"No one needs my notes."

"You used to want to meet everyone on Earth, Adina. If you publish you won't meet everyone, but you will meet a lot more. Or at least, your thoughts will."

"I've met more people since then," Adina says. ". . . and no longer want that."

"I don't believe you. I'm not going to try to persuade you. Think about it."

"It would take years to organize my notes."

"They're in perfect folders and you know it."

Adina tells her she's recently met a pianist who can see sound. As if summoned by the mention, he texts.

"A pianist who can see sound," Toni says, in that way she has.

*

Wine! It's the worst!

Wine is a liquid people pathologize in the way they talk about it, sell it, in the vessels they put it in. Red wine tastes like a dark-walled library and white wine smells like a woman looking away.

IF IT'S TERRIBLE, WHY DO HUMANS DRINK IT?

Because, like many things humans enjoy, it frees them from their bodies. Other examples are blankets and robes. People are forever yammering about some great robe they encountered in a hotel.

*

Miguel wears a puffy orange vest over a flannel as if at any moment he might go camping. It scares Adina that he is awake like she is. One night he stands in the rain on her stoop listening to her thrash the Beatles. He decides to leave.

"So long," he says. "Eames birds," he says, "is what your voice looks like."

If he leaves, I won't forgive myself. She apologizes and asks him to stay which is embarrassing after trying so hard to make him leave but she promises a beer and a grilled cheese and brings him upstairs, her apartment shaking from a passing train. Butternut unfurls a spirited cheer for this boy taking off his dark jacket and she doesn't know if her little dog is a prophet or a traitor and Miguel says it's the best he's ever had about the grilled cheese and she says, really, the best, okay, and he says, "I mean it, sister, best ever," and Adina knows she will have to deal with every ugly thing she's been ignoring to be half as good as he deserves and this makes her tired in advance and he says we can finish them in the morning about the dishes so they lie in the blue light of Caress Hair Braiding that makes everything in her bedroom seem aquatic and she asks, has he ever heard of Martin's Aquarium in Northeast Philadelphia? and he says no, he's never been to Philadelphia but doesn't sound afraid of it or the shape she can't get rid of that it makes in her, how it sharpens her remarks and pulls down the sides of her mouth, and she grows more tired because of what she'll have to explain maybe even the Very Big Thing she's only told her mother and Toni—she wishes she could call Toni now—he says, he'd like to hear about it if she feels like sharing and she says, it would take decades, then begins with the tails of the show-off betta fish and the soft green nets but these don't make sense unless she tells him about her mother and the Flying Man and how she's never experienced a new life level without pain, some brutal shedding, and she thinks, Oh no, she thinks, All for the want of a grilled cheese! which doesn't apply but is the kind of logic one exhibits when finding oneself on the shaky-glittery brink of something that's probably going to fuck her up in a way that if humanity or entropy or Andromeda is kind will turn out to be important, will at least not hurt, at least, not much, will maybe bridge the distance between her and everything, between her and herself, and he says green is big terrain, you know, about the soft green nets, so what color—frog or lentil or emerald or lima bean or lily pad or pine needle or grass?

*

Adina types the last old transmission into her Word document. She is finished visiting herself at younger ages. Years of learning and failing in a stack of pages five inches thick. She can't decide if that's absurd or admirable, as she emails the document to Toni.

The work has transferred into a pleasant stiffness in her wrists that makes her proud. Walking home from the train, she passes a produce market. The heads of cauliflower admire her. She admires them. The chives are cheers.

"Brie?" a kind-faced farmer says.

"No thank you," she says.

"Bread?"

She no thank-yous down the street, enjoying the bargain the sun makes with the shop windows, 7 train whistling above her.

*

Adina bakes Miguel lasagna from a centuries-old recipe she finds on the internet. It requires a trip downtown for a particular cheese and several phone calls to her mother. She wants to fill him with soft dough until he half-closes his eyes and makes the humming sound that signifies joy.

Her mother is pleased. "This is the most Sicilian you've ever been."

He arrives carrying a box wrapped in string. Their bodies are too big for her small kitchen. They jockey around each other until he sits at the table and arranges his legs where he will have space to stretch one then the other.

The lasagna is so-so. The noodle preparation was rushed and produced tiny knots in the final product. Miguel says he can't remember a finer meal. He plays an up-tempo song of violins clashing over guitar and they take turns dancing with Butternut.

"It's from the Voyager's Golden Record," he says. "What do you think?"

Was this a signal? Was he an other? The song is frenetic, raucous. What message did the astronomers hope it would convey to the extraterrestrials?

She says, "It's loud."

✶

Later, he slides his hand underneath the waistband of her jeans. It's the first time someone has pressed her there. She nods, waits to be overcome by passion. He tries different pressures and speeds.

"So interesting." It's not the right thing to say.

He says physical chemistry can take time. Sex like anything else changes with a relationship. She wants to ask him what he meant when he said he was also an alien. He knows a lot about sex and relationships. Perhaps this is his assignment, to report on human romantic connection. She can see why he'd be chosen. His body contains a nimble energy, offering his hand when getting out of the car, closing the door behind her, placing his palm on the most delicate part of her back. Even the way his mouth forms certain words is attractive. "Fellini," he says. "Clitoris."

Why does she think of Amadeo in this moment, his feigned surprise upon fishing his own penis out of his underwear. The tiny gasp. Again and again. Look who decided to join us! Every so often, Adina will be filling the candy jar at Landry Business Solutions or watching her clothes tumble at the laundromat, and the image of Amadeo's penis will flash into her mind. An angry mushroom. Shame heats her. Again and again, Janae finds her gaze above the crowd. Dominic walks her home amid the shattering beach sprinklers, the fractured boards, the watermelon rinds. Circumcised, purplish skin with a disparaging point of view.

*

Sarah Glide has early multiple sclerosis that hasn't yet begun to affect her everyday life. She is fair-skinned and can wear the pale pinks and sand-colored tones from the preferred side of the color palette. Adina assumes the serious diagnosis paired with enormous talent means Sarah Glide will be kind, in the way humans are when confronted by the headlights of death, prioritized.

But at a backyard summer party, someone plays a song from her college days and Adina sings along. Sarah Glide's voice keens through the crowd's din, "Did you hear what Adina sang? 'Simeon the Whale.' It's 'Send me on my way!' Adina! Why would it be 'Simeon the whale'?"

It is a hot, airless city evening. Miguel has disappeared into the kitchen to find ice. The summer-dressed strangers who surround Adina hold cups the color of a cartoon fire.

"I thought it was a song about a whale," Adina says.

"You're so cute," Sarah Glide says. "Everything you say is so weird!" Adina has learned the human tendency to pronounce mean words cheerfully. Sarah Glide is smiling, tan, and pretending to be one person but Adina knows she is six girls in jean jackets and high ponytails, even as her virtuoso voice makes the word five syllables: *We-ee-ee-ei-rd*.

*

Toni's boss wants to publish Adina's chapbook in a limited run to correlate with an art book fair the following year. Toni tells Adina as if she is delivering grave news, correctly predicting adverse reaction. "No one will read it," Toni promises. "The run will be discreet."

"How many?"

"Five hundred." Toni says the number as if it is paltry.

"Five hundred?" Adina yells.

"Any other author would cry if I said their run would be that small. You will have creative input into everything from the cover to the launch."

"Launch?" Adina says. "I never should have sent them."

"You never should have," Toni says.

*

Dominic says Bruce Springsteen's music is about hiding who you are, donning a disguise, making deals with women named Mary near the river, always living in the unlit part of town.

"It's a queer metaphor," he says.

He, Adina, and Toni are streaming down the Belt Parkway to Coney Island. The word for what they are is queer, Dominic says.

"How is Adina queer?" Toni says.

"Not having sex is queer. There's more than one way to not have sex with a cat."

Adina winces and Dominic apologizes. He forgot to put his bathing suit on under his shorts. He can do it in the car but they have to promise not to look. He sinks to the floor of the back seat, pulling his shorts off.

"I will be so bummed if the Wonder Wheel isn't open," Toni says. "Massive disappointment. Speaking of, Dominic, is that a nipple piercing?"

"I said, don't look!" Dominic yells.

They arrive at sunset when the clouds are pink check marks and flies stir over the boardwalk's discarded hot dogs. Adina and Dominic shoot water into the yawning mouths of plastic animals. No one wins. "It's built that way," Toni says. "So you always feel like next time, next time."

They buy tickets to the Ferris wheel. As the hard steel cage locks around them Adina hooks her fingers around Toni's wrist.

"Don't worry," Toni says. "It's not like flying."

Slowly, they ascend to the top where the broad swath of littered beaches comes into view, rides jolting forward and back beneath them. Wind whistles across the cage. After two revolutions, Dominic says, they will have to disembark, so get a good whiff. Sour apple and warm skin. After the ride, Adina dry heaves in the bathroom where girls fix their tube tops. Outside a couple dressed in head-to-toe denim and platform sneakers make out against the gate. He palms the back of her head, pulling her closer. Behind them, the Atlantic Ocean grieves but the boardwalk is merry. Everyone wears flip-flops because no one has to hurry.

"I'd trade places with them in a second," Toni says, meaning the couple in denim. "Who wouldn't?"

"I wouldn't," says Dominic.

"I wouldn't," says Adina.

*

Misogyny, like Roman Catholicism, is an institution built on faith. It has hierarchy, jokes, language, periodicals. Its believers insist on a theory with no proof. With proof to the contrary, even. Built into the system of maintaining the status quo is an ingenious method of casting aspersions on nonbelievers, and reasons why the "proof" must remain unseen.

The Beatles sing about vanilla desires and in reward the world turns them into an institution. This institution has hierarchy, jokes, language, periodicals. They go to India and "discover" yoga. Yoko Ono shows up, ideal for othering: petite, Asian, maker of hard art that dares to venture beyond the idea of holding a girl's hand. She makes the mistake of having a white singer fall in love with her. He leaves the Beatles and Yoko is blamed for bewitching him. The blaming of Yoko Ono for the Beatles' breakup becomes an institution: It has hierarchy, jokes, language, periodicals, and unquestioning believers who turn her into a verb: To Yoko something means to ruin it.

These people fail to imagine John Lennon happy.

But it was Yoko Ono who had the magic. Once you understand this, you see these institutions everywhere. And when you realize you're living inside an institution in which actual artists are shunned while inferior artists are rewarded, where someone says, "If there'd been no Yoko Ono we'd have four more Beatles albums," and to avoid argument someone else says, "Totally," then you can no longer pretend to live in a functional system, you will never again be able to close your eyes to the unique and tender bodies harmed every day by so-called rational small talk. Yoko Ono was the artist and, like every artist, she was also a key to greater understanding.

*

Miguel lives in an attic apartment on the Lower East Side.

He makes tortillas from scratch and fries them on a griddle he inherited from his grandfather. They make out on his mattress on the floor for what feels like a long time. She tells him it is okay to put his penis inside of her.

Does this hurt? No, I like it. Am I leaning too hard on you? No, I like it.

They seem to enter a single body that advances in stages up a long chute. Her arms are covered in goose bumps. He finishes on her stomach. This is the first time she's seen semen. *I've heard a lot about you*, she does not say. She studies it as he leaves the room to find a towel. It appears sentient, active. She scoops up a fingertip, smells it, tastes it. Oceanic. He returns with a beach towel. Adina doesn't break or even bleed.

They hold each other under the slanted ceiling. His voice is loamy. "Did you finish?"

She doesn't think so. She doesn't feel expunged the way he is, nodding off. She decides to use this intimacy as a place to put the question she's been longing to ask.

"On that first night, you said you were an alien. Will you tell me more?"

"It's hard to talk about." He gazes toward the ceiling. This is a secret he's waited to share. Her thighs ache, her blood pounds. "Sometimes I feel like I'm in the mix, but I'm also on the outside, watching. I don't understand why these things called people do what they do. It's like when I saw *E.T.* I thought, exactly. That's me."

Adina's voice is quiet. "That's me too."

He clasps her hand. "We're aliens, Adina. We're on the outside, but we're the real ones. They're the freaks."

Her excitement snags, catching up. "Figuratively?"

"Drones," he says. "Lemmings." He rests his head against

her shoulder and closes his eyes. On a poster taped to the ceiling, the most famous actress on Earth holds a cherry between her teeth. The figurative alien slips into sleep.

Adina attempts to salvage meaning. She wants him to stay awake and explain. She says, "*E.T.* was the first movie I saw in the theater."

From the vestibule of sleep, he says, "*E.T.* was the first movie everyone our age saw in the theater."

*

You lied, she faxes. *Miguel isn't an other!*

WHAT IS MIGUEL?

The person I thought was like me!

YOU WANTED TO BELIEVE.

When two people have sex, they place themselves against each other. Whatever parts they have they touch or rub or insert into or next to whatever parts their partner has. The friction causes an accelerating arousal. Sometimes, liquid comes out. It is simple and crude.

IS EARTH SUITABLE FOR US TO LIVE?

She assumes this reply is a joke, but when she writes back, *The parking is awful. You'd have to move your spaceship twice a week*, the response is decidedly sober.

THERE IS NOT MUCH "TIME" LEFT.

What do you mean?

She waits for an answer, repeating her transmission throughout the night, concern growing. *What do you mean?*

In the morning, A YEAR?

She faxes back, *I have a year?*

The reply: A YEAR?

As if she is asking herself.

*

During a routine mammogram, a mass is detected in Toni's breast. More images are ordered. Adina joins her for the follow-up visit.

The technician, arranging Toni's right breast between two clear plastic slides, says, "In the image a mammogram produces, regular breast fibers look like a cloudy day."

"Cumuloft or cirrus?" Adina says.

"Cumulous," Toni corrects her.

The nurse does not have a sense of humor. Adina wouldn't want to joke either if her job was to press breasts against hard plastic, frown over X-rays, and leave the room without explanation.

*

Adina watches a movie with a despondent female character and a soundtrack that consists of one trembling note of a violin.

She texts Toni: AM I AN ADULT NOW?

Toni texts back: YES YOU ARE VERY OLD.

*

It has been a month since her superiors have asked about Earth and Miguel has been using the continuous present:

You are always leaving crumbs on your side of the bed. Toni waits for results. The burner under every area of her life has flipped on. In weeks, her notes will be published under the title *Alien Opus*. Adina wants to tell Miguel her big thing before the launch. One night, a good dinner emboldens Adina.

"What would you say if I told you I was from another planet?" she says. "And that I was here to take notes on human beings that I fax back to my superiors. And that it's possible one day they'll signal to me that it's time to go?"

Adina explains the activation, the fax machine, the Night Classroom, roller coasters. His face is arranged in its pleasant listening expression. Finally, she takes a long sip of tea and sits back, satisfied she has told him everything and ready for his questions.

"I believe you," he says. Then he asks if she wants to watch the movie about the troubled cop who reluctantly rejoins the force after his daughter is murdered or the movie about the troubled astronaut who reluctantly accepts a space mission after his daughter is murdered.

✶

"The ultrasound confirmed the doctor's suspicions and they want to do a biopsy," Toni says over pizza. "There is a mass that shouldn't be there and it either has very distinct borders or really weak ones. I forget which it has and which one we're rooting for."

Adina assumed the tests were formalities they'd get through then rejoin their healthy lives. "We're not even forty."

"In other news," Toni says. "My ob-gyn assures me my ovaries are perfect. Gorgeous, she called them."

"But your breasts?"

"Overcast," she says. "Chance of rain."

Seventy-five percent of biopsies turn out to be benign, Adina reads to her over the phone later.

"So, I guess it's a matter of how lucky do I feel?"

*

That winter, snow falls constantly, urgently. Adina volunteers to dig the car out because she likes sweating in the cold and she wants to be away from Miguel who stays over most nights.

She cannot explain why she doesn't want to have sex with him. Or why, when they have sex, she feels like she's wearing a turtleneck three sizes small. It bothers him, he makes jokes about it, the jokes bother her.

Adina sits in her dug-out car drinking coffee from a glass, waiting for the windshield's ice to melt and listening to an astronomer named Jerry compare the Milky Way and Andromeda to fried eggs lying back to back. He uses this metaphor because humans involve eggs whenever humanly possible. Humanly. Alien-ly. Doggily.

Gaya is a space observatory currently measuring how the stars and planets are falling into the center of the Milky Way, which is spread in a thin layer across the sky.

"Half of the weight," Jerry says, "comes from mass and half comes from dark matter."

The newscast contains nothing that is news to her. Frustrated, she silences Jerry, and wonders for the Sagan time why she lives in a place whose lights obscure the night sky. Why was she sent to an obscure spiral arm thirty thousand light-years from the center of this croque madame? The developing arts district of the galaxy. What is she supposed to learn from this backward place and its backward people with their supernumerary limbs and organs—who haven't even advanced past the body? Who still send letters with stamps, literally and metaphorically? If these letter-senders are her planet's only hope for survival, the word for how quantum doomed they are does not exist in mundane three-dimensional space.

Miguel emerges from her apartment with Butternut, holding a cup of something steaming she knows is for her. The little dog hurls his ecstatic, furry body into a snowdrift, is immediately confused by what has happened to him, does it again. Miguel searches the street for her. She cannot hear him but reads his lips when he says, "There she is."

*

In 2015, SETI astronomers spot an object of almost impossible brightness—the brightest ever seen in ancient space. A quasar is a nucleus of extraordinary luminosity powered by a black hole. This one is 12.8 billion light-years away and from only 900 million years after the Big Bang. From an interstellar perspective its birthday is practically the dawn of time. It's 420 trillion times more luminous than the earth's sun. A wise, old quasar. Adina pictures the animated owl from the Tootsie Pop commercials cartoon. This wide, wondering quasar with horn-rimmed glasses is detectable with even a relatively small telescope.

*

Adina and Toni sit on the bench in the doctor's office, holding hands without realizing. The doctors diagnose the lump in Toni's breast as late stage-three breast cancer. Totally workable, they say. Six weeks of chemo, then radiation, then surgery, then we'll see.

Waiting for the elevator, Adina tries to think of words to make this anything other than the worst day of Toni's life.

Toni speaks for her. "I guess as it turns out, I'm pretty lucky."

Adina asks if she'd like to get a drink but Toni wants to go home. At her apartment, she says she'd like to be alone. The door shuts between them.

*

Adina calls her mother from the street and says that the doctors used the words *bing-bam-boom,* and *no big deal* when what they said was, *cross that bridge when we come to it,* and *too soon to tell.*

*

The Something Else she first encountered in college, the occasional rummaging drag, visits more often. During these episodes, Adina's body is a lumbering, boxy suit. She walks down the street negotiating with her heavy legs. Such outdated tools. The Something Else feels distinctly linked to her human carapace and not her extraterrestrial origins. She longs to be relieved of her body. She longs to compel across a space like a wish. You're barely finished making it and you're already above the tree line, pumping into the incalculable banks of clouds.

*

Adina takes the train to Pulverize and performs a joyless two miles on the treadmill. Over the bank of pulsing bodies, a television reporter says that unfortunately what they thought was a new planet was a shadow on someone's computer monitor. Bing-bam-boom, no planet. Benign. Everyone is getting everyone else's desired results. In the locker room, Adina bargains: If she throws her towel and it makes it into Pulverize's laundry basket, Toni will be fine. Women enter wrestling with sports bras, toweling off, misremembering locker combinations. Adina is unable to move. Eventually, she places the towel lightly on the top of the laundry pile, moves her body up the stairs to the street where humans rush toward or away from the train, disappear down steps, slide by on buses. We're so tender, Adina thinks, our puny bodies cannot withstand any of this, how do we get through even one day?

*

Miguel and Adina attend a party at Sarah Glide's apartment. Her space is small but fastened to a private patio surrounded by trees. Adina is in the kitchen politely declining a stout beer when she hears a familiar and unsettling sound: her mother's name. Unmistakable. Two quick spirals on the descending line. A short, digital throb then a whirl. The whirl: the interim sound in *Mario Bros.* when moving to a new level. Closing doors on a *Star Wars* ship. A sound that grants access: her mother's name. Or, what humans would refer to as mother. The closest Planet Cricket Rice equivalent would be benevolent manufacturer.

Adina is so moved that she wants to share this news with Miguel and the party. She believes even Sarah Glide will understand. Adina walks toward the open patio doors and proclaims to the humans sitting outside,

"That's my mother's name."

Sarah Glide raises her voice so everyone can hear. "Wow, Adina," she says. "I knew you were weird but I didn't know you were the child of a bird."

The party titters. Miguel, sitting at the table, laughs. Seeing Adina's frown he says, "Aw, it's a joke."

Sarah Glide waits for Adina to explain. To get out clean, Adina is required to lie and say that's not what she meant. But lying baffles Adina. Sarah Glide baffles Adina: a human comprised of saying one thing and meaning another. In between the two currents, Adina doesn't sense much substance. Yet she commands a group.

Adina's failure to explain creates a double offense (saying it then not being ashamed of it) that doubly obligates Sarah to punish. Apparently, she's been keeping a log of Adina's weirdnesses. How bad Adina is at shaving. How she botched her legs so terribly she had to cover it up with makeup foundation. Sarah Glide knows to keep her tone unapproachably jovial, to avoid the words that would evoke sympathy or null her authority—ethnic, poor, sensitive—so no one can challenge her. She's manipulated her thread into the knot of the group so expertly that if she gets pulled, they all come undone.

Finally, Miguel's quiet voice. "All right, Sarah, we get it."

Adina stands in the doorway, one hand out as if to brace herself. The giddiness over a family sound, the knife feeling of this girl listing sins Adina has committed against the world. She remembers in high school on her birthday holding a thick bouquet of balloons. So far away from both mothers.

The veery thrush in the trees is undaunted. She calls. She calls and calls.

*

When they are in pain, human beings sing "Amazing Grace." It has transcended religious, cultural, and racial context and is about the basest of human cultures, which is suffering. The more we live, the more we lose, the more we believe we are lost. The song says, if you remain elegant you will be found. It might take a while. You may have to chill in misery for longer than you feel is necessary. Hang in there and you will receive grace. Grace is unmerited kindness. Unmerited because you are a wretch which is a synonym for human which is a synonym for flawed. Grace, a place to store loss.

*

Adina leaves her bed where Miguel is sweetly snoring and fumbles toward the family room couch in the dark. She hears Butternut's paws landing on the floor as he follows her. He presses his front paws onto the couch, to tell her he wants up. She lifts him. The curve of his back tucks into her chest. He falls asleep. Every so often, he sighs and readjusts his body to a more comfortable position against her. Adina stays awake in the joy of these recalibrations.

Dogs, she faxes, *are the best we can do.*

✶

Toni insists that life proceed normally as she receives treatment. Plans for the book launch move forward. The publisher asks Adina to send an author photo and bio that will be printed on the back cover. Miguel takes a picture of Adina with Butternut on her lap. She writes: *Adina is an alien. This book is a memoir.*

She figures it is better to err on the side of honesty. She didn't learn that on Earth. But she learned it.

✶

Adina is wondering how to tell Miguel she does not want him to stay over as much when he returns from outside, carrying a box. Inside are fifteen copies of her book, spines gleaming, *Alien Opus: A Memoir in Stories.*

"What is a memoir in stories?" Adina says. Butternut comes over and sniffs the pile.

"No idea," Miguel says.

✶

When they are lonely, human beings reach out with their holding parts. If no one is around they reach out with their thoughts. They write sentences on paper to express their desire. This makes them feel less alone because they have created another person on the page.

Are we alone? astronomers ask the universe with their rudimentary instruments.

Humans want to find aliens so they feel less alone. They don't know there is nothing lonelier than an alien.

The reply fax squeaks through the machine.

HOW CAN PEOPLE FEEL ALONE IN NEW YORK CITY?

✶

Adina, Miguel, Toni's boss, and Adina's mother sit in a storage space behind the room where Adina will give her contractually obligated reading for *Alien Opus*. It is not unlike the backroom in Landry Business Solutions where they store reams of paper. That morning, Delilah said she'd try to come but no promises. Since being left to die in the women's bathroom, she no longer possesses the desire to pander.

Toni's boss wears three different animal prints. This is called power clashing. Adina has seen floral and stripes in spirited discussion on the subway. She identifies cheetah on her sweater, tiger on her heels, but cannot place the last print.

Toni arrives with Audrey and news. A writer for a popular online magazine was intrigued by *Alien Opus* and has featured this reading on a popular list. This list was picked up and spread around other people's networks in an unlikely and disturbing eruption.

"There are more people here than we anticipated," Toni summarizes. Then, seeing Adina's concern, assures her, "It's a good thing."

Adina's throat feels heavy. "How many?"

*

They enter the main room, a renovated church with tall columns and high windows. Humans fill the pews, lean against walls, shuffle to allow others to pass, reposition themselves so more can fit. There are more humans in the overflow room behind this one, who want to listen.

Toni's boss walks to the podium and introduces Adina. Adina thinks, walking to the microphone, cow. She loses her footing at the podium and puts this word into the microphone: Hello. The microphone takes it, adds twelve layers to it, and carries it to those hustling to sit. Even though it connects her to this room of strangers and the room behind it, the effect of the amplification is one of privacy. She can say anything into this instrument and it will make it accurate or, if not accurate, true.

"My name is Adina and I'm an alien."

The audience reacts with bright, strong applause. In the front row, her mother's face is tight with a smile, Miguel's flushed in surprise.

"Upon seeing someone they know on the street," she reads, "human beings lower their eyes, hoping that person won't see them. But if the person walks by without saying hello, they will wonder whether the person saw them and didn't say hi. Did they not see me? They will consult other human beings who weren't present in that moment and who couldn't possibly weigh in."

A disturbance in the front row: A woman can't control her giggling. Other audience members around her titter. Toni gives Adina a thumbs-up.

"'I'm sure they didn't see you,' the other human will say. 'What does it matter? You didn't want to talk to them anyway.'"

The woman in the front row is still laughing. Adina hears chuckling from the other, farther room. She likes how the microphone adds whispery filaments to her voice. She likes how she can make them expand or diminish by using her tone.

"The offended human being will stew. They will stand in front of the mirror and assure themselves they deserve to be seen. Though they didn't want to get pulled into conversation, they wanted to at least be acknowledged. Sometimes it is hard to be human for reasons that don't make sense on a medical chart.

"Maybe in some inner private chamber they don't think they deserve to be seen.

"'I fucking see you,' they will insist into the mirror. 'There you are.'

"Meanwhile the offender continues their life, unaware. When their name comes up in conversation the offended will say, 'Oh nothing,' in a way that will mean that person is trash, but will refuse to explain.

"The offender will be given an award for achievement in ophthalmology or seeing through walls. (One of the most frustrating parts about being human is that the person who is the worst will be universally lauded for being the best.) Magic occurs. In the offended's life, everything transforms into being about eyes and vision, or, conversely, invisibility. Everything is shaped like an eye. A classroom of misbehaving pupils. A bouquet of iris. In the supermarket, a child will accidentally collide into the offended and they will yell, 'HELLO! I AM NOT INVISIBLE. I AM IN THIS WORLD.'

"The child will wheel around, frightened. Its mother will pull it by its tiny arm into the protection of her coat, soothing it with stories or sentiments meant to educate. Things like, 'Some human beings don't like when other people seem happy.'

"If only that person had said hello."

Adina steps away from the microphone. The audience hits their hands together again and again.

*

Toni says she knows the reading was a success because at the end she heard the audience make an oof sound that means they were punched in the emotional gut. She says the delivery in addition to the words was what made the woman in the front row giggle. The doctors say she will lose her hair after chemotherapy, not during, as many people think.

Adina is a nervous mix of shaky-glittery. They walk to a nearby restaurant and sit on a back patio.

"How do you feel?" her mother asks over french fries.

Someone stops at their table. "I saw your show," he says. "I really liked the bit about saying hello. Hello," he says, "just say hello."

"Thank you." Adina returns to her french fries.

The man, looking confused, leaves.

"Adina," her mother says. "I think they're going to make you do it again."

*

What is the story implied by wearing an animal print? Lookit, I have murdered a cheetah. Now I will wear its skin to Pilates.

*

Dominic and Adina take turns driving Toni to the sprawling hospital perched on the East River. Every other Wednesday, Adina waits in the car while Toni receives her treatments.

Toni says, "Chemo is quite a thing. They pump you full of poison then send you home."

*

Feedback from the reading arrives in exclamatory emails from Toni and her boss. Some audience members stayed at the venue for half an hour to discuss the book with one another. Reading groups formed. They were disappointed there was no Q&A, so we'll have to have one next time, Toni says. More humans empathize with her alien experience than anyone anticipated. Adina is convinced there are others faxing in their midnight bedrooms and navigating the loneliness that comes from distance.

I need to know, she faxes.

OR PERHAPS YOU JUST WANT OUT OF YOUR RELATIONSHIP.

She crumples the reply and throws it into the trash. It's easy to hurl observations when they are centuries away. They don't know what it's like to manage responsibilities to her publisher and Landry Business Solutions, who have added inventory to her job. She must spend two Saturdays a month counting staples and screws in the break room. To care for Toni, diminishing every day under the chemicals.

She yanks the fax's cord from the wall. A sense of righteousness when she watches the green light die. She covers the machine with a towel.

*

"They're trying a new kind of chemo," Toni says. "Those jerks can't get it right." She is making curry shrimp.

"This time will work," Adina says.

"Nevertheless, for all of your work and prayers and rides, I thank you. From the bottom of my gorgeous, perfect ovaries."

Adina is unable to eat. When she gets home, the fax machine looms silent under the towel. She ignores the urge to transmit her anxiety to her superiors. She keeps it to herself, allowing it to agitate her singular, private mind.

*

Alien Opus sells out. Because Adina has no online presence, someone makes a web page where fans can compare notes—hers and theirs.

Another reading is scheduled to coincide with the second

printing in the spring. This time, Toni insists, there will be a Q&A. Adina visits several department stores to find a suit like the one Carl Sagan wore to deliver his "lost lecture" on his sixtieth birthday.

✶

The Good Place is a television show about humans who die and find themselves in a heaven-type place.

Adina and Miguel watch until they reach the last season. Adina explains to Miguel that she cannot watch the final episode because of *Cheers* and the Worst Feeling. He explains that avoiding experiences because of fear makes them feel bigger than they are. She is panicking over something that, if faced, would turn out to be minuscule. It is called integrating one's shadow self. Instead of avoiding a fear, you move toward it.

They watch the final episode. The characters have reached actual heaven after several seasons of madcap adventures. But they tire of it. Humans can only have their ideal day so many times before it gets old. Their superiors decide they can leave heaven whenever they want. To disperse into stars or dust. One by one, during the last episode, they say their real goodbyes.

After it is over, Adina walks to the kitchen and pours herself a glass of water. She drinks it soundlessly, standing at the counter. As she replays each character's goodbye, dark buttons press against her heart and throat. She drinks another glass of water, tears coating her cheeks.

"Are you okay?" Miguel says. "You haven't said anything

in over an hour." He'd enjoyed the episode in a that's-that kind of way.

Adina retreats into the bathroom and draws a hot bath. She throws up a polite amount of water into the toilet. She climbs into the bath and is overcome by chills.

Miguel is outside the door. His voice is quiet, stable. "I'm sorry. I'm sorry."

She emerges from the bathroom and stands over where he half-reads a magazine on the couch. She removes her towel and points to where hives have grown. Cinnamon-colored peaks that itch and burn: She is pleased to have a physical mark to show him because he doesn't seem to believe in anything he can't see.

*

A hairdresser comes to Toni's house and lops off her hair in strips. Her head is surprisingly lumpy.

"You never know what shape head you have until you get cancer," the hairdresser says.

They practice tying scarves. The hairdresser holds Butternut and jogs around the room. She stops, addresses him in a serious voice. "Did that feel like you were flying?"

*

Adina makes a nonfragrant pot of rice that Toni smashes her fork into but doesn't eat. She lilts to one side on her chair. Sometimes the drugs make her piercing and irritable but on this night she's nostalgic. "Guess who I bumped into a few weeks ago? That girl who took your scholarship. She was named after a state?"

"Dakota," Adina says.

"She said I looked tired."

"Is she on Broadway?"

"She's a corporate lawyer."

"Of course she is." They laugh. The girl who took Adina's scholarship did not even use it. It's not an of-course-she-is situation but adds up in human math, where people like Dakota take because they can. "I mean, what was I going to be? An actress?"

Toni pulls her cardigan tighter. The worrisome stars of her collarbones show through the faded material, her drastic elbows. "I know what I look like, Adina."

"You look fine, the same."

"Don't be the person who can't level with me."

"You look tired."

"Thank you for being honest. Honesty is my thing these days. I'm high all the time so I can't be held responsible." She tells Adina she called Audrey the night before and said embarrassing things about her body. "Filthy things I can't remember. She loved it, said I should have gotten cancer years ago."

*

Failures of imagination:

That summer in the airspace over San Diego, pilots report unidentified space craft at thirty thousand feet, higher than they've ever seen. They noticed after their radar was upgraded from their 1980s-era machines. The footage shows objects traveling at supersonic speeds, halting and reversing in an amount of time scientists believe is impossible.

The Pinta Island tortoise, a poised-looking subspecies that lives in the Galápagos Islands, is declared extinct. It had poor dispersal tactics and could not outrun hunters or outcompete goats for vegetation.

Every solar system has a planet capable of producing water and that is roughly the same size as Earth. How many of these planets produce societies that destroy them? In her particular set of years, Adina has watched humans back into a trap everyone could see. In a newspaper clipping, the tortoise cranes its distinguished neck, staring back from the forever space of extinction. It looks like it would take everything you say too literally but would lend you money if you needed it. Biologists consider assigning human qualities to animals verboten. Adina understands, it's hard enough assigning human qualities to humans. Biologists fail to imagine the Pinta Island tortoise. Adina supposes that humanizing an animal risks making one feel obligated to try to save it, or at least examine one's own participation in making it extinct.

*

At Landry Business Solutions's Halloween costume party, Delilah is dressed for a regular day at work.

She says, "I am a serial killer. We look just like everyone else."

Adina is also dressed for a regular day of work, black jeans, button-down black shirt, and sneakers.

"What are you?" Delilah says, then answers herself. "Oh right, an alien. I read the book."

*

Arguments over *Alien Opus* have erupted online, Toni tells her. A popular magazine publishes an editorial saying truth doesn't matter. Another decries the article, several more debate niche points from the other two. Popular book trade publications take sides or slyly defer. A WNYC personality leads a reading group that discusses the memoir chapter by chapter. Why doesn't she write about sex or motherhood, more feminine subjects? One of the callers, an elementary school teacher, diagnoses Adina as autistic. "Removed from society," she says. "She is a reporter. That's why her transmissions are episodic, matter-of-fact, and don't have an overarching story like a novel or miniseries." Readers don't know how seriously to take her. Some think she is playing a role. Others beg her through online forums to get help. Each theory has merits and flaws, but who are they talking about? Not her. Some other, more public Adina.

*

The spring reading takes place at a downtown bookstore lit by tulip-shaped string lights. The bookstore is at capacity. Its meadow-wide windows overlook the rain-slicked street, where people without tickets gather. One waves when she steps onto the podium. Dominic sits in the front row with his new boyfriend. Ted is thin, attentive, the kind of person who would catch you up to a conversation if you arrived late.

Adina is halfway through her reading when she senses movement in the middle of the audience. A petite person with a bold haircut raises a sign. It is well-made, thoughtfully lettered: I BELIEVE IN YOU.

Will she react? Does she see it? The people outside motion to one another and at the sign. Adina continues, aware of her mother panic-blinking in the front row. People snap photos with their phones.

Adina finishes. As she leaves the stage, Toni, head wrapped in a polka-dot scarf, reminds her about the Q&A.

Adina sits in the provided chair. "Does anyone have any questions?"

Several hands ascend.

"Are your superiors happy with your work here?" a man with wet hair asks. The words on a page would read as neutral, but he speaks with the ironic tone of the camp that thinks she's a performance art construction. This plus the crowd's kinetic, argumentative energy plus the fact that she has not communicated with her superiors in a while adds up to a jagged feeling of being a fraud.

"Excuse me," Adina says. She stands and leaves the stage.

*

Adina sits behind a table and signs books. Miguel scans the line unhappily. He says he will take her mother and friends to a restaurant down the street to wait for her. Adina watches them leave. Her mother wears a new plaid dress and smiles into everyone's eyes as she moves through the crowd. Miguel frowns, waits for an excited reader to pass. He is in a business of being applauded and congratulated. Every time he leaves his piano bench he is subsumed into the light of admiration. Why would her reading bring him discomfort?

"He's very handsome." A woman holds out a copy of the book to sign. "Is he an alien too?"

*

After dinner, Miguel asks Adina how long she plans to keep up the "schtick." They've accompanied her mother to her hotel and are back at her apartment. The little dog is playing with his toys.

After a spiraling conversation that lands far from its original intent, he says, "Maybe the part of you that wants to be alone is bigger than the other parts of you."

Adina stares out of the darkened window after he falls asleep. She can feel the fax machine covered on her desk, as if it is her own body underneath the beach towel. Still, she is tired of asking questions and sharing her most intimate thoughts and getting little to no support. She pulls out a notebook and pen.

*

Living in New York, she writes, is like sitting at a nine-million-person blackjack table. We work together against the dealer.

If you call on 11 (request a fresh bagel to be toasted), the table scowls at you. You can trust the group. If a group of New Yorkers are walking against the light, you can cross. If a group of New Yorkers avoid a subway car, it is covered in feces. If a group of New Yorkers leave their cars parked on ASP day, alternate side of the street and parking meter rules have been suspended. Like it or not, you're part of the team. Uptown or down? Express or local? Yell *Hold the train*, and at least three New Yorkers will wrench their hands between the closing doors. Life in New York is a series of no-look passes. Not true in cities like Philadelphia where, if humans are participating in an activity, much more follow-up is required.

*

"So long," Miguel says. "I'm leaving." He is going to Los Angeles to record music with a friend. She is relieved she won't have to witness his punctured pouting when she doesn't want to have sex.

"For a week," Adina adds.

He hesitates, nods. "Maybe when I get back we can talk about next steps."

Adina says she's not sure whether she's ready for next steps.

He readjusts the strap of his bag to a more comfortable place on his shoulder. "I'm sorry," he says. "I don't want to wait anymore. This distance hurts. There's a part of you that will never give yourself over. To me."

"That's probably true," Adina says, and he says, "It is true."

"Do you," Adina says, "think I'm lying about . . . ?"

"Being from another planet." He pronounces the question like it is an answer. "I think it has to do with trauma. Being hurt as a kid." He says, "Even if it is true, I'd have to wonder why you got involved with me in the first place. Was it to have a love experience to write about? For your notes?"

"So, you wouldn't be like, 'Cool, I'm happy for you.'"

His eyes widen. "Happy for you?"

"Like, 'Adina, you must do what you need to do.' Like in *Close Encounters*, or *E.T.* or *Contact*? Stories where someone has a higher calling and everyone around them gets it."

The 7 train hurries by. A plane flies overhead. "Those are movies!" he says over the noise.

"Sometimes movies are all we—"

"This is my life," he says. "It would not be like in *Contact*."

They stand across from each other long enough that Adina no longer feels her own body but his. His bag strap digs into her shoulder. His belt is too tight around her waist. Adina can hear the little dog chewing his toy. Sometimes even his mouth sounds annoy her. Life is often one thing plus an opposing feeling. Miguel's gaze contains surprise and pity. She tries to make her voice tender enough to hold his anger and her hope. "So long," she says. Eventually, she is alone in the room.

*

The empty apartment feels malevolent. Adina takes the little dog outside where pink clouds perch above the 7 train platform, delayed like everyone else. Late afternoon sun fills the neighborhood. People perform errands in sitcom-kitchen lighting. The neighbor who dresses her trio of plastic stoop geese in seasonally appropriate attire walks by. "Hello, sweetheart, how are you today? I like your hat."

"It's very necessary." Adina points to the sky.

"You too," she says, continuing down the street.

Adina returns to her apartment and scrubs the tub with three kinds of bleach. She lets it sit, soaps it up, lets it sit. She washes the sink, scrubs the tiles, wipes the mirrors until they shine. She ignores her sad countenance in the mirror as the sound of scraping metal fills the apartment. It must be 7:30 p.m.

She returns the cleaning agents to the cabinet beneath the sink and sees the mouse. Mournful, caught, it pretends to be the sponge it's sitting on. Adina kicks the cabinet shut. She paces the family room as the little dog recrosses his front paws, places his chin on the top one.

She leaves a message on Miguel's voicemail.

"Mouse," she says. "Help."

She thinks of the mouse's cold black eyes. Roger, she decides.

*

Adina falls asleep on the couch, bleach stiffening on her hands. She wakes, Butternut curled by her feet in sleep. There is no light in the room. It is 3:00 a.m. She has missed his dinnertime. She turns on every lamp.

The kitchen feels staged, as if Roger has taken every item out then replaced it, an inch to the side. There is a stand-in quality to the rug, the mugs too orderly in the rack. The chairs are the wrong color. Twitching under the hutch is Roger. A succinct gray mark on the pale pink. The city is quiet, the kitchen is quiet. Roger makes a sequence of fluttery clicks that follow an elliptical pattern then cease. After a few moments of silence, he calls again. Adina has no doubt—he is transmitting into the night. For help, she thinks, though she does not want to empathize. Believing he's alone, he scuttles into view. The full measure of his back, the grabby hands, tufted ears.

*

Miguel does not mention the mouse but emails a picture of his desk in Los Angeles. Two screens, a keyboard, a cup of pens, a rose, the kind of rubber eraser that punishes the paper, a snarl of headphones. Adina knows that distance blurs feeling and intent. This is his way of bridging that distance. This is a borrowed desk. Adina imagines Miguel at a party of producers and musicians chatting around a pale pool somewhere called Los Angeles.

Who gave him the rose?

*

Adina cannot stay in the mouse-infested apartment. She and Butternut drive home to see her mother.

"But what is one for?" she insists. They are eating gingersnaps at the half-moon table. Butternut is asleep on her mother's lap.

"One what?" her mother says. "Man?"

"Husband. Boyfriend. People want them so much but I can't understand what they're supposed to do. They take so much energy."

"A husband," her mother says. "What is a husband for." Her expression fuzzes, sharpens. She pushes herself away from the half-moon table and, holding Butternut to her chest, walks into the other room with unsure steps. "A husband." Whatever she's piecing together bewilders her and settles a suspicion. Though it is about Adina it doesn't seem to require her. An idea she's been tending alongside her actual daughter. Her thoughts continue around the room as her body follows, sitting on the edge of a chair before moving to the couch, then the other chair, before standing in the doorway in a purposeless stance.

"Am I supposed to follow you?" Adina says.

Her mother sits on the couch and pats the area next to her. "I've been so intent on raising you strong that I messed you up in a different way. I was taught complaints go up, so I never wanted to share how hard things were. For example, I never told you, but we didn't have a lot of money."

Adina does not know whether her mother is joking.

Her mother sinks against the couch, shaking her head, a small smile. Butternut, annoyed by the movement, transfers to Adina's lap. "You knew. Of course you did."

"We shopped in the alley behind House of Bargains. The stuff they were throwing away."

"Jesus, that's right," she says. "The alley. What was I even trying to do? Protect myself. I just wanted to get through with you intact. If you don't know what a man is for." She removes her glasses and rubs the bridge of her nose. "You've been around the wrong men. I haven't shown you how to be a partner. I'm sorry."

Adina tells her mother there is nothing to be sorry for.

That she's happy she ended up with her as a mother. A strange, complex, honest mother is as good as what anyone else had. Better.

"Now that you're an adult I should relax but I'm still always worried." Emotion halts her, so she nods at Adina. That's it.

"Most families would hug now," Adina says.

"We'll do it. We'll hug."

She holds out her arms and Adina moves into the embrace, a stiff gesture that jostles more than it soothes. They release each other.

"How's Miguel? Do I want to ask?"

Adina says she is living only with a mouse named Roger.

She says, "Oh no, Roger!"

Their favorite comedian hosts *Saturday Night Live*. They eat popcorn from separate bowls and laugh at the same parts. Toward the end of the show, only Adina is laughing. Her mother is asleep, head resting against the chair's soft wingback. Adina and Butternut watch what her mother calls the shitty end bits alone.

*

In her own kitchen, she sets a mousetrap.

Miguel has not called. Perhaps he is too busy giving roses to every woman in Los Angeles. Sticking his penis inside them. Or maybe they will no longer respond to each other's emergencies, real or imagined. Or from, of course. The rose could be from someone. She opens a cabinet and imagines a tiny sneeze.

"God bless you, Roger."

Adina eats chicken over rice at the bar across the street. The Tour de France is being shown on the television above the bar. Streams of metal and flags. Thin, muscled, brightly colored bikers careen around the mountains. She goes home, where the little dog stands at the foot of the kitchen counter, gaze fixed toward the ceiling.

"What's up, bud?" Adina says, turning on the faucet. Roger leaps from the strainer. Adina screams and palms the faucet off. Roger bats against the sink's slick sides then freezes.

She wraps herself and the little dog in the covers and falls into a troubled sleep.

The next morning Roger is dead in the sink. His hunger made him desperate enough to come out of the wall. No different than Adina signaling over and over to her superiors.

Sweeping him into the dustpan feels too intimate. But if Toni can suffer a second kind of chemo, she can sweep up a dead mouse. He was longer than she thought, and grayer. She disposes of all of his vulnerable, sympathetic parts.

*

Normally Toni wants to go home after treatment, but this Wednesday she requests takeout from their pizza restaurant. She waits in the car while Adina runs in. When Adina returns, Toni's head is pressed against the window, staring up at the sign that is draped in unlit string lights.

She says, "I wish those were on."

*

Miguel stands in the doorway holding his bag against his side as if afraid to enter.

"It's like we were raised on two different planets."

"Figuratively?" she says.

At the end of the halting, gentle conversation, neither of them is anyone's boyfriend or girlfriend. She waits to bolt the latch after he leaves the building so the last sound he hears of her is not one of unwelcome.

Miguel releases a sad, almost inaudible breath. He is outside on the sidewalk underneath the flight path of a brightly colored jet yet Adina hears him.

She takes the good tea down from the shelf, arranges the chamomile leaves in the tea decanter, lets it steep for the full ten minutes, removes the decanter from the steaming water, sits at the kitchen table. She uses the good honey. He never read her book. Growing up he never noticed the lobsters in the aquarium. Different planets: a telling phrase. Is it odd that he came closest to understanding her while leaving or does it make complete sense?

The project of romance in Adina's life has concluded. She feels sorrowful and relieved. She will relocate her love for him like a spider from her house, gently. In the end, they break up for a common human reason: They don't believe in each other.

✶

Adina pulls the fax machine out from the bottom shelf. She uncovers it, uses the towel and glass cleaner to remove the dust from its creases, and connects the plug. The machine whirs on. She is relieved to see the certain, green light.

For me to do my job correctly, I must get close to human beings. So they show me who they are. So I can learn more about who I am. However, getting close to a human means putting them and myself in danger. I risk hurting them and being hurt. I'm here as a student and will one day have to leave. So I build what Yolanda K. calls emotional moating. Humans beam their lights to me but I'm too far away to see. It is an extraterrestrial and human quandary.

Help. Please advise.

No response.

*

Cars are not attached to anything. They are free to collide with other bodies whenever they want and wreck each other. This would not happen with my bumper car system. Cars would be attached to poles linked to an overarching mechanism, as they are in bumper cars. The worst that can happen in a bumper car is you make a strange face when you smash someone. A strange face that makes the other person think you are uglier than they thought and that maybe there are other ugly things they don't know about you. But they forget in the next second when they are smashed by someone else. It doesn't hurt, though, as much as real cars. It doesn't hurt as much.

No response.

*

Human beings, she faxes the next day, *develop counterintuitive connections to unexpected things, like inanimate objects, and things they thought they hated and wanted to die, like mice.*

No response.

✶

Worry unzips Adina.

As it turns out the nostalgia I feel at final episodes is only the Second Worst Feeling. The first is breaking up with someone because you are incompatible.

The 7 train passes. Everything trembles. She leaves a message for her mother, for Toni, but no one on Earth or beyond is responding. Are they brooding? Holding a grudge over her impetuousness?

Is this punishment?

✶

Adina finds herself in the uncomfortable position of chasing her superiors' attention. Because their interaction has always been one-on-one and personal, she's never had to seek external support but now she scours the internet and newspapers for extraterrestrial news. She watches footage of UFO sightings and press conferences ranging from serious to absurd. In Arizona, seeking to capitalize on their town's most recent UFO sighting, a political official conducts a press conference in a full alien costume. She checks on TRAPPIST-1, the first exoplanets, anything that might explain this cosmic silence.

Adina longs to return to the Night Classroom. She misses

Solomon, the Flying Man, Martin's Aquarium, Reel to Reel Video. She misses Mrs. Leafhalter, who was cold but who taught her the different ways women fold their legs. Upright, hard fold, ankle cross. Adina notes each type every time she's on the subway. Mrs. Leafhalter wasn't vicious, she was a single woman living her life, the way Adina is. If she'd understood sooner maybe she'd have made better decisions at key moments and wouldn't be missing her and everyone she's ever met, even the terrible ones who ripped important things from her like wire from a wall. Adina doesn't want to be younger, only to be sitting at that Wildwood table when her biggest problem was how to get in with the *J* girls, the afternoon Mrs. Leafhalter chided her mother over butter.

*

In her hospital room, Toni tries and fails to read James Baldwin. Machines hem and bleat around her. Dominic texts his boyfriend. Adina writes and reads out loud. "When you hit ten years in New York . . . ," she says.

"When you hit ten years . . . ," Dominic says.

"Something about roaches," Adina says.

"They force you to eat a roach!" he says.

"Stop making me laugh," Toni says. "It hurts." She says there's a photo online of the girl Miguel is seeing. "She's ugly in a manipulative way. Do you want to see?"

Adina says no and returns to her notes. "When you hit ten years in New York . . ."

"You have to share your apartment with a family of flying roaches," Dominic says.

A doctor arrives, fiddles with a few of the machines, asks Toni how she's feeling.

"Bald," Toni says.

The doctor leaves.

"When you hit ten years in New York, they surgically replace your heart with a roach. But you get to choose the roach." She says, "Will I make it to fifteen?"

Dominic moves from his chair to sit on the edge of the bed. "Of course you will."

Adina says, "But will the roach?"

"Roaches outlast everything," Toni says. "They're like our cousin who's been shot like a hundred times. All the wrong people."

"All the wrong people what?" Dominic says.

"Have the luck."

"Your cousin is the worst," Adina says. "He can bum out an entire party."

"I'd rather be awful like he is and have good luck," Toni says. Negativity has crept into her spirit. Illness gives her the right.

"You agree, though," Adina says.

"About our cousin? He's the living worst."

Adina says she's changed her mind, she would like to see the photo. Toni opens her laptop and finds the right page. Adina and Dominic lean over the photograph of a regular girl in a party hat, smiling. Miguel stands behind her casually holding a glass of wine.

"I don't get the manipulative thing," Adina says.

Toni shrugs. "It takes a girl with brothers to see something like that."

*

In the hospital convenience store, a man wearing scrubs is buying everyone flowers.

"I just had a daughter," he says, pointing to the ceiling. "She's up there right now. Sleeping with her mama. I've never done anything good. Yet she's perfect."

*

Human beings design irrigation systems that carry water billions of miles but cannot invent an ironing board that opens without sounding like a metal seizure.

No response.

*

Are you cold? her mother asks and Adina says, "Always."

They are at Shop & Save, doing a big shop for Toni. She's eating less so the cart is filled with things for the body: blankets, hot water bottle, *National Enquirers*. A camping family reports being probed in New Mexico. Adina has long since abandoned hope that news of her superiors will be delivered via tabloid. The descriptions are too crude, too designed to titillate. If her people had visited anyone that person would experience only an almost imperceptible rearrangement, akin to the sensation of not knowing whether the train or the platform is moving. This would not be interesting to the *National Enquirer* readers.

"Because of the jaundice thing," her mother says, pricing a bag of pistachios.

"What jaundice thing?"

"They had you under a light for days when you were born. You were puny. I nearly died having you so, thankfully, I was too out of it to understand the magnitude. The nurses had to drag me half-conscious to the nursery. Robe hanging off. I was a mess."

Her mother continues. "Spend your first week on Earth under a lamp you go searching for heat the rest of your life." She scrutinizes the bag of nuts. She has finished her bachelor's and will be the first person in the family with a master's degree. She says, everything is math. The shape of Queen Anne's lace, bees. Everything can be explained except for why pistachios are the most expensive food in the world. She hurls the bag back onto the shelf. "No matter where I go they're like a hundred dollars."

*

The longer her superiors remain silent, the more Adina is convinced they're not responding because they can't. They've been taken over by violent colonizers or have blown themselves up. Adina lies awake, red-eyed and panicky.

*

The quasar owl chills in vast, distant space. For the black hole to grow to such a staggering size in less than a billion years, astronomers posit, it must have been pulling mass from its surroundings at the maximum rate. Is that where her faxes have been going? Transmissions about Yolanda K. sinking into its bottomless interstellar pocket? Widening with every observation—bodega cats, chemo, highway signs that tell you falling rock but don't tell you what to do about it, each experience enriching the churning understanding. Maybe Adina's pain is what's making the limitless mass glow brighter until schoolchildren in China can glimpse it with regular telescopes. Her information will be a lighthouse, guiding scientists to greater discoveries, more black holes, more stars, more extraterrestrials perched on doomed planets yearning toward the beacon.

The lamplighter planet was Il Piccolo Principe's favorite because it contained 440 sunsets a day.

Scientists don't have a theory to explain how this giant luminosity remained hidden for so long. But Adina wouldn't underestimate the human tendency to ignore whatever they don't understand.

✶

In Palau, an island country in the western Pacific Ocean, jellyfish live in a lake connected to the sea by a subaquatic tunnel. Over the years the tunnel is filled in by erosion. Separated from the ocean, the jellyfish lose their capacity to sting. They don't need it; they have no predators. For years the harmless jellyfish live peacefully in the secluded lake. Gradually, El Niño conditions create a new climate and a decimating drought. The jellyfish begin to disappear. The lake closes to visitors.

The jellyfish rebound. The lake reopens. There are enough jellyfish to guarantee a quality experience, the newspaper promises. Adina watches a video of the friendly ghouls pumping in the clear, bright water. They must swim around the lake constantly to follow the sunlight, trailed by their luminescent tentacles. Golden, stingless, isolated, yet, because of social media, simultaneously overexposed.

*

After a dinner of egg noodles and butter, Adina plays R.E.M. and dances with Butternut. He stands on his hind legs and she clasps his front paws. He takes tiny steps to the right. Tiny steps to the left. In bed, they watch a movie where an actor known for her rap career plays a young woman new to Cincinnati. She is tough. She will make it.

In the morning, Adina cannot find the little dog. He is not in bed, or on the carpet next to the bed, or in the kitchen drinking water.

"There you are," she says, relieved to see him sleeping underneath her desk. A quarter-size amount of throw-up gleams beside him. Adina crawls underneath the desk. He is already gone. His body is rigid and cold. His teeth are bared, attempting to ward off whatever was happening to him. It gives him a vicious appearance so unlike how he was in life. She places her arms around him and they lie together for what feels like hours. Wall Street traders arrive to work and fathers on every planet love their children and florists walk the Chelsea Market flower stalls, but her little dog does not wake up. He must have woken sometime in the night, found his bed in the darkness, curled into sleep, and turned to stone.

*

"Heart attack," the vet says over the phone. "Or stroke. It was quick. Nothing you could have done."

The vet says she can put him in the freezer until she is ready to say goodbye then call someone to transport his body.

"I can't hear you," Adina says. "Did you say put him in my freezer?"

*

Adina wraps Butternut in the crocheted sweater her mother made for him. His body has swollen in death so she must cut the sides to make it fit. She swaddles him in the blanket bought the night she ran around the city making room for him in her life. She removes the ice cube trays, bags of frozen peas, half-eaten carton of sorbet, and an almost-empty bottle of vodka from the freezer, and slides him in. At least he is still in the house. They are still together.

*

The doctor says, "You don't have to fight anymore. You can go home."

Toni turns to Adina, her brothers, Audrey, her mother and stepfather, crowded around the hospital bed. It is to them that she addresses the question. "What's that supposed to mean?"

"It means the fight is over," the doctor says.

"Try something else," she says. "Another set of chemo. Needles. Whatever."

Her care changes from curative to comfort. It is not possible, Adina thinks, to lose her little dog and her best friend within days. This is called bargaining. Everything is possible. Everything exists.

People assume the dying are peaceful but Toni is angry until the drugs take her under. Her family and Adina and Audrey surround her as her chest expands and contracts. Fills and diminishes.

Adina doesn't know if she imagines or intuits this: A spark of light grows in the center of Toni's chest. As if it has always been there. The light spreads into her arms and legs. It contains the spaciousness of sunlight. It moves beyond Toni's body and onto the bed. It runs over the floor and encompasses everyone in the room. No one moves. Toni's mother is still tilted forward, eyebrows knit into a grimace, brothers slumped against the walls. Adina and Dominic clasp Toni's warm hands. The bleating of machines outside, the rustle of bedsheets, the hard soles of Audrey's boots as she returns from the vending machine to encounter the room filled with light that spills out of the door and into the adjoining corridors, filling the many floors. It moves into the parking lot and street. Adina's ears and cheeks heat as if she's blown up a giant balloon. It's the kind of light you picnic in, that makes for great pictures, that signals end of day. It keeps going. It fills the city where they grew up. The Mustang, their childhood homes, and farther, the city where they moved, the buildings that housed their first jobs, dating experiences, everything that served them and did not. Toni's chest rises and falls. There is a choking sound as if she's struggling to breathe. "She's in pain!" her mother cries, but the nurses assure her it's only upper airway congestion. Air hunger, they call it. More upsetting to hear than to feel. Nothing is hurting Toni anymore. Her lungs fill. Her brain is still. Her heart continues. Adina remembers that the heart was the last organ to be operated on by doctors. At the end of the century, every other organ had been dissected. The heart is self-sustaining. Areas that are farthest away from it get cold fastest. The brain cannot function without the heartbeat but the heart can function without the brain. The light continues. Out through the troposphere, to where Adina's original frequency is still broadcasting, out and out, until it reaches everything and everyone. This light that began in Toni's chest that fills, diminishes, then does not. The heart is still. The body, no longer in pain, is still. The light does not dim and continues to travel.

*

The day they tried to buy earrings at the fancy mall. Adina remembers eating egg rolls on the trunk of Toni's car, a duck bleating somewhere in the dark. Toni would always cut them in half, eat the insides, and save the crispy exoskeleton for last. She preferred to end with what she liked best.

When someone dies, where does the way they eat egg rolls go?

No response.

BLACK HOLE

(DEATH)

The subways have the gall to run. The 7 drivers announce each station in clear, strong voices. The LIRR is on time. In unfair morning light, the halal meat vendors load their trucks. Adina's neighbor's stoop geese are bespectacled and headed back to school. The gosling carries an apple. New York City could have ground to a halt, at least for a moment, but alternate side of the street and parking meter regulations are in effect. Emilio is still selling round rolls two for a dollar. His daughter is still seeing the boy he dislikes, even though that boy owes her money, and what is he—her father—supposed to think about a man like that?

*

Yolanda K.:

When you're sitting on the couch eating guacamole and listening to Beyoncé I want you to think of me. Reach like it's the first time you've reached for anything. Imagine your abs cinched up like one of those old handbags. This is called the zipper. It means zipping up the goodness of the practice. One lunge for your mother! One lunge for your father! I care about your abs! But this is about your brain! Go deeper. Stand on the ceiling. Think about that! GO THERE. This is called the zipper. This is called the zipper.

*

Every human dies. But the bad news is that every day they act like they don't know they're alive. They lie or behave inconsiderately or cheat. Each one is a little death. Humans experience many little deaths before the final one.

No response.

*

The funeral reception is held at Toni's childhood home. The yard is cleared of old cars. The living room table is covered in plates of cold cuts, lettuce, hoagie rolls, cold salads. Toni's publishing friends surround Adina and her mother and ask if there will be a sequel to the memoir.

"I've never seen her more excited about anything ever," one of Toni's fellow editors says. "She called you a genius and she called literally no one that."

"We grew up together," Adina says.

They've been waiting to meet her. The internet has generated theories that she's a CIA operative or a bored housewife. There are Believers and Nonbelievers, websites, Instagram and Twitter handles dedicated to mining the memoir for clues.

"Clues about what?" Adina says, and they are surprised she doesn't know. "I'm not really online."

"You really are an alien," one of them says. Her expression a familiar mix of confusion and wonder.

Matteo, once a wild turkey agitator antagonist, has grown into a civilized, sweatered man holding a jar for a woman spreading mustard on a table of sandwich halves. This must be his wife, delivering precise swipes to each slice of bread. Adina misses whatever Toni would say about her. Dominic has brought his boyfriend home for the first time. On a regular visit, this would create a hurricane in the family climate. But on this day, it barely registers. Dominic asks Adina to follow him to the living room where they can be alone. Grief has de-clarified him, as if someone has used an eraser to smudge his features. Gray whiskers bloom at his temples.

"Don't be mad but she left you something." He pulls a small box from his bag and hands it to Adina. Toni has become the "she" in their heads. They no longer have to say her name.

Adina leaves it unopened and balanced on her lap. "What is it?"

"She didn't want you to be mad."

"You said that. Mad at what?"

"Maybe open it at home when you have some quiet."

Before rejoining the party, he pauses at the door. "It's amazing to know," he says. "That you're never going to be totally okay ever again."

At the food table, Adina asks Toni's awful cousin what kind of cheese it is they're eating.

"Brie?" he guesses. "It's gross."

She asks how his job is going and he tells her it'd be better if his boss wasn't always riding his balls.

Editor friends, writer friends, old friends. Adina is taken into a hug before she realizes it's Audrey, skeletal with sadness. Toni's mother, smiling, distracted in the corner, pulling strands from a blanket. Her health has improved. For the first time anyone can remember, she does not need the assistance of a wheelchair. The irony of losing her daughter when her own troubles have receded. Good news at bad times brings no joy. Tufts of yarn lay beneath her on the carpet.

Adina's mother kneels beside her. "Marianne," she says. "Hello."

"Térèse," she says. "Good to see you."

Toni's boss wears all black. No animal print peeks out from her sleeve. Even her pocketbook is a serious gray. Adina leaves the reception and drives. The boulevard is sequined in red and gold trees that reach far above the heads of the pretzel vendors hollering across the medians.

*

Beautyland has been renovated. Its friendly, messy sections have been corralled into an orderly arrangement of shelves. It smells like an inexpensive, not unpleasant cranberry candle.

The perfumery section is untouched, to Adina's relief. She climbs the steps expecting to see the man who was always vacuuming. Instead, a woman wearing a complicated apron stands behind the counter, glaring at a stack of tickets. The walls are still a sun-bleached carrot, the aisles the same tired ivory. Adina realizes the perfumes are not the brands you find in department stores but those marketed to working mothers who don't want to pay a lot or create too much fuss. The fancy-cheap brocade boxes, the caps like faux-gold hats. Adina can afford any of them. Why had it seemed so opulent and untouchable? She hates this store for making her mother feel intimidated and wishes that rotten-apple man were around so she could spray him with every off-brand scent.

Her mother texts: WHERE ARE YOU.

Adina stares at a display of control-top pantyhose. The clerk approaches. "Do you need help finding anything?"

She says, "Do these come in Misty Taupe?"

The woman sorts through the stack and finds the package.

Adina follows her to the cash register. "I used to come here as a girl," she says. "With my mother."

The woman says many people have been visiting to check out the recent renovation. Adina is pleased. She doesn't want to be the only person who remembers this place. "Recent?"

"Until a few months ago, it was exactly the same. My aunties lived in this neighborhood," the girl says. "They'd take me here too."

They smile at each other. "It was time," she says. "For an update."

She wears a short skirt and cropped sweater and has what they call it. Adina wears a long coat, her hair arranged in a bun. She remembers the doctor who explained her speech impediment to her mother. The word rabbit. She is a machine that is malfunctioning in the form of memory overload. She no longer believes the neighborhood maxim to show it if you have it. But she does believe in having it. She does still long to have it. When had it all changed?

Her mother texts: WE'LL WRAP UP CAKE FOR YOU.

"What brings you back?" the girl says, handing Adina her purchase.

Outside, an early winter breeze moves through the dry leaves. Soon these back-to-school decorations will be replaced by pumpkins and turkeys. Then Christmas trees and Hanukkah candles, then New Year's cherubs then cupids, candied eggs, flags, fireworks, beach balls, then back-to-school. Suburban lawns, city retailers, stoop geese. Humans, do not fear, this is what season it is.

"Beautyland," Adina says.

The clerk wears the unmistakable expression of the neighborhood: So?

"Auto World. United Skates of America. Seafood Shanty. You ever notice how weird the names are around here?"

"They're named after places," she says. Adina's sentiment is too obvious to take seriously.

"Well," Adina says, "they are places."

"I mean, they're named after places to sound like places. Places you know."

"So you think you've already been there?" Adina says.

"No, no, no," the clerk says. An unmistakable *l* tags the word. Nawl, nawl, nawl. "So you think you're home."

Adina counts her change. She thinks about it on the ride back to the reception, where people file to their cars. Inside the house, strangers give her recommendations for a movement teacher, a life coach, and a therapist who specializes in grief.

She finds her mother and hands her the pantyhose. "I bought you these."

Her mother opens her mouth to ask a question then stops.

"I haven't worn these in years," she says. "They were always crap."

They say goodbye to Toni's family and friends. Dominic insists on carrying their bags to the car so they can hold thick cake slices shining under cellophane.

"You should probably go online and see what they're saying," he says. "Your book is getting to be a thing."

"Get with it, Adina," her mother says. "Join the twentieth century."

"Are you on Twitter?" Dominic is impressed.

"I'm no dinosaur," her mother says.

Adina turns on the wipers to rid the windshield of errant leaves then they wave to Dominic. He lifts one foot comically into the air. Then the other.

"What's he doing?" her mother says. "Dancing?"

"He's trying to make us laugh."

In the rearview mirror Adina watches his smile fade. His shoulders regain their familiar hunch. He pulls himself back into himself. Matteo and Christopher emerge from the house. They each put an arm around him and stand on the lawn long enough for Christopher to clap him on the shoulder, long enough for Matteo to say something that makes the other two wince. It was meant to be funny, Adina can tell. Dominic held in the middle, the brothers turn and walk back to the house.

*

Adina returns to New York, drops her bags in the hallway, and says hello to the little dog, still in the freezer. The box

Dominic gave her sits on the kitchen table as she cooks chicken and rice.

After dinner she unwraps it, surprised to find a regular-looking phone. One of the models with a giant screen. There is only one icon on its homescreen: Twitter.

Adina places the phone at the back of the silverware drawer and slams it shut. She leaves the house and walks three blocks to her neighborhood dry cleaners. It is not the best dry cleaners or the closest; it is the only one she knows. The kid at the counter seems surprised to see someone walking through the doors so late.

"Picking up?" The clothes rack moves behind her. Coats chug by. A brightly colored dress.

Adina says, "Dropping off."

"Dropping off?" The kid's braces flash under the store's pendant lamps. Adina has seen her around the neighborhood, skateboarding with her friends. Not the one ollying the library's railing but the one covering her mouth in awe.

Adina slides out of her sweater, unzips her skirt, and steps out. She stands in her underwear and blouse, which she unbuttons. Under her blouse, she wears a cloth bralette. The kid watches then, as if remembering etiquette, hastens to fill out a receipt. The kid collects the sweater, blouse, and skirt, confusion creating a stitch in her eyebrows. "Rush?"

"Nah," Adina says.

An older woman, the kid's mother Adina guesses, emerges from the back. "There's a storm coming," she tells the kid and Adina. "Later this week, they said."

Adina walks quickly home in her bralette and underwear.

The night is cold but there are only three blocks to walk. In front of her building, the halal meat carts wait in line for their turn to be stored in the back. They ornament the street like coins.

"You need a coat, honey," a vendor says. "Too cold for that shit."

*

Four days pass. Adina stops into the dry cleaners after work. The kid holds Adina's receipt in front of her like a flashlight until she identifies the correct clothes which she unhooks and hands to Adina.

Adina pays, leaves, walks home. She enjoys the sensation of the cold clothes flapping against her like a wild wing. She reaches her apartment, walks upstairs, ignores the snubbed feeling the unfriendly fireplace stirs, hangs the clothes in her closet. She sits at her desk and listens to a party outside for the length of one failed joke. She returns to the hallway, lifts the cellophane from the clothes, pulls them from their hangers, walks downstairs and outside where she folds and arranges them on her stoop. Sweater, blouse, skirt. Trashes the wrapping.

In the park, the ducks swim in close circles for warmth. When she returns, people are holding up the clothes, considering. Not wanting to dissuade them, she walks to her bodega where Emilio is stacking soft drinks. She chooses a fudge bar from the flat freezer.

"Time for a treat?" he says, ringing her up.

"There's a storm coming today," she says. "In a few hours."

The sky is clear except for one bright cloud. He nods as if he doubts it but wants to trust her. "Anything's possible."

*

Human life is quick. I do not mean: Life is short. I mean: The reason we feel like certain significant days happened only yesterday is because they did. Many of us have bodies that age preposterously out of proportion with how young we are. It's like aging in theater time. We're all seven-year-olds hired to play the parts of adults. A decade is not long. Two decades is not long. We say it is because we weigh it against the end of our life span. Our life spans are short and do not give us time to feel temporally in proportion.

No response.

*

Death's biggest surprise is that it does not end the conversation.

No response.

*

A weeping season.

First in private places like the shower. Then wider, weirder: Braced on the windowsill by her hip bones, thrust into midair and hovering over the halal meat cart's courtyard, where rubbery parts fitting machines that no longer exist are junked. It is a new climate. There are so many kinds of rain.

Broad swaths that linger for days, succinct squalls that begin upon entering an empty elevator and end at the desired floor. The tears come from another location, storm fronts that originate far away. Like everything that happens regularly, weeping becomes routine. She can do other things alongside it like talk on the phone to her mother or prepare a meal. One day she catches sight of her flattened face in the mirror, shirt soaked through. It makes her laugh.

*

One day the tears, perhaps sensing their pointlessness, halt.

*

One day, Adina quits her run halfway through. The next day, she walks her usual route, promising herself she'll run it the next day but when that day comes, she enters the park in her running clothes after work, sees a woman hustling along the track, and leaves. The next day, she passes the park on the way to work, unable to look. The next day, she sees the trees from where she drops a bill into the mailbox. The next day, she collects mail from her doorway and retreats into her apartment. The Something Else has grown and comprises everything. No trace of her unaffected self. It is a long weekend. The next day she spends in bed. The next day she spends in bed. The next day she spends in bed.

*

The therapist says, “Put a smiley face on what you're afraid of.” The life coach tells her to make a budget. The movement teacher tells her to trust the universe. Adina imagines a 747 with two eyes and a mouth. She drags the cursor down a column to arrange an auto sum.

“Which one?” Adina says.

The movement teacher stretches in front of a mirror, eyes on herself. “Which one what?”

“Universe?”

“This?” she says. “One?”

“Andromeda is colliding with us every moment and in a relative blip will crush the sun and planets and everything we've ever known.”

“I hear that you're struggling,” the movement teacher says.

The therapist says they should meet twice a week. The life coach promises organization will do what feelings can't. The movement coach says, “Stay in the discomfort of this moment,” and places her hand on the area between Adina's neck and breast.

Dogma's self-regard is exhausting. Adina opts out after the free initial sessions. She prefers Yolanda K., whose advice borders on body shame but who asks, “What would it take for your ass to flourish?” Who possesses a seemingly limitless array of Wonder Woman outfits. She likes that at the end of class, they help each other return their mats and dumbbells. She likes that Yolanda K. has thick thighs and wide, round hips and that during a new year class showed up wearing sunglasses and said, “No maximum anything today” and led them in gentle stretching.

*

The Anthropologie model has added outfits to her anguish. In agony in seaside shorts, an occasion cape, cotton crepe maxi, reimagined merino, a skirt in peekaboo stripe, burnout pocket tee, slim jeans in indigo rinse. Cocktails on the lawn, groping hat-in-wind. Caught in midwail, she is a fixed response to life's horror. It comforts Adina, scrolling by.

*

Human beings, Adina faxes, *rip their addresses off old magazines when they donate them to hair salons. This is how criminals find their victims: They search stacks of* People *magazines. If they find one where the address has been left on, they think: What a fool. I will go to her house and murder her.*

No response.

*

Adina remembers the night she told Dominic she'd never been lonely. How he believed her, and said it was so great.

Andromeda, entropy, or whatever force is glue and the stuff glue bonds, must have been listening and laughed her/him/them/itselves senseless.

Adina was lonely even then, under those frozen trees, saying those idiotic words. Perhaps she's never been anything other than lonely. Loneliness is a composite feeling: ironically unable to exist alone. It can contain anger, hunger, fear, jealousy. Adina had misidentified it for homesickness for her planet but it also meant restlessness when one is not in the place they long for. The most content she ever felt was with Toni and the little dog. Where are they? Where are they?

✶

Anyone questioning whether god exists need only consider the brevity of a dog's life span. If there was a god, let alone a benevolent one, dogs would have life spans similar to parrots. We'd have to provide arrangements for them in our wills. We wouldn't have to see their muzzles fill with gray at age four. We'd never have to find them in the morning, turned to stone.

Adina lines the paper into the tray and is about to press the wide send button when a word leaps from the page. When had she started using we instead of they?

✶

Maybe her superiors are ignoring her faxes because they do not understand why one individual or one dog would be more significant than another. Planet Cricket Rice does not have a process that is analogous to aging and death. The closest human equivalent would be akin to the life cycle of a star: stellar nebula, massive star, red supergiant, supernova, black hole.

Adina feels a tang in the middle of her rib cage: loyalty on behalf of the individual. The most American she's ever been.

In *Il Piccolo Principe*, the rose explains that even though

Earth contains fields of her, she is special because he has nourished her. Adina faxes this chapter to her superiors.

✶

What am I supposed to be doing?

✶

Her superiors have always been a religion she was forced to believe in without seeing. She worries a plague or chemical or philosophical war has eviscerated her planet, killing her familial multi-souled sentiment. She imagines her faxes lying unread on plastic feeders in what would be their equivalent of an empty office down their equivalent of an empty hallway near their equivalent of an empty reception desk where their equivalent of a receptionist answers their equivalent of a phone.

✶

Finally, one day, a sublime sound: the squeak of the fax machine.

A sheet of paper ekes out. Adina can barely read it through her tears. It is a professional business letter from a tanning salon owner in Minnesota, writing to inform employees of a new protocol. Each client must be escorted to their appointed tanning beds. No more pointing down the hall and staying behind the counter.

This must be an elaborate cover, Adina thinks, dialing the salon's phone number. A woman answers immediately.

"I'm here," Adina tells her.

"Great," the woman says. "Are you outside?"

"I'm in New York," Adina says. "Where are you?"

"White Oaks. Near the Hello Pizza. Not the old one, the new one. Do you have an appointment? We're running a promo on tanning gel."

Adina hangs up.

*

As hope thins, other beliefs flourish.

Adina visits the library and googles her name. Dozens of discussion pages appear where users with names like Alienator12 and SpaceJunkGrl debate her identity. Book groups hold heated online discussions. Readers divide into two main factions: Those who believe she is on Earth to take notes on human beings fueled by a benevolent, multi-souled planet, and those who think she is a troubled person whose mental illness manifests in prose. Why not both? argues a poster named CelestialJane. Commenters are curious about her body. In one conversation, readers debate whether she has genitals and, if so, what they look like. Under her clothes, TheMartianBookworm insists, you'd find slime and fizz and bubble. Skin but also sinew. Two contradictory things can be true, CelestialJane insists. She is 100 percent mortal, 100 percent everlasting. Almost every reader agrees she is reclusive. No one knows where she lives except SaturnSteve, who makes multi-platform proclamations that he was on a spaceship with her in the 1970s being probed on conjoined gurneys.

Adina signs off, leaves the library, and walks into a pharmacy where the sympathy cards youarenotalone cross an entire wall. Alone, Adina walks home through the park, too distracted to notice every unlit streetlamp turning on. A little boy points it out to his mother who struggles with an overstuffed bag.

*

One of the most underwhelming human American expressions of support is: *Congrats*. Its brevity cancels its sentiment. If someone truly cared about their friend's achievement, they would finish the word. Instead, congrats: *You are not worth ulation.*

However, *Congrats* is warm compared to its sinister cousin platitude. The closest Adina comes to giving up on Earth exists in the moments after she hears someone say it: You are not alone. Printed on sympathy cards, advertisements, even, most troubling, materials meant to dissuade those with suicidal tendencies.

Whatever else Adina feels after Toni's death, she is definitely alone. In summer, when her neighbors perform their errands in the sitcom-kitchen light of late afternoon, during cold evenings spent with a silent fax machine, during holidays when no one calls: Alone. To be told she is not alone denies what she knows. Alone is not the bad news. Alone is reliable. Alone has been loyal to her like a boyfriend. The bad news is platitudes! Having the basest understanding of your situation questioned at a vulnerable time! *You are not alone* is meant for the person saying it. It is the opposite of sympathy.

Not true, you snobby cow, the greeting cards insist, you are connected to others by thought. Everyone cares, though they don't call, write, follow up, or say so. You are not alone, metaphorically.

Adina argues: What a human in a dark room who has lost the ability to see themselves or others does not need is a metaphor. More effective would be to say, If you feel alone, you are. I'm sorry I cannot join you in that dark space but I won't offend you with a metaphor. Yet. Grief is a bad mirror. It shows you manipulated images of yourself, your will, and the future. It cannot show you how the small work you do will add up to yourself. Inch by inch.

⁎

Adina sautés shrimp in butter and listens to *Glassworks*.

She slides the unused frozen shrimp next to the little dog in the freezer.

"Hey buddy," she whispers. "We're still together."

⁎

Adina's mother enters a period of self-renovation. She calls to find out how she did as a mother.

"You were always doing taxes," Adina says. "Like always."

"True," she says. "I took a freelance job filing other people's taxes. You know that, right? You like that fancy high school you went to? That was because of other people's taxes. It's like when you wrote that all we ever ate for dinner was chicken. Little girl, I made pasta every night. What other facts are you misremembering about your childhood?"

Adina makes an excuse and gets off the phone. It's a bad day when someone corrects your perceived slights.

*

Adina compliments the dog owner on his well-mannered poodle and he thanks her and asks what her dog's name is.

"Butternut." This poodle's bark sounds like someone sanding paint from a vinyl ship bottom. In long, thorough strokes.

"And where is Butternut?" he says, as if he is a kindergarten teacher leading her through a lesson.

"The freezer."

*

Adina boils water for spaghetti and listens to *Glassworks*. Toni's boss calls to tell her the second printing of the book, expanded to include more recent notes, has sold out its ten thousand copies.

"I know you said you don't want to and I've tried to wait a respectful amount of time but we are fielding massive interest. Would you be willing to do another reading at a slightly bigger venue?"

Adina declines, hangs up, and spends the night reading about the mantis shrimp that can see a zillion colors. Later, she sits on the front stoop holding the little dog's tiny sweater against her cheek. Every so often the passing 7 train dismantles her.

*

Adina visits the park for the first time in months. Sitting on a rock she senses another presence and is startled to find a turtle. Yellow hatch marks accessorize its shell. It gazes at her with tiny, uncurious eyes. Walking home, she listens to "Barracuda" and wonders what it feels like to live above and below water. At a corner, she moves her shoulders to the music. A little girl holding her mother's hand dances with her. Her mother stares at her phone, unaware. They are waiting for the light to turn green so they can cross. Adina points at the little girl who points back and keeps dancing.

*

Her mother calls to ask if she feels better than yesterday when she called to ask if she felt better than the day before.

How can Adina ever be certain that she is not some dream she's having, unconscious at three?

"Maybe no more phone calls for a while," she tells her mother.

*

A veterinarian arrives in a truck to take the little dog away. Butternut will be cremated and Adina will receive his ashes in two to three weeks. The little dog feels lighter than the five pounds he was when he was alive. She places his body in a box adorned with bodega daisies. The man drives away with Butternut. Adina cries through a roll of toilet paper.

She misses his orange-and-white body beating happily beside her, traveling four strokes to her every two. He never lay coldly next to her after an argument, never subtracted himself when his ego was bruised. He even left Earth peacefully so she never had to see him in pain.

*

At the same time Adina reads the name Keith in an email, Santino is in the conference room asking Delilah if she's ever heard of Keith Haring. The day before, the clerk at the wine shop was named Keith. She remembers Keith Nguyen who was always referred to as Keith Nguyen.

If she still believed in her superiors, she would consider this a signal. Instead, she thinks, sometimes it is simply Keith o'clock.

*

"Please consider another reading," Toni's boss says on her voice mail. "Your book is really, really popular."

*

Grief plus aging reduces the cartilage in Adina's face. Even Yolanda K. notices, yelling over Rihanna:

"Your cheekbones look amazing! What are you doing?"

"Thank you!" Adina yells back. "Dying!"

*

When you reach fifteen years living in New York, she faxes, *they surgically replace your heart with a bagel. You're allowed to choose which kind as long as they have it in stock. Sesame sells out first. If you choose everything, they wrap it in its own bag and keep it away from the other organs. This city will break your bagel again and again, but thankfully it also shoves a criminal number of napkins in the bag so you can clean up your sorry mess.*

*

"On the train yesterday, a pirate got on at West Fourth and off at Jay Street–MetroTech. He carried a sword and a scabbard. I couldn't think of a joke."

"The Arrrrrrrrr train," Dominic says over the phone.

This is a happy moment, Adina reminds herself, though she does not know why.

*

Adina dresses, leaves the house, and walks to the bodega to ask if there are any bagels left. There are.

"Plain or everything?" Emilio says.

"Plain." She has rehearsed.

She pays and leaves. At home she toasts the bagel and puts

turkey on it. This is more than she did the day before. She remembers a friend in college who adopted a beagle and called him Cinnamon Raisin Beagle. It is a good day. A sandwich!

The next day, Adina dresses, leaves the house, and walks to the bodega to ask if there are any bagels left. There aren't. She has not prepared for no bagels.

She blinks at Emilio for a beat too long. His face switches from neutral to worried.

"What did you say?" Adina says.

"I said, 'hopefully the sun will stay around forever.'"

Outside, people walk in slow motion sending what they think are kind words through water, but she can't hear them. She thanks him, goes home, takes off her clothes, and does not eat anything. She can't imagine anything braver than leaving the house.

*

Please come get me, she faxes.

*

"Raise your hand when you hear the tone," the doctor says.

Adina nods. A few moments pass—in silence, she assumes. "Any tone," he says.

"You bet."

Finally, he slides his headphones off and smiles. His loud swallow disgusts her.

"I hear you swallowing," she says hopefully.

She has lost a chunk of her hearing. "Aging," he explains.

"I'm only forty."

The clopping sound of the little dog's claws on the kitchen's linoleum floor. His bark at the doorbell. His breathing in the middle of the night. Toni's tendency to say things in a comical lower register when she wanted Adina to laugh. What was there to listen for?

The doctor places a wide-mouthed apparatus onto her chest. On the screen, amid a galaxy of cells, they watch her heartbeat.

"It's healthy," the doctor says. "Only a murmur."

Adina says, "It's broken."

"What it sounds like are panic attacks, not cardiac problems."

His skepticism does not surprise her. Not being believed has become a hobby.

"Has anything changed in your life?"

Adina can't think of anything. She's been living in the same apartment for years. "I mean, my dog died."

"That's significant." He scribbles onto her chart.

"And my best friend. Died too. My boyfriend and I broke up. And I haven't spoken to my . . . family in a while. I keep trying to connect but they're not responding."

The doctor blinks. "Those are some changes."

He says there's a word for her aversion to sound. *Misophonia*. That the condition had been maligned for many years but has recently become slightly less maligned. "People report feeling rage when their loved ones clear their throats or eat. The clicking of a pen can launch them into fits of impassioned yelling. Some have berated strangers."

Adina is surprised and pleased to receive this word. A

human explanation for it all along! She wonders what other rational human qualities she wrote off as extraterrestrial because of a human's tendency to other what they don't understand. She receives new gear. A silk pillow, a pamphlet on meditation. Misophonia. An evil sorceress. A faraway land.

Some years age you and some make you young. Maybe she will grow young again the following year.

✶

Please, please come get me, she faxes. *I'm done done done.*

✶

Even grief can't stop the seasons.

Everyone is horny that it's spring. They're pointing out buds. They're reporting on trees. That one is about to bloom! Let's stand here and wait for it. Thank god the death and sadness and gray meadows and coldness are over and the Earth is metaphoring itself into abundance. Life will always start anew! Check out the babies strollering over the bursting earth. Everyone is superpsyched, oversprung.

Toni believed she shouldn't say everyone when what she meant was certain people.

Adina wants to do the opposite of forget the dead. She wants to pin them on her sweater. She's not afraid of the sadness that coincides with remembering that someone named Toni lived. These new humans stroller over the death it took Adina forever to fall in love with. Nothing new can replace what takes years to build.

✶

Eventually, grief numbs Adina's desire to notice. She does not take notes on her cheekbones, or bagels, or stoop geese, or her coworkers' tendency to use *i.e.* when they mean *e.g.* She shelves the human urge to differentiate and name, and allows every person, ritual, and object in her purview to roam freely, uncollected by her thoughts.

✶

Sitting on the surface of one of the Earth-size planets orbiting the ultracool dwarf star, you'd receive two hundred times less light than you'd get from the sun, but as much energy, because you'd be closer. The views would be stunning. Other planets would appear bigger than Earth's moon. If you lived there long enough, Adina reasons, you might begin to assign certain attributes to these heavenly bodies. That planet over there rules love, you might say. That one? Malice. Clean your house when that one is hidden. Call your boss when that one is full.

✶

One afternoon, Adina and Dominic listen to fellow moviegoers crunching in the hushed twilight of matinee previews. Every popcorn-filled mouth pushes a needle through Adina. She braces, anticipating the concussion of kernels. Cleared throats. She focuses on the advertised movie: A dog is trying to make it cross-country with the help of an otter.

"Don't otters have to be in water?" she asks Dominic.

"Maybe they stick to river routes."

"What river goes east to west?" Adina says. The explosions of saliva and popped corn continue.

Dominic says, "If you expect accuracy from Hollywood, you're going to remain disappointed."

"There are so many mouth sounds here."

Dominic suggests moving out of the city, but if she does, how will Butternut know where she is?

*

When she returns home, it's all over the news.

Astronomers at the University of Hawaii have detected the first interstellar object within the Milky Way. Named Oumuamua, it is longer than it is wide, cigar-shaped, described as a "red and extremely elongated asteroid." Ooo-moo-a-moo-a. An aquarium sound. Oumuamua is progressing more slowly than it should. This means that it has traveled from very far away, a place more slow-moving than—the phrase echoes in Adina's mind later as she tries to sleep—*what humans are used to.*

Oumuamua: The Hawaiian word for "messenger," or "scout."

*

Enlivened by the discovery of Oumuamua, Adina faxes her superiors for the first time in months.

Are you there? Did you send Oumuamua? she faxes. *Is it time?*

She ignores the unspoken rule to remain rational and emotionless and adds: *I quantum miss you. I miss you in the deeper level of reality where distance has no meaning.*

✶

One hour passes without reply. Adina walks outside where the neighbor who dresses her stoop geese in seasonally appropriate attire stands on the sidewalk, glaring at a sheet of paper. An anonymous neighbor has left a letter of complaint. The geese have been wearing their raincoats for too long.

"'It is no longer spring,'" the woman reads aloud. "'This is not appropriate. We rely on you.'" She folds the letter, baffled. "Who relies on ceramic geese? Who writes a letter like this?"

"Someone upset about other things."

She gestures to the geese, outfitted in clear plastic with red polka dots, holding matching umbrellas. "I ordered autumn outfits but they haven't arrived."

"You have no responsibility to anonymous letter writers," Adina says.

"And yet."

✶

That evening, still no response from her superiors. An astronomer is interviewed about Oumuamua on the news. He says, "It's possible that the civilization is not alive anymore but sent a spacecraft long ago. We ourselves sent out Voyager 1 and Voyager 2. There could be a lot of equipment out there. The point is that this is the very first object we found from outside the solar system. It is very similar to when I walk on the beach with my daughter and look at the seashells that are swept ashore. Every now and then we find an object of artificial origin. This could be a message in a bottle. We should be open-minded."

*

Things the Yoga Instructor Who Is Subbing for Yolanda K. whispers:

A very famous sage, the actor Burt Reynolds, once said, "Forty years is a long time to suck in your stomach." Practice being cool with it. You are a lowercase *t*. You're a crescent moon. You're a wet rag, kind of. Take your ankles in your hands. Reach toward your outstretched leg. Soften into your appendix. Salute the unseen work you've done to get to the mat.

At the end of class, the students chill in savasana as he places a cool towel on each person's forehead. Adina stares into the twinkling irises of string lights that hang above her, feeling pleasantly wrung out. Instrumental music plays.

"Take as much time as you want," the Yoga Instructor Who Is Subbing for Yolanda K. says, and leaves.

One by one, people leave the room.

*

On the drive to her mother's house for Christmas, Adina listens to a radio show about blowing your nose.

Toni's boss has called again. The fourth and fifth printing

have sold out. Her voice has lost her peppy veneer and she is pleading. Would she please consider doing a reading in the new year?

"It shouldn't be hard," the rhinologist says. "Whatever you can't get out gently can stay inside."

Adina remembers it took her longer than most children to learn how to blow her nose. She remembers being too young to have memories. Entering her neighborhood, she can't drive a block without having several. This is where she worked as a waitress. This is where the homes sank.

"Don't overthink it," the expert says.

*

Her mother's radio breaks. They travel to the less-fancy mall to get it fixed.

"This must be the last RadioShack," her mother says when they enter.

A clerk helps her find the part while Adina looks at a wall display of fax machines. The sign reads: RETRO COMMUNICATION.

In line, her mother explains to the clerk why it's important to not give up on an old radio. Craftsmanship, ingenuity, and loyalty. He agrees, says they still get customers every day coming in for transistor radios, even rotary phones. A commotion near the mall entrance distracts him. A jarring, collective chugging sound.

He calls to a clerk at the front of the store. "What's going on up there, Sal?"

"It's the fax machines." Sal points to an unseen area on the wall.

Adina and her mother follow the clerk to the front of the store where the wall of fax machines chirp and gasp out reams of paper. Adina's pulse leaps in her wrist. Page after page.

The clerk collects one and holds it up, frowning. "They're blank."

✶

On the ride home, her mother tells Adina she stopped in to see Toni's mother the week prior. "I can't imagine what that woman is going through. I remember when you were sick as a kid. That was bad enough. Such a scary time. I was five seconds from taking you to the ER and I had no insurance."

"It was a cold," Adina says. "It was only a week."

"It was much more than a cold and it was well over a week. I'd come home at lunch and you'd be feverish on the couch. But one day you finally got better. The clouds parted. I went into the bathroom and cried."

✶

The visit strengthens a shelf in Adina. Perhaps, finally, grief has released its grip.

As long as no one charms the waiter. As long as no one corrects anyone else's use of lie and lay. As long as no one listens to her story wearing an expression of bemusement and concern, waiting until she's finished to say, *There's a lot of answer in those questions.* As long as snow doesn't fall from the gutter to the ground. As long as nothing shines. As long as there are no dinners of fried chicken and honey. As long as no one asks the waiter, *If this isn't the most popular pizza, what is?* As long as the elevator remains silent between floors. And no one prefers a rainy day to a sunny. Or dances in place while waiting for the train. Or says no without looking up. When the subway moves, as long as no one turns to the person next to them and says, *Can you believe this thing was built by nuns?* As long as no one thinks highly of her or forgives her too easily. She called one night after reading Adina's finished notes. It was before dawn, even New York City's vendors were asleep. She said, *Sometimes the best person to show you your life is a newcomer.* As long as no one plays '90s hip-hop. As long as there is no music at all.

*

In March, a knock on the door.

A police officer stands outside, holding a small book. "We found him!" he says. He seems to expect big praise. Receiving no response, he clarifies, "The man who robbed your apartment." Adina is quiet for so long he checks the address against one written in his book. "Your apartment was robbed?"

"A really long time ago."

The officer is pleased. He raises his voice over the halal meat cart screaming by. "He confessed. To this house and a few others in the neighborhood. After we caught him doing a big job across town. Thought you'd want to know."

Information conveyed, he turns and walks the path toward the street.

"He took a pillowcase," she calls. "I didn't have anything worth anything."

"Damage is damage."

He's right. She felt exposed for weeks. Cut in some part of her she didn't realize was soft. She looks at the sky for a long time, a pale wrist of moon.

*

One day, a ten-minute laughing jag. One full day without a stomachache. Adina reminds herself, we are sad. Toni is gone. Sorrow feels familiar and comfortable. But she orders a velour jumpsuit online and it arrives, too big. And the company makes returning it so easy. All she must do is peel off a label and affix it to the original package and drop it at a FedEx hub. There's one next to her bodega. And the bodega has whole wheat sesame seed bagels left from the morning. New York and the internet feel like miracles.

Emilio says, "You look beautiful today." He has purchased the store after years of saving.

Adina says, "How's Veronica? How's business? How's life?"

She eats a bagel and walks home through the park, remembering how she and her mother had to invent family histories to get House of Bargains to accept returns. A woman in front of her chooses the prettier remote path so Adina takes the remote path too. A few yards in, the woman pauses to gaze up into the canopy of a tree. When a New Yorker does this it can mean only one thing: Cool bird. There it is, red-orange and tweeping above their heads. Adina drifts down the hill to stand beside the woman. She is shorter than Adina, which is rare.

"Do you see the cardinal?" The woman's hair is tight gray curls. "Mating season."

Adina and the woman stare at the small red bird. A passing boy trips then regains his balance. Adina worries the commotion will disturb the bird but it stays.

"Not a cardinal," the woman corrects herself. "It doesn't have the right head. I'm not sure what that bird is."

The bird, now untitled, seems farther away. "Wrong head," Adina agrees.

The bird flies down the lane and disappears into a different set of trees.

"It heard us talking about it," Adina says.

The woman smiles and walks away. In this moment, Adina is certain of two things: It was a pleasant exchange, and she is finished living in New York. The former's unarguability has made the latter visible, the way a steady hand draws out a timid child.

*

The first run is painful. She quits at the hill. The next is impenetrable. She quits at the hill. On the next run she makes it through what had been her shorter route then quits, kicks dirt, laughs over how bad she is.

"What's the dream?" Yolanda K. says.

"To master gravity," Adina says.

"That's where you have it wrong. Gravity's your friend. It allows you to fall with grace. It's the earth that's stopping you."

The next day, Adina's feet don't hurt, her side doesn't ache. She plays Rihanna on repeat and makes it to the hill without feeling spent, then she is over it, treading lightly, almost skipping, down the lower paths. She finishes. Supine on the grass, she looks through a hole in the tree canopy. The yellow leaves are loosing themselves over the field. Damp earth soaks her back. She looks up. Unhurried cumulus clouds travel through the canopy window. It was a wobbly run no real runner would be proud of but she is not a real runner. She looks up, filled with simple pride that like cancer has arrived alone. It is not accompanied by her past. It is not in addition to her grief. It is not underlined in fear. It is fall. Everything in the park is in love with gravity. After months of wasting sorrow she has finished a hard run and she is alive and lying on the Earth, looking up.

*

Breaking news out of Cambridge. The chair of Harvard's astronomy department has examined Oumuamua's "peculiar acceleration" and concluded that the object "may be a fully operational probe sent intentionally to Earth's vicinity by an alien civilization." She suggests that astronomers might communicate with the civilization that sent it. She is frustrated they saw Oumuamua too late in its journey to photograph it. Oumuamua was ejected from its home star's realm while its planets were taking shape. It is either a scout or a comet or a dead planet. She is searching for the slingshot planet, the one that could have delivered such a gravitational kick, sending the object into the depth of space. So far where there should be a planet near each of these possible dwarf stars, there is nothing. Astronomers identify four possible home stars for Oumuamua that had their close encounters between one and seven million light-years ago.

"Quite a window," the newscaster, who understands nothing about time, jokes.

✶

Adina shuts off the television and sits in silence. Dead planet. Her dark suspicions that her planet has been annihilated are confirmed. Adina knows it wasn't ejected. It left. Oumuamua was a survivor craft meant to scoop her. She missed her ride. The object appears too far to return. Adina is stuck in an obscure spiral arm, thirty thousand light-years away from the center of a minor galaxy. The lobby of the community pool, watching the headlights of other family cars scan her. The sad glances of the receptionists. No one is coming to get her. She is like everyone else. On her own.

✶

Adina "wakes" to find herself seated on a white couch in a white room, facing a wide movie screen. Solomon glimmers next to her. She tries to wrap her arms around them. She feels a current of gentle air as a tinkling of birds at dawn fills her ears. They beam, pleased by her attempt. A film begins.

It is the Johnny Carson interview with Carl Sagan from 1978. Adina is confused. Her superiors had rebuffed, ignored, or responded lukewarmly to her faxes about him. She realizes: They are attempting to speak her language.

She knows the interview by memory. Silky long bob, black suit, polka-dot tie, sitting in front of a realistically painted forest scene. Johnny Carson is perturbed that there can't be anything faster than the speed of light. He owns several sports cars and probably wants to believe that someday he will do it. Carl Sagan says that several astronomers, like Johnny, took exception to Einstein's theory of relativity. Men don't like limits. If it were possible to move faster than the speed of light, Carl says, circumstances would change. Effects would precede causes. The light turns on before you even reach the switch. The egg uncooks.

The interview fades from the screen. The chief astronomer on the Oumuamua research team appears. He says that he believes Oumuamua could be the aliens' way of sending a cosmic message in a bottle, the way humans did by sending Voyager 1.

Solomon conveys that though the astronomer is correct about the message, his reasons are incorrect. They are not trying to communicate with every human, only those who belong to them. Adina's people have been forced out of their solar system and have buzzed Earth. It is time. A word appears on the screen that makes Adina jolt in her "seat." DEACTIVATE. Solomon shimmers urgently, purples and blues spark out, anticipating her questions. She doesn't have any. She has never figured out why humans say one thing and mean another, but death she understands.

✶

Adina wakes with full memory of her visitation, feeling like a mailbox stuffed with mail. A sound in the other room has awakened her. Clear, famous, her favorite sound on Earth. The fax machine rumbles out a message.

SUMMARIZE EARTH IN ONE WORD, the transmission reads. DEACTIVATE.

Do you mean sentence?

WORD. THEN DEACTIVATE.

I don't want to leave anymore. I want to stay.

OH WELL.

It will not be like the movies. There will be no fleet of pearlized spaceships hovering a dolphin's jump over the Atlantic. Every second Oumuamua retreats farther. If Adina waits too long they will be out of range.

✶

Toni's boss sounds shocked to hear her on the other line. "I'm delighted. Though, based on the popularity of the book, we will need an even bigger venue."

Adina says, "How big?"

✶

Voyager 1 becomes the farthest human-made object from Earth. It is considered a relic. Astronomers shut down its systems to preserve energy. If Voyager ever falls into the hands—or anything that could be considered a holding part—of extraterrestrial life, it will hopefully have enough power to deliver its news.

Adina's human joints pop and click. Her hair thins. Her breasts ache. Grief has thrown a blanket over her senses. She imagines Voyager hurtling through space as, one by one, its lights turn off. They are sibling probes in middle age. Both launched in 1977, intended to communicate and collect.

How can Adina express the composite nature of her location in one word? She hopes deactivating will allow her to regain what humans call consciousness inside Oumuamua, back in the collective fold of her people. She hopes her light turns on. If it does, when will she be?

Yolanda K. says, There is no reason to be anything other than optimistic.

Will she be Earthsick? Perhaps she can only know whether this planet was her home after she leaves it.

*

It is winter. Adina's mother's garden is sleeping. She guides Adina around the plants and bushes, pointing to what will be. Lavender, zinnias, lemon basil. She has graduated with a master's in education and has been promoted to vice president of HR, the position she used to assist. For the first time in her life, she is doing okay with money. Tulips, daffodils, butterfly bush. She remains stymied by the success of the roses as if they arrived by bus during the night, as if she didn't encourage them from seed, confess to them, research and dispatch their enemies. Portulaca, Siberian iris, crepe myrtle. Every day her mother checks to see if it's still there and it is.

"Savings," she says. "After all these years. I can't believe it."

The grass is dead. The ground is unforgiving. Chives, black-eyed Susans, hyacinth bean vine. Her mother steps around each plant's potential like a woman in love.

*

Adina's publisher rents a Brooklyn synagogue for her reading. That night, Adina and her mother arrive in a cab to find a line stretching around the building and down the street.

"Adina, what on earth?" Her mother's dress is dark with tiny roses that blink like stars under the streetlights. She walks quickly to join a man standing near the front entrance. The door swings open to welcome another group of people, throwing light onto his silver hair and beard.

"Charles," she says. "This is my daughter."

"I read your book," he says. "I didn't understand most of it but I could tell it was good."

Adina laughs, his forehead reddens.

The green room sparkles with platters of food, wine carafes, a smattering of editors, everyone's good mood. Toni's boss wears a sweater and prairie skirt in matching tiger stripes. Adina asks why these readings occur in religious spaces and she says they're the only ones large enough to accommodate her readership.

Some of the editors believe her story and some don't, this is no different from any other social interaction. Still, everyone lifts their glass and makes encouraging remarks. "Can you believe this turnout? Whoever would have thought an indie press book would capture the imagination of so many people?"

"Me," her mother says, eating from a pile of cookies stacked on Charles's plate. Her gray hair is gathered into a bun at the nape of her neck where a diamond clip winks. Her accent contrasts with the editors who speak like Midwestern weathermen. It is a shining sound. Charles moves a cookie from his plate to hers.

"Did you always believe her?" an editor asks, then clarifies, "In her, I mean?"

"She almost killed me when she was born, did she tell you that?"

"Your mom is so funny," Toni's boss whispers into Adina's ear.

Charles and her mother find their seats in the front row. He helps arrange her cardigan on the seat back. He places his arm around her. A work coat and new-looking sneakers. Adina knows he will haul her mother's trees and bushes and praise the tiniest growth in her lilies. Dominic and Ted arrive, wave to Adina onstage. The synagogue's lights dim.

Toni's boss walks to the microphone. "Let's give a big round of applause," she says, "to someone who has traveled so far to be here." The audience titters.

Animal prints, Adina realizes, are not meant to imply *I killed a cheetah*, but *I am the cheetah*. This happy thought propels her to the microphone.

*

"The moan humans make when they listen, especially when another human confides a painful feeling. Anything over rice. When a human asks another human running late if they'd like them to order a drink so it's there when they arrive. Thin tomato slices dusted with oregano. Dominic, when he was left out of things like passing the joint, used to say, 'What's my name, Skip?' The moment of silence under an overpass when driving in a storm. Control-top pantyhose. The rosebushes behind the Mobil station that bloom like they're in Versailles. The ripples in my hair after sleeping in a braid. Going to see a movie in bright afternoon and emerging when it's night. The word yet: because it allows you to believe more than one thing. Yolanda K. pretending to dance on top of a pyramid, waving a yoga mat like a cape, 'doing' Diana Ross, the dog in the park in the sun catching the ball and bringing it back, flashing between his people like a gem. The night Toni said, 'Let's wear our weather earrings and go to Whole Foods and say things like, "I just love ramps, don't you?"' Fridays on the subway, when suitcases spring up like violets, as people leave, as people arrive, then again on Monday, as people return, as people leave. I have never lost my beginner's eye for the city, never stopped looking at the skyline when the 7 emerges from the tunnel for the aboveground stops. My little dog standing on his hind legs, dancing. Wine, blankets, and robes because they take away the body. A body is a hard thing to have.

"I was sent here to report on the human experience and have failed. I haven't used my life enough. Even the word itself, human, means flawed. It means everything is technically correct but some unanticipated trouble has fouled it up.

If the assignment had been to be human, to fail, then I succeeded. But if it was to create a comprehensive document of life on Earth, I was always doomed. Language is pitiable when weighed against experience. My deepest loves and sadnesses fell outside the realm of articulation and never reached the fax machine. There was always an unattainable aspect to my work, which they must have known, otherwise they would have sent someone less sensitive. There is no way of succeeding or failing that the word human doesn't allow."

Adina senses movement in the middle of the room. A man raises a sign: I BELIEVE IN YOU.

Adina continues. "By far, those who cause the most damage are humans who promise to be some kind of home and are not."

In the front row, a woman raises a sign: YOU ARE A FRAUD.

"By far, my favorite human emotion is joy. Because it is so misunderstood. Because it contains all the others."

Signs ascend in the pews and at the back of the auditorium. Dominic and Charles turn in their seats. Believers outnumber nonbelievers. No, a few more signs: LIAR. ALIEN GO HOME. Some signs offer confusing, third-party opinions. BETTER WAGES FOR TEACHERS. EAT MORE KALE. Adina's mother does not turn; other people's opinions of her daughter do not matter. She knows her daughter's heart because it is her heart. She keeps a steady gaze on her daughter, faltering at the podium.

Adina says, "Should I continue?"

*

Adina removes the phone from the drawer, turns it on, and clicks the Twitter icon.

Toni has used her official author photo, the little dog on her lap, and has written her bio: *Adina Giorno is an undercover, asexual alien reporting on human behavior.* There is a blue checkmark next to her name and her account follows only one other: Martin's Aquarium in Northeast Philadelphia. She has six hundred and fifty thousand followers. Her mother, Dominic, Audrey, Santino, Delilah, Miguel, her neighbor who dresses her stoop geese in seasonally appropriate attire, Heather, Melissa, and Phyllis from the diner, Keith Nguyen, Mrs. Goldman, the woman Miguel is dating who Toni said was ugly in a manipulative way. A profile picture of a woman pumping iron: Yolanda K.

Adina paces her apartment, remakes her bed, returns to the phone, and opens the page. She types: HELLO.

*

Adina sits on her bed, mug of tea braced between her knees.

She imagines every human she's ever known entering her room one by one. They pause by her bedside. She smiles, seeing their particular gestures and movements clearly—Dominic with a shy knock, okay to come in? Audrey, confident, striding. Even those she was not supposed to want to see again she welcomes. Her father, Miguel, Dakota. They visit and move on. Outside, wind swirls through Queens and rattles her finicky windowpanes. Adina sits cross-legged and welcomes each person. Did each one—wherever they were physically—know they had stopped in? She hopes they are in the middle of a good meal, repairing a car they like, tromping the woods, negotiating with the stubborn roots of a rhododendron. She touches them, thinks highly of them, apologizes, forgives them. Every human, singular and exact, is bound by pain and a finite life span. Every human shares the same hometown. Her cheeks warm as if she has attended a party where her dress had been a hit. The wind outside, the tea in her mug.

"It's enough."

✶

Replies arrive so fast the phone can't differentiate each one so it produces a guttural wheeze.

Hello! Your work means so much to me and my . . .

OMG! I've been hoping you'd . . .

We've been studying the grade-school chapters and . . .

Thank you for . . .

Adina reads the messages late into the night. When the sun appears over the whistling 7 train, she sends a final tweet:

THANK YOU.

She turns off the phone and leaves it with her things.

She faxes her final, one-word transmission and leaves it in the feeder.

✶

In the beginning there was Adina and her Earth mother.

Maybe that's why at the end, awake in her bed, sunlight striping her through the blinds, her mother's coat occurs to her, how it smelled as they stood in the House of Bargains return line concocting their story, on one of their endless errand days. Adina had to join her because her mother was the only thing she had. It was so boring under those hissing lights, pretending to be too tired to stand, leaning against her mother's side, searching for a chicken to boil. Every earthly need handled. In memory, Adina's mother pauses the work of a sponge to scratch a tough spot. She had been in her thirties then, not old. An afternoon of errands, her mother's coat, the word vestibule, and the winter dark. Was it ever anything but winter in childhood? Did they ever eat anything other than chicken? Her mother's coat was a shade of eggplant impossible to replicate, barrel-shaped buttons, descending in puffy waves from her neck to the floor. It embarrassed Adina when she wore it to pick her up at school. The coat that smelled like Moroccan oil, pencil eraser, and moss, the coat that kept her warm.

*

The human life span was perfectly designed to be brief but to at times feel endless. A set of years that pass in a minute, eternity in an afternoon. Yet in the same way competing weather fronts produce a climate that's right for a tornado, brevity versus eternity (the push-pull that contains everything) is the condition for romantic love, sorrow, betrayal, joy. Countless meaningless profound transactions. Adina understands the agonized hope that springs toward the closing door. She should have traveled more. Like most humans, she'd been a homebody, preferring to repeat the same routes. To reach the end of your life and wish you had time for a few other roads—

what could be more human? One life span is too short to try to love everything she wants to try to love, do everything she loves as many times as she can. Adina hasn't experienced romantic love like the ones portrayed in movies, or a more realistic love like the ones portrayed in more realistic movies. But to love a mother who grew alongside her. A friend when she left the Earth. To love a dog. To love vocation. To love humans, even those she didn't know. These loves were transcendent. They changed her. Like so many things, it was the good and bad news.

*

Adina will ride the Staten Island Ferry to the middle of the icy harbor. Other vessels will gleam inside the intimate fog.

She will travel with her mind still lit by human concerns. Her mother, the previous night's reading, but in transit her thinking will broaden. Maybe her people have discovered how to move faster than the speed of light so effect will no longer follow cause. Maybe the sadness she experienced on Earth was because everyone she loved was already gone. Maybe some part of her will proceed forever into the past and another will hover in space, a period at the end of a sentence not yet written. Maybe the circumstances leading to the sentence are just beginning to form. She had always felt like she was waiting for everyone to catch up, after all, as she accrued notes and lost home after home. She was American, in that she rarely traveled. Alien, in that she was remote. Human, in that she never admitted how remote she felt. As she leaves, she'll discover the last human sense to depart is hearing. Her final connection will be an everysound of an orchestra tuning, a chorus of violins, chains husking over the dock, the bleat of barges in the fog, an oboe. She will miss Earth, the planet that contained every human she ever loved. Only her casing will remain.

"It will look as if I'm dead," the Little Prince said to the pilot. "But that won't be true."

Adina will enter the absolute corridor where death is merely a diminishment of a solo perspective. As her star's point of view dims, there will be a sensation of one light joining many. A glittering, infinite expanse.

Hello, she will say. *I'm so happy to see you.*

Hello, Adina, we will say. *Welcome home.*

ACKNOWLEDGMENTS

Claudia Ballard, my loyal, peerless agent, Jenna Johnson for her faith-shaped guidance, Lianna Culp and the team at FSG, Phyllis Trout and Brian Brooks, Julia Strayer, Steph Opitz, Amy Brill, Courtney Maum, Halimah Marcus, Elliott Holt, Mira Jacob, CJ Hauser, Claire Vaye Watkins, Manuel Gonzales, Thomas Morris, Tsering Wangmo Dhompa, Annie Liontas. For their kind early reads, Brandon Hobson, Tommy Orange, and Kaveh Akbar. Ramona Ausubel, thank you.

Carl Hall at Crunch, whichever writer on *The Good Place* named the clam-chowder-themed restaurant "A Little Bit Chowder Now," Prospect Park's running track, every treadmill in every hotel across America, Brian Lehrer. Those who passed over me for awards, jobs, and distinctions of any kind, thank you. The Inutterable Magic of Keeping One's Head Down and Listening Only to the Work. The gentleman in the Ft. Hamilton subway station who when he realized I did not have an umbrella wordlessly handed me his, then flipped his collar and strode into the rain like some unassailable god.

My teachers, my brothers (related and not). My students at NYU, the New School, the Institute for American Indian Arts, and beyond. The University of Vermont's End-of-Life Facilitation program, and Catland Books. The Cabins Retreat, the Munster Literature Centre in Ireland, and Yale University. The Dodson family.

Those who love and were made better by Adina Talve-Goodman: 1986–2018.

My first reader, Helene Bertino, and every flower in her garden. Marcello, and the poet Ted Dodson.

Antoine de Saint-Exupéry, and all fellow pilots.